TRACKING TRISHA:

DRAGON LORDS OF VALDIER
BOOK 3

BY S. E. SMITH

Acknowledgments

I would like to thank my husband Steve for believing in me and being proud enough of me to give me the courage to follow my dream. I would also like to give a special thank-you to my sister and best friend Linda who not only encouraged me to write but who also read the manuscript.

—S. E. Smith

Science Fiction Romance

TRACKING TRISHA

First E-Book Publication June 2012

Cover Design by Melody Simmons

Synopsis

Trisha Grove enjoyed her job as a pilot for Boswell International but realized something was still missing from her life—her family. She is ready to call it quits and head back home to Wyoming where her father lives. She never expected her last flight for Boswell would end with an unplanned trip out of this world. Trisha isn't sure at first what is real and what isn't; all she knows is that she is determined to get back to her dad no matter what it takes.

Kelan Reykill is the fourth son in the royal line of Valdier. Commander of the *V'ager,* one of the largest Valdier warships, he prides himself on his strict self-discipline, his ability to remain in command in any situation, and his skill at handling any challenge. That is, until he meets a stubborn human female from the primitive planet his older brother sought refuge on. Now, all he can think about is how to get the female into his bed and under his control while staying in one piece.

When she is taken from him, Kelan will track Trisha to the ends of the universe and farther, because he knows one thing. She is his true mate, and he will do anything, kill anyone, who tries to harm her.

Contents

Prologue

The large buck moved cautiously through the dense forest. It paused looking around. A shiver passed over its tan coat, and its ears twitched back and forth trying to detect the slightest sound that was not natural to its habitat. Its large, dark brown eyes searched the nearby brush looking for the danger it could sense by not see. Taking a tentative step forward, it suddenly whirled and jumped quickly over a log, disappearing into the surrounding forest. A muttered curse exploded from the lips of the figure lying silently on the ground. The man slowly rose out of his hiding place, a large hunting knife in his hand. He hadn't eaten in three days. As he stood up, brushing the leaves and branches off his shoulders and legs, a sharp impact to the center of his back threw him forward, and he lay still, knowing he had just been killed.

"Last target down," Trisha said softly into her mic.

She calmly tucked the bow back into the harness clipped to her side and began working her way down the large tree she was in. Even as she moved, it was almost impossible to see her small form as she stayed in the shadows and covering of the branches. She jumped down the last couple of feet and moved to the man who lay prone on the damp, forest floor. Walking over to him with her pistol held tightly against her, she looked at the red stain spreading over his back. *A clean kill,* she thought. *Severed spine, arrow straight through the heart, no sound.*

"Good job, baby girl," a deep voice replied with pride. "That makes ten for ten. Tag target and come on in."

Trisha grinned as she bent down and touched the target. "Tag, you're it," she said.

The man groaned as he turned over and looked up into the shining dark, brown eyes of the girl standing over him. His only consolation was he had been the last one tagged. The bad thing was The bad thing was he'd been tagged by a twelve-year-old little girl. He was never going to live down the ribbing from the other guys in his squadron.

"Daddy says we can come in now," Trisha said as she reached out a hand to help the soldier who was going through an intensive wilderness survival training program with Trisha's dad.

"What gave me away?" the man grumbled as he slowly got to his feet again.

"Your stomach," Trisha replied with a grin. "You should have eaten those bugs two days ago or some of the fish left over from the grizzly yesterday. They weren't too bad."

The man just grunted as he rotated his shoulders trying to ease the pain where Trisha shot him with the arrow. The tips were designed with an ink pack on them so when they hit the target, it was noticeable to the instructors. The problem was it still hurt like hell. He would be sporting a softball-sized bruise for at least a week.

"How did you know about the bugs and the fish?" The man asked as he tried to look over his shoulder to see what kind of shape he would have been in if she shot him with a real arrow.

"Oh, about an hour after you left I found your trail. You left some really good tracks, and it wasn't too hard to follow you. Anyway, I watched you as tried to decide if you were going to eat them," Trisha replied as she stepped over a log. "By the way, I severed your spinal column and the arrow would have gone into your heart, killing you instantly."

The man shook his head in wonder. What kind of father would teach his little girl how to track, hunt, and kill for fun? He heard of the father/daughter team from some of the other Navy Seals who had gone through the training. None of them ever made it through the first time without getting killed. Very few, if any, ever made it through the second or third time. Once they made it through, the father would send them in again, only this time he would send his daughter in after them. None ever survived.

"Why didn't you kill me earlier?" The man asked. He followed the small figure in front of him without questioning her whether she knew where they were at, much less where they were going.

"Oh, I like studying my prey to see how it thinks. Daddy says you can learn a lot about a person by studying the way they react to things that are going on around them. You did a good job once you realized I was tracking you. I liked how you used the river to try to cover your tracks," Trisha said turning toward a narrow animal trail.

"Thanks," the man grumbled again.

Dante Rodriguez listened as Trisha explained all the things she noticed him doing right and pointed out some things he did wrong. He shook his head thinking it was hard to believe he was listening to a twelve-year-old. She seemed much older. She moved with an easy grace and confidence which told of her knowledge, experience, and comfort at being in her present environment. He remembered laughing with the other nine guys in his squadron when his commanding officer told them they were going to participate in a wilderness survival camp held by Grove Wilderness Guides, a private company that worked out of Wyoming. The guys all joked that if they could survive basic training and Camp Coronado, they could survive anything. Obviously, the U. S. Navy Seals never expected they would be up against the skills of a very talented twelve-year-old girl.

"Daddy!" Trisha squealed suddenly and took off at a run. Dante watched as her slim shape was engulfed in a hug by a huge bear of a man.

* * *

Later that night, Trisha lay on the roof outside her bedroom window. Her dad was saying good-bye to the last of their clients, and she was waiting for him in their favorite spot. Her eyes lit up as the big, muscular frame of her father crawled through the narrow opening without a sound. A moment later, he lowered his huge frame down next to her, and they both stared silently up at the night sky.

"You did real good, baby girl," her dad said in a gruff voice. "Your mom and I are real proud of you."

Trisha smiled as she stared up at the twinkling stars. "Which one is she on tonight?" Trisha asked softly.

Her dad pointed to a bright spot. "That one," he replied just as quietly. "Your mom's on that star tonight looking down on you. Can you hear her? She's telling me what a beautiful young lady you are turning out to be and how proud she is of you."

Trisha smiled up at the star her dad pointed out. "I'm glad. One day I'm going to fly up there and find her," Trisha said before she turned her head to look at her dad. "And when I do, I'm going to take you with me."

Trisha's dad, Paul, kept his eyes focused on the star he had chosen tonight. He didn't say anything, he couldn't. His throat was tight from holding in the tears at the innocence in his only daughter's promise. Since his wife died from a brain aneurysm when Trisha was a year old, it was just him and her. Every night they would lie out under the stars and pick a different one. He reached over and gently cupped Trisha's small hand in his larger one.

"You do that, baby girl. You do that and I'll be happy to go with you," he finally said.

Chapter 1

Trisha Grove grimaced at the faint scars marring her flat stomach. One large and a half-dozen smaller ones fanned out in different directions. She pulled the black top of her uniform down to cover them and turned away from the mirror. She pictured a nice, sturdy metal filing cabinet in her mind. Once she had a clear vision of it, she mentally put all her bad memories in it and locked it securely, throwing away the key. The damn thing always found a way to open itself up, but it was taking longer and longer for it to do so, she thought in satisfaction.

Trisha pulled out her black canvas duffle bag with the Boswell International logo on it and packed two changes of clothes, one for work and one for play. Not that she did much playing any more. *Oops,* she thought to herself with a self-reproving smile, *forgot that one.* After packing her bag, she walked back over to the mirror and pulled her light brown hair up and braided it into a rope. Her hair was extremely curly from the top all the way to the tips. She tried cutting it short once and found out that was a huge mistake! She ended up with an Afro that would have made the comedian Carrot Top proud if her hair had been red. After that disastrous style decision, she let it grow out, thinking the weight of it would at least allow her to braid it or put it up into her current favorite style of the braided rope. She studied her face for a moment with a sigh. She had to admit that at twenty-eight, she wasn't half bad—at least with her clothes on. At five foot six, her slender frame was well-proportioned. She was a little big on top but not so much that it became a problem when strapping into a cockpit. Her almost waist-length hair framed her long, narrow face. She had a straight nose and lips that were not too full but not too thin. Her biggest asset was her dark chocolate-brown eyes. They were so dark it was hard to see her pupils most of the time. Her dad still told her they weren't brown for nothing whenever she would give him a hard time, she thought with a grin. Her eyes darkened as she realized she was long overdue for a visit with her dad. She should have gone last month, but she was running out of excuses to give him about why she still wasn't dating anyone.

*Sorry, Daddy, I can't give you those grandkids you've been wanting, the doctors say it is too dangerous. No, I'm not seeing anyone. I've been too busy with work. No, I haven't heard from Peter since the divorce—and your little private conversation with him. Yes, I know there are other men out there who...*Trisha slammed her mind closed. *Enough!* she told herself fiercely. *It's been three friggin' years. Get over it!* Trisha pictured a deep black hole and threw all those bad memories into it, sealing it up with a huge metal lid. As an afterthought, she opened it up just enough to toss Peter into it as well before resealing it. *That's much better.* Trisha chuckled.

Picking up her bag, she looked around to see if there was anything she might have missed. As she headed out to her SUV, she glanced up at the dark skies. Yeah, it seemed to fit the mood she was in. She pulled out of the parking garage under her apartment building and grinned. At least she was flying today. The weather forecast said it was scheduled to clear later this afternoon. She and her best friends, Ariel Hamm and Cara Truman, were scheduled to take an artist back across the country in an experimental business jet that was just about ready for full-scale production. She and Ariel had been test-flying it all over the world. It was a beauty, with state of the art navigation and instrumentation. The sleek design was built for speed, and so far, it handled a diversity of environmental conditions beautifully.

Trisha's cellphone rang as she was pulling onto the freeway heading toward the private airfield owned by Boswell. Trisha frowned and muttered under her breath when a car nearly clipped her left bumper. Bad weather seemed to bring out the worst drivers.

Trisha pressed a button on the steering wheel connecting the call. "Hello, Ariel."

"Hey, Trish," Ariel said. Trisha grinned as she heard the breathlessness in Ariel's voice. She'd bashed another alarm clock from the sound of it.

"Miss your wake-up call?" Trisha asked with a grin. They'd both slept in due to their late night in the training simulator at Boswell's research facility last night, and Trisha wouldn't have been surprised if Ariel had gone straight from the research lab to the no-kill kennel where she volunteered. Ariel really should have been a vet, Trisha thought as she changed lanes.

"My damn clocks are always breaking. I don't know why I even bother buying a new one. They don't last more than a week before they stop working," Ariel grumbled under her breath. "Anyway, I was looking at the weather forecast, and it looks like a go for early to mid afternoon. I know Abby was anxious to get back home. I haven't heard from Cara, but she should be in. I know she was in either Detroit or Philadelphia, I can't remember which one. Anyway, you know how she is on a flight. We'll be lucky if she doesn't try to dismantle the damn thing at thirty thousand feet for the hell of it. Oh, and Carmen is coming too," Ariel added quickly at the end.

Trisha bit back a chuckle. She knew Ariel would not appreciate her humor right now. Carmen was a sore point with Ariel. If the truth was known, Trisha could relate to how Carmen was feeling. Carmen had lost her husband three years ago in a traumatic way. Trisha thought Carmen was doing pretty well considering what she went through. She refocused when she heard the pause on the other end of the line and knew Ariel was waiting for her to reply.

"That's great! I haven't seen Carmen in a couple of months. Do you think Cara has forgiven us yet for the blind date we set her up with last week?" Trisha asked. She grinned when she heard the relief in Ariel's voice as she changed the subject to something less stressful.

"I hope so, or we may be flapping our arms all the way to California," Ariel said with a laugh. They had learned a valuable lesson—never set up a blind date for someone who is not only ADHD but smarter than Einstein, especially when you are drunk. The poor guy ended up having an asthma attack in the middle of the restaurant. Neither Ariel nor Trisha, who were two sheets to the wind, realized it until he finally got enough breath to ask the maître d' for an ambulance.

"Anyway, I'm on my way and should be there in about twenty or thirty minutes," Ariel said.

"Sounds good, I'd like to check over the controls again. I know we've been in the simulator a lot this week making sure we are comfortable, but I want to recheck a few things," Trisha said.

They talked for a few more minutes before hanging up. Trisha knew she needed to make one more phone call before she flew out. She wanted to set up a time to meet with her dad so she could finally explain what she was planning to do. Pressing the pre-programmed number, she waited for his deep voice.

"Hello, baby girl," Paul Grove said softly. "How are you doing?"

Trisha felt the smile curving her lips. She loved her dad so much. "I'm doing good, Daddy. I'm missing you."

Paul Grove laughed. "Okay, when are you coming so we can head up into the mountains for a few days?"

"How do you know me so well?" Trisha said with a sigh.

"We're two of kind, baby girl. Give us the outdoors with room to roam and the peace and quiet of the world around us, and we can solve all the world's problems," Paul

Grove responded with a chuckle. "So, with those words of wisdom said, when are you coming out?"

"I'm doing a test flight to California for Boswell International. I should be back sometime tomorrow. I put in for my vacation starting on Monday. I'll be there sometime late Monday afternoon," Trisha said. Trisha used the word "vacation" instead of "resignation" because she didn't want her dad to worry and didn't have time to explain her decision. Some things were better said in person.

"Sounds good. I don't have any clients lined up until the end of the month. I'll keep my schedule clear. How long are you planning on staying?" Paul asked gruffly. He didn't want to admit to how much he missed Trisha. He knew she had her own life now, but it didn't mean he didn't miss her.

"I'm off until the end of the month. I was thinking we could talk when I get there. I wanted to run a few things by you," Trisha replied softly.

"Of course, baby girl. I can't wait to see you."

"Thanks, Daddy, I'll give you a call before I leave on Monday. I love you," Trisha said.

"I love you too, Trisha," Paul Grove said. "Be safe."

"Always!" Trisha responded lightly. She was feeling better all ready.

Trisha disconnected the call and focused on the rest of the drive to the airport. There were a lot of things she needed to think about. She needed to talk to Ariel. Trisha decided it was time for a change. She had given her resignation to Boswell International and was going to join her dad back at Grove Wildness Guides. After her accident, she realized she would never make it into the space program. She would never be able to touch the stars. She hoped that staying active in a career devoted to flying would have been enough to satisfy her, but there was still something missing. She finally realized she missed her quiet nights with her dad and the freedom of exploring the woods and mountains. But what she missed the most was the sense of being a part of a family. It was time to go home.

* * *

Trisha was working inside the jet by the time Ariel got there. She could hear her and Carmen outside but decided to stay focused on what she was doing. Ariel would take care of the outside inspections. Trisha was the pilot on this flight and Ariel was the co-pilot. They often switched back and forth.

A little while later, Trisha heard Cara's cheerful voice in the hanger. *Uh-oh,* Trisha thought as she listened. *Cara's on a caffeine high!* She couldn't help but grin. Cara was so much fun. Trisha and Ariel adopted her several years ago as their surrogate little sister. Cara had been going through a difficult time with one of the engineers at Boswell who was being a real dip-wad to her. When he showed up late one night at Cara's apartment and started to get a little physical with her, Trisha and Ariel, who were visiting Cara at the time, ended up escorting him out none to gently.

They told him in explicit detail what they would do to him if they ever saw him near her again. The jerk transferred overseas shortly afterward. Trisha chuckled as she remembered the look on his face as they walked him out.

Trisha stood up and stretched, trying to ease some of the tension in her shoulders. She decided she would see what Cara was up to before contacting the tower to see if they had permission for take-off. She'd checked the radar about an hour before, and it looked like the worst of the storm was passing through. It should be an easy take-off once they were given clearance.

Cara looked like she was just finishing up as Trisha stepped down the steps of the jet. "Hey, Trish."

Trisha turned as she reached the bottom step and walked toward her. Trisha gave Cara a big smile. "Hey, Cara. Welcome aboard! Is this your first flight on the new Phantom Series?"

"Yeah, I'm really looking forward to putting her through the ringer," Cara said. "Carmen coming too?"

"Yeah," Trisha said softly watching as Ariel headed toward her sister. "Ariel got permission for Carmen to tag along. We're heading to California to take home an artist the Boswells had commissioned to do a piece, and Carmen needed a lift," Trisha said. She pulled Cara's tool belt from her. It looked too heavy for Cara's small frame, but Trisha knew better. Cara was tough as nails when she had to be. Glancing back one last time at Ariel and Carmen, she turned to head up the stairs of the jet telling Cara softly under her breath, "She's still not doing too good."

Forty minutes later, Trisha received permission for take-off, and they were soon airborne. The next six or seven hours would have been boring, but Trisha decided she wanted to put the new jet through through its paces since they were making such a long flight. She wasn't quite ready to tell Ariel about her plans yet. She decided to tell her on the return flight. She figured she wouldn't have to worry about Carmen trying to kill her sister when she blew a gasket after she heard Trisha was giving up flying for a living.

Chapter 2

They landed back in Shelby, California a little after eight that night. The skies were beautiful with the stars twinkling up above. Trisha picked the brightest one and silently told her mom about her plans to return home. Trisha could have sworn it actually winked at her. Taking it as a good sign, she let the stress melt away. Trisha groaned as she stood up slowly, stretching. One thing she wouldn't miss about being a pilot were the cross-country and international flights where she sat for so long. She was still having problems if she was stationary for any length of time. She knew the stiffness would never go away. That was another deciding factor in her decision to resign her position at Boswell. She was just pulling her jacket off the back of her seat and was about to reach for the cabin door when Ariel put her hand on her arm stopping her.

"You know I'll understand whatever it is you're hiding from me, don't you?" Ariel said softly, looking into Trisha's eyes. "I know something's wrong. I'll always be there for you."

Tears burned the back of Trisha's eyes. She should have known Ariel would notice she wasn't herself lately. "I know." Trisha took a deep breath before blurting out what she had been afraid to tell her best friend.

"I've resigned my position at Boswell International, and I'm going home to work with my dad," Trisha said in a rush. Her heart was pounding as she waited for Ariel's response.

Ariel lifted an eyebrow at Trisha before she burst out laughing. "Is that all? I thought you were like, dying or something! So, when do we start?"

Trisha looked at Ariel in stunned silence. "What do you mean, when do we start? We who?"

"Me and you. I know your dad could use some help. He has called me at least once a week to get help with the paperwork ever since we left home! Remember, I was his bookkeeper before we left to join the Air Force. I've been doing all the major bookkeeping for the past ten-plus years," Ariel said with a grin.

"W-what?" Trisha stuttered. "He never said a word! I had no idea he was having problems."

"Not problems, necessarily. He has always hated doing the books. He would rather be out in the woods chasing the greenhorns. I've been talking to him for months about coming home but didn't want to leave you. I'm tired of all the traveling. Since things bombed between me and Eric, I thought it was time for a change. I asked your dad a couple of months ago if he would hire me if I came back home," Ariel said with a relieved grin before she turned and walked out the door of the cabin.

Trisha just stood looking at her best friend's back in stunned silence. They had grown up together in the small town of Casper Mountain, Wyoming. It had been Ariel, Carmen, and Trisha against the world. Since Trisha was an only child, having two other girls close to her age was wonderful. Ariel and Trisha were in the same grade while

Carmen was a year behind them. Ariel started working for Trisha's dad, doing the bookkeeping between her junior and senior year of high school. Both girls took college classes online while in high school and received their Associates degree by the time they graduated.

They were both just starting their sophomore year in college when Ariel and Carmen's parents were killed in a car crash. Trisha was sure the only thing that got Carmen through the rest of her senior year was having Trisha's dad there, and Scott, Carmen's high school sweetheart. Carmen and Scott got married just days after they graduated high school. Ariel and Trisha decided to go into the Air Force since both of them wanted to get into the space program. Ariel didn't make the cut—but Trisha had, at least, until the accident.

Trisha shook herself. She wasn't going to go there. She had been there a thousand times, and it always ended the same. She gave a cynical chuckle. *Isn't that the definition of insanity?* she thought to herself. *Doing the same thing over and over and expecting a different outcome.* Shaking her head, she walked through the cabin and followed Ariel down the steps. She chuckled softly as she remembered hearing Cara opening the door to the jet almost before they had come to a complete stop.

Abby was looking at Cara with a somewhat hesitant look when she and Ariel walked up to them. Trisha wondered if she thought they were supposed to be tipped or something. She looked that uncomfortable. Cara, on the other hand, looked like she was trying to think up some reason not to get back in the jet. Trisha had a feeling Cara would have strapped herself to the top of it if she could have managed it. Trisha didn't tell Cara, but both she and Ariel knew about Cara's claustrophobia. They'd already decided to stay for the night. There was no sense in wearing them both out and stressing Cara to the point she would drive them insane.

"It's really late for you to head out tonight. Would you like to stay at my place for the night? It's a little ways up the mountain, but it is really beautiful. I have an extra bedroom if you don't mind doubling up and an oversized couch that makes a great bed," Abby said, looking nervously back and forth between the three of them.

Trisha was just about to open her mouth to agree when Cara burst out in obvious relief. It took every bit of self-discipline inside Trisha not to laugh. Ariel rolled her eyes while she tried to hide her smile.

"Sounds great to me!" Cara said excitedly. "I'd go bonkers if I had to get back in that tin can tonight. I'd love to meet your man. You said he had some brothers? Any chance of meeting them between tonight and tomorrow morning? I love meeting new guys. I'm trying to break my record of driving them off. I think the longest any have put up with me has been ten minutes."

Trisha and Ariel laughed. "Ah, Cara, I think that Danny guy lasted twelve. What do you think, Ariel?"

"Oh, at least twelve, maybe even thirteen minutes," Ariel added.

Trisha winced. She was the one who'd snagged Cara's last blind date. It was not one of her shining moments. She decided to surprise Cara at dinner with a physics professor from the local university who lived across the hall from her. Cara had not been very happy with her choice. Grimacing, Trisha admitted she couldn't really blame Cara for that. The guy treated all three of them like they were imbeciles. Cara quickly turned the tables on him when she began her recitation of Stephen Hawking's theory of black holes (in exquisite detail) and how relationships could be correlated to it. The poor guy ended up having an asthma attack in the middle of it. It wouldn't have been so bad, except Trisha was well on her way to a really good hangover and was totally oblivious to his distress. She had given her notice at Boswell that afternoon and was celebrating a little early. Imagine her surprise when Ariel hadn't been in much better condition. Cara, being the only sober one of the group besides the physics professor, took one look at both of them and started laughing. Trisha knew, even as drunk as she was, that Cara was collecting blackmail points for future use. The last thing Trisha wanted to do was remind her of it.

"You two are nuts. You were so drunk," Cara said, laughing, "you can't even remember his name. It was Douglas. 'Not Dougie.'" Cara's perfect imitation of the outraged physics professor had Trisha and Ariel laughing so hard they had tears in their eyes.

"Oh yeah, good ol' Dougie," Trisha said, wiping her eyes. "How could we forget?"

Trisha looked at Abby and smiled. She knew her next words were more for Cara than for them, but she would never admit it. "Unlike some people we know, Ariel and I both need at least eight hours of sleep more than once a month to survive. We would love to take you up on both of your offers."

Abby frowned. "Both of my offers?"

"Yeah, bed and brothers." Trisha, Cara, and Ariel smirked.

Trisha went along with the joking about the brothers, but inside she winced. She was a lot like Carmen. She wasn't ready for another relationship yet. Trisha snorted silently. Maybe she was more like her dad. Her dad never did find another woman to replace her mom. Her parents married very young, younger than she and Peter, but theirs was a soul match. Her parents had been married a little over four years when her mom died suddenly. Trisha's dad turned all his love and attention on their infant daughter. Trisha knew her dad had a few affairs over the years but nothing that ever lasted very long. He never became serious about any of the women, no matter how much they tried to pressure him into making a commitment. She asked him once about it, but he just gave her a sad smile and said he hadn't found another woman who lit the same spark as her mom. He told her that if he ever did find another one like her mom, he would snatch her up so fast she wouldn't know what hit her. He and Trisha laughed and made a list of all the things he was looking for in a woman. She agreed that they had never found a woman who met all of the characteristics on his list. Trisha realized she had been looking for that special someone, too. She thought at the time it was Peter, but she had obviously been mistaken. Trisha jerked back to what was going on around her when Carmen came up silently behind them.

"I appreciate the offer, but I think I'll skip. I had transportation delivered earlier. I think I'll head out as I slept most of the trip," Carmen said quietly as she came up as if out of nowhere.

Trisha listened as Cara excitedly told Abby it wouldn't take long for her to get her stuff. Her focus, though, was on Ariel. She was worried about her. She knew better than anyone how much Ariel worried about her younger sister. Three years ago, neither one of them thought Carmen was even going to live. Ariel didn't renew her commission in the Air Force so she could stay at the hospital during those first critical weeks. Between Trisha's recovery and what happened to Carmen, Ariel's hands had been full three years ago, Trisha thought with regret. Damn, but she needed to keep her thoughts focused. If she wasn't careful, she would turn into a grumpy old lady.

"Okay. It'll take us about ten minutes or so to close everything up," Trisha said, glancing worriedly at Ariel.

Trisha turned and headed up the steps of the jet. It wouldn't take that long to get ready. They just needed to lock the jet down and get their bags. Trisha reached up into the storage unit near the front of the cabin and pulled her and Ariel's bags down. Gripping one in each hand, she turned to head back down the steps. She met Ariel at the bottom of the steps. Ariel secured the door to the jet before she turned back to Trisha and reached for her bag.

Handing Ariel her bag, Trisha murmured, "She'll be all right. It just takes time."

Ariel's eyes were bright with unshed tears. She cleared her throat before she responded, "Yeah, but how much time? It's been three years."

"It's been three years for me too, and I'm still not ready," Trisha replied softly. "She lost someone very special to her, Ariel. Not all of us heal at the same rate. Just look at my dad. You just have to take it one day at a time and hope it will get better," Trisha finished, looking off into the darkness with a haunted expression.

"I'm sorry," Ariel said, pulling Trisha into a one-armed hug. "Sometimes I forget you can understand what Carmen is going through better than me. Thank you for being there for the both of us."

"Hey, what are sisters for?" Trisha said with a grin. "Now, enough of all the sober, depressing stuff. I am sick of feeling bah humbug. Let's concentrate on all the fun we are going to have messing with the greenhorns. I think the Navy is still sending their Seals to my dad for training. I can't wait to see their faces when I tag them."

Ariel giggled at the thought. "You are so bad! You know they are going to need therapy after you mess with their heads, don't you?"

Trisha was just about to reply when she heard a popping sound. She and Ariel had been around enough gunfire to recognize it immediately. Both of them dropped their bags and took off at a fast run toward the parking lot where they had heard it. Trisha squeezed through the fencing first, followed closely by Ariel. Trisha breathed out a sigh of relief when she saw Cara and Carmen together. Her gaze searched frantically for Abby. She heard the sound of tires squealing and turned in time to see the taillights of a pickup truck leaving the parking area at a high speed.

"Shit, what happened?" Trisha asked.

Carmen spoke up before Cara could. Her expression was dark and deadly. Trisha could tell she was pissed. "Some asshole waylaid Abby. From the little I was able to gather he isn't too happy she didn't choose him instead of this Zoran guy. He stuck her with something and has her cuffed. I'm going to follow him. Keep your line open. I might need some backup." Carmen took off running toward a motorcycle hidden in the dark between two hangers before anyone could say anything.

"We need wheels," Ariel muttered darkly as she watched her sister take off after the pickup truck.

"On it," Cara said shakily before she ran across the dimly lit parking lot to Abby's truck. Trisha watched as Cara deftly unlocked the truck and had it running in a matter of seconds.

Cara face lit up with a big grin when she saw Trisha's raised eyebrow. "I used to have a problem with taking vehicles for a spin."

Trisha just shook her head as Ariel jumped into the truck, scooting over to the middle so she could get in. In a hand-to-hand confrontation, Trisha was still better than Ariel. Her dad taught her how to fight, sometimes not exactly fairly. He knew if she was out in the woods alone, sometimes for days or weeks, with some of their clients, she would need to be able to defend herself in any circumstance. Some of their clients did not like to lose to a woman. Paul Grove said it didn't matter if you were a male or a female when it came down to fighting for your life. You either knew how to fight to live or you died. He made sure his little girl knew how to fight to live.

Trisha listened intently to the conversation between Ariel and Carmen. When Cara threw in one of her off-the-wall comments, Trisha couldn't help but respond. Only Cara would be able to think of working on something mechanical while in a high-speed chase.

Trisha rolled her eyes when Cara commented on Abby's truck acceleration. "Only you would be thinking about something like that while chasing down bad guys in the middle of nowhere."

"Hey, I can work on more than one thing at a time," Cara said right before she took a turn on two wheels instead of four.

Trisha wasn't the only one letting out a long string of expletives she'd learned while in the Air Force. Ariel was keeping up with her pretty well while Cara just laughed. Trisha wasn't sure she wanted to know where Cara had learned to drive like this.

Chapter 3

Kelan Reykill sat in the commander's conference room aboard the *V'ager*, the Valdier warship he commanded. It was the largest and most sophisticated ship in their fleet thanks to his brother Trelon's constant upgrades. He was studying the reports that were brought to him with a frown. He wasn't concerned about the reports pertaining to the planet below them. Zoran already warned them about the primitive planet he had taken refuge on. Zoran told them to come in using extreme caution as the inhabitants of the planet were unaware of other life-forms that existed outside their galaxy. Trelon already made sure they would remain undetected. Kelan wasn't even worried about when he, Trelon, and a few others transported down as they would be more than capable of defending themselves based on the information the reports contained about the planet's military. They could simply transport out and be out of the solar system before the military even knew they were there.

No, what worried him was what happened to his older brother, Zoran. Kelan seethed as he read over the report on his brother's capture and torture. He was in constant contact with his other two brothers back on Valdier. Mandra and Creon knew Zoran was captured by a group of Curizan warriors, but something just wasn't adding up. They had been at peace with their former enemies for well over a century. It didn't make sense. He knew the members of the royal house of Curizan. Ha'ven, leader of the Curizans, was his brother Creon's closest friend. Well, as close of a friend as Creon would admit to having. He knew

Creon saved Ha'ven's life during the wars, and that was one of the factors that brought it to an end.

Why would they have taken him to a remote military base that had been abandoned eons ago? Why did they want to know the secrets of the symbiotic relationship between a Valdier warrior, his dragon, and his symbiot? Others had tried in the past to gain such knowledge by trying to capture a warrior's symbiot. Every time it ended with the captor being killed by the symbiot. It was this knowledge that gave the leaders of Valdier the power they needed to open their planet to trade almost three hundred years ago. By then, the end of the Three Wars between the Sarafin, the Curizan, and the Valdier was coming to a close. Trade agreements and peace treaties were signed. In exchange for possible mates, the Valdier would trade some of their powerful crystals to the Curizan. The Sarafin were promised the first-born daughter of the King of Valdier would be mated to the first-born son of the King of the Sarafin. Unfortunately, Kelan's father, who wrote and negotiated that particular treaty, did not inform the Sarafin that females were few and far between for the Valdier, especially those of the royal house. The treaty was signed over a century before, and so far, the Valdier had no problems with the Sarafin. In fact, his brother Trelon was a frequent visitor to their spaceports and did a significant amount of trading with them.

Kelan rubbed his stomach in irritation. Ever since his brother Zoran introduced them to his true mate, Abby, Kelan's dragon had been acting up. Kelan always prided himself on his ability to deal and negotiate with his more primal half, but ever since it laid eyes on the dragon's mark on Abby's neck, it was a constant battle to get his dragon to calm down. He wanted to get to the planet and find his mate. *If one true mate can be found on this primitive planet, then so can another. Mine!* His dragon growled in annoyance. *Go, now. Find my mate.*

Will you just back off! Kelan growled back in anger. *We have more important things to do. Plus, there is little likelihood of finding a mate on this planet. You know how our symbiot is! It is so picky, we have never even been able to have sex with a female if it is in the same room that we are.*

Kelan's symbiot looked up at him with a low snarl and showed its teeth. It was in the shape of their huge werecat, a creature known for gutting its prey and eating it while it was still alive. Kelan's dragon snarled back, for all the good it did either of them. The symbiot could tell through the bands wrapped around his upper arms what his dragon was doing, but it merely snorted before lowering its head. It knew that when it came to the final acceptance of a female as a true mate, if the symbiot did not accept the female, then the dragon would not accept it. And if the symbiot didn't accepted the female, and the dragon refused to breathe the dragon's fire into her, Kelan knew he was totally screwed. There was no way he would ever have his true mate without all three of them accepting her.

Kelan threw the report down on the table in front of him with a growl. He didn't have time to waste on fantasies. If he hadn't found a female yet out of all the females he'd bedded on Valdier—*and Curizan and Sarafin and a few others*—his symbiot added through images with a yawn…Kelan snarled loudly at his symbiot in response. His symbiot stood up slowly and shook before turning its head and walking out of the room. Kelan ran his hands through his hair, wishing he could get rid of his dragon as easily as that. It was tearing gouges inside him like a werecat sharpening its claws. He needed to remain focused on the situation at hand. Closing his eyes, he sought the calm he was renowned for having before he opened his eyes again with a steely determination glittering from them. First things first, get Zoran and Abby. Next, return to Valdier and find out what Mandra and Creon have discovered. Last, kill the bad guys. A smile curved Kelan's lips as he found his center again. His dragon could just go take a long cold shower until they were done.

* * *

It was dark by the time they transported down. They decided it would be better to use the cover of darkness. The darkness did not affect them. They simply let their dragon come to their aid as it could see in the dark just as well as during the day. Kelan studied the meadow where Zoran landed initially. He had to practically tie his dragon down to keep him under control. The only thing that worked so far was the threat of not leaving the warship and sending another in his place. Only then did his dragon finally calm down and behave himself. His symbiot walked around the meadow exploring in a slow, disinterested manner. Kelan noticed a change in his symbiot lately and was concerned. He never heard of a symbiot losing its will to live, for its very essence was attached to his own, but his was spending more and more time simply lying around watching the other symbiots and their warriors. It no longer actively sought the company of the other symbiots on the warship like it did before. He made a mental note to ask Zoran to look in the Archives of Knowledge to see if there was any reference to the symptoms his symbiot was displaying. Zoran, as ruler of the Valdier, was the only one to have access to them because they were said to explain the origins of the symbiot.

Kelan walked over to where Trelon and Zoran were. He was so deep in thought he didn't notice the immediate change in Zoran until Trelon made a comment. Glancing at his older brother, Kelan studied his face trying to see if there was any difference in him now that he had a true mate.

"Zoran, all is well?" Trelon asked.

From the dazed expression on Zoran's face followed by the fierce relief and joy, he would have to say yes; there was definitely a change. He had never known Zoran to be anything but stern and reserved. Now, his whole face changed as he responded to Trelon's question.

Zoran looked at Trelon as if coming out of a daze, a huge smile on his face. "She has returned."

Kelan grinned at Zoran. Trelon must have also noticed the same change because he was wearing a huge grin as well. Kelan fought back a chuckle as he watched Zoran's dragon fight to come out. He wanted his mate. *He isn't the only one who would like to see his mate,* Kelan's dragon said sarcastically. Kelan barely hid his jerk of surprise. Since when had his dragon learned how to be sarcastic? What in the hell was going on? First, his symbiot was walking around looking like he had killed its best friend. Now, his dragon was giving him lip. Since when did he start losing so much control over the other parts of himself? He never lost control! He was known for his strict self-discipline. In fact, his ability to remain in command in any situation, no matter how difficult or dangerous, was still discussed with awe among the warriors. And, he was known for his skill at handling any challenge, no matter how impossible it seemed. He had proved himself time and time again before, during, and after the Three Wars.

Yes, but none of those skills have helped you find us a mate, have they? his dragon retorted angrily.

Shut up, will you? Kelan thought furiously. *Just keep your focus on getting Zoran and his true mate off this planet, or so help me, I won't let you out for a month once we get back.*

It wasn't much as far as threats went, but it was the only thing Kelan could think of to shut his dragon up for a few precious seconds of peace. Kelan's symbiot just walked over and lay down at his feet, ignoring the conflict going on between Kelan and his dragon.

Zoran's face creased into a smile, and he said in a relieved tone, "Soon you will meet my true mate."

Kelan watched as his younger brother picked on Zoran. When Trelon playfully punched Kelan in the arm, wanting him to grab Zoran, Kelan just shook his head with an answering grin. It had been a long time since they had wrestled with each other. All five brothers were very close growing up, often getting into trouble together. Their father and mother tried futilely to separate them on more than one occasion when they had been particularly mischievous. That never stopped them, though. They simply shifted and took off for the dense forests that covered their world. Kelan chuckled when he saw Trelon reaching for Zoran. Zoran suddenly became very still, frowning in concentration.

"Abby will not be returning alone. There are three females with her," Zoran grumbled.

"Perhaps she brings our true mates to us," Trelon teased. "I, for one, am not ready, but perhaps Kelan, Mandra, and Creon might appreciate having one. I still have much to taste before I settle for one female."

Kelan choked out a laugh and grabbed Trelon around the neck, imaging it was his dragon's when the damn thing roared out excitedly at the idea of meeting its potential mate. As Kelan fought to control his dragon, he couldn't resist ribbing Trelon. "You believe yourself a bull dragon to satisfy so many females. It takes that many because none could ever put up with you for long."

Trelon responded to Kelan's comment just as Kelan knew he would, by trying to take him down. Kelan may have been slightly taller and a year older than Trelon, but Trelon was definitely broader and more muscular. Kelan had just twisted to break the hold Trelon was trying to get around his neck when he heard Zoran's roar of rage. In a flash, he shifted and called to his symbiot. Golden armor swiftly covered his arms, legs, and chest. He rose into the air, prepared for battle.

* * *

Kelan listened intently to the conversation between his two brothers. At first, he regretted sending the other warriors back to the warship. If necessary, he could call to them to return. Until he knew what the issue was, he did not want to endanger any of his men's lives. When Zoran explained his true mate had been attacked, he began forming strategies to get her back. It appeared there was only one male involved that they knew of. There was no need to call for additional support. One primitive male would be no match for the three skilled warriors. Kelan notified the *V'ager* via his symbiot to be prepared for a swift departure and to prepare medical just in case it was needed for Zoran's mate. He was not concerned about the welfare of the male who had taken her. That one was already dead as far as Kelan was concerned.

* * *

Trisha gripped the armrest with one hand and put her other hand on the dashboard to try to keep from being tossed around. Cara was doing a great job of driving, but it was still scaring the shit out of her. Both she and Ariel were cussing up a blue streak. When Cara made the turn onto the gravel road, Trisha began wondering if it would be a good time to start praying again. She was doing the best she could to keep the taillights of Carmen's motorcycle in sight. Since Carmen was running dark, the only time they could see her was when she hit the brakes, which didn't seem often enough for Trisha's peace of mind. *She must be traveling like a bat out of hell to be so far ahead of us,* Trisha thought. When the truck slid dangerously close to the trees on Trisha's side of the truck, she didn't say a word, but the sweat beading on her forehead was enough to show it was closer than she was comfortable with. A flashback to her own accident was enough to make her swallow down the nausea that threatened. She couldn't lose it now. She had to keep control until this was over and Abby was safe. Focus on Abby, she kept telling herself.

Trisha could see Cara was fighting to maintain control of the pickup truck. When she didn't see Carmen's taillights, she became worried that Carmen might have taken a spill and was lying in the middle of the road where they couldn't see her. If they came upon her suddenly, there would be no way to avoid hitting her.

"Do you see her?" Trisha asked anxiously, voicing her fears. "I can barely see a thing. I would hate for Carmen to wreck in the middle of the road and not see her until too late."

"She's fine. I think I saw some brake lights up ahead through the trees," Ariel bit out between bumps. "God, Cara. Do you think you could hit any more ruts?"

Ariel no sooner finished her sentence when she was thrown into Trisha. Trisha couldn't quite contain the groan that escaped her when her head hit the passenger side window hard. She knew she was going to have a nice knot on her head. The bad thing was she couldn't even let go of her grip long enough to rub it out. Gritting her teeth together, she pushed back the pain. She had gotten pretty good at doing that, she thought with a dry sense of humor.

Trisha bit back a laugh as Cara responded to Ariel. She wasn't about to say a word. Cara had a long memory, and Trisha didn't want to be on her bad side. She was still waiting for the payback for the blind date. In fact, Trisha wouldn't have been in the least bit surprised if Cara didn't pull over and tell Ariel she could drive if she thought she could do it better.

"I'm doing the best I can. It is darker than shit out here, and I don't think this road has ever been graded! You try driving over twenty miles an hour on it and see if you can do any better," Cara said crossly.

Yup, Cara is pissed, Trisha thought. When she heard the sound of metal scraping, she cringed.

"I can fix that," Cara said loudly over the screeching.

Trisha bit back a chuckle and just shook her head. Knowing Cara, she would too, and it would be even better than before. That thought had no sooner left her brain when she saw a flash of bright blue light. She turned around to see what it was just as Cara called out.

"Son of a bitch! What was that?" Cara gasped.

Ariel twisted around to trying to see out the back window. "I don't know. You didn't hit the gas tank or anything did you?"

"Of course, she didn't," Trisha bit out tensely, gripping the dashboard harder so she wouldn't be thrown into the side window again. "That would have been us, otherwise. Just don't give her any ideas!"

Trisha turned around in time to gasp as another flash lit up the night. Her eyes widened as she saw Carmen's motorcycle lying on its side behind the pickup truck of the man who had kidnapped Abby. They were about twenty-five yards ahead of them.

"Holy shit! Did you see that?" Cara asked looking up through the windshield.

Trisha's eyes were focused on the struggle going on in the truck in front of them. She could see inside the cab as the light came on when the driver's-side door opened. She watched as the man leaned over Abby. After a moment, he began pulling her out of the truck by her hair.

"Oh, my God. Abby!" Trisha cried out.

Trisha struggled to open the door to the truck just as it rolled to a stop behind the pickup in front of them. She ignored everything else but the need to get to Abby. She almost fell as her feet connected with the uneven surface of the gravel road. Trisha bit back a curse. She was still stiff from the flight and was having difficulty getting her muscles to work right. Biting back a cry of pain, she forced herself to move out of the way so Ariel could climb out after her.

"Where's Carmen?" Ariel called out frantically as she slid out of the truck.

Trisha gave a cry of alarm as she watched three huge creatures surround the man who had pulled Abby out of the truck. Within seconds, more of the bright blue fire appeared and surrounded the man. Trisha watched in horror as the man was engulfed in flames, his silent screams were frozen on his face for just a moment before his body dissolved into a pile of ash.

* * *

Kelan kept Zoran in his sights as he followed him to Abby. He flew fast and silent, his huge body moving in a graceful rhythm while his keen eyesight looked down through the dark forest below for any sign of Zoran's mate. Kelan watched as Zoran suddenly dropped down out of the sky, shifting at the last possible moment so he could land in the back of the pickup truck holding Abby. Kelan swerved up and over some trees before he fell back behind the other strange transports that were following Zoran's mate. He spewed dragon fire behind the last transport causing several large trees to explode and effectively block the road. He would have just destroyed the transport, but he wanted to find out what they wanted with Zoran's mate first. Did they know about Zoran? Were they helping the man who had taken Abby? He circled around and was coming in for a landing when he saw the man who was holding Abby raise a weapon and fire point-blank into Zoran's chest. Cold rage gripped him for a moment as he watched his brother collapse. He let out a roar. To attack one Valdier warrior was to attack them all. The man and any of the others who were helping him were dead. They just didn't know it yet.

Kelan moved in to land just as a dark shape appeared out from the side of the road and tackled the man with the gun.

Kelan's head jerked around when he heard Trelon's voice. *"Kelan, do you have a fix on the others?"*

"Yes," Kelan replied, focusing again on the other transport. He could already see Zoran was moving again. He should have known better than to worry about his older brother. The corner of his mouth twitched into amusement as he saw the exact moment Zoran's symbiot finished healing him. *"The other transport is coming up fast, and there is one who is fighting the man who harmed Zoran. Perhaps we should let that one live if he wins,"* Kelan responded.

Kelan landed next to Trelon just as Zoran stood up. He watched silently as the face of Abby's abductor changed from triumph to horror as Zoran sentenced him to death before he shifted. Blue flames poured out of Zoran, engulfing the human male in dragon fire. Within moments, nothing remained of the human but ash.

Kelan carefully cataloged the scene around him as he prepared to finish off the other humans. The one who tackled the man lay prone on the ground. Kelan could smell the blood and could tell from the heartbeat the man would not survive for long. His head turned as the other transport drew to a sliding stop, and he watched as three figures slid out of it. The one closest to them was tiny. Kelan's keen eyesight noticed right away that the figure was a female, not a male, and she was armed with some type of metal bar. He ignored the weapon. He could disarm her in seconds.

His gaze swung to the other two figures as they came around the side of the transport. In that moment, his life changed forever.

Chapter 4

Trisha vaguely heard Cara call out to Ariel as she moved toward Abby. Trisha stood frozen in place as Ariel pushed past her and ran to where Carmen was lying in the dirt. Her eyes flickered between the three huge shapes. Trisha moved cautiously toward Ariel, who was kneeling on the ground next to Carmen. Trisha could almost hear her father's voice in her head as she approached the massive figures. *Always assess the situation, baby girl. Make sure you know what you are getting yourself into before you make a move.* Trisha tried desperately to think about how she could assess this one! Her father never taught her how to deal with creatures that could breathe fire and had huge wings. Her mind tried to flit through some of the movies she had seen to see if any of the scenarios in them might actually work. She was definitely drawing a blank here. She would give anything to call her dad and ask for his advice. He would know what to do. He always did. She absently patted her uniform to see if she actually had her cellphone on her. She didn't, of course. Her uniform didn't have any pockets on it. The designer said it messed up the sleek lines of the design when Trisha and Ariel requested some pockets be included in the female uniforms. Her cell phone was in her jacket pocket which was lying on the tarmac back at the Shelby airport.

Trisha's eyes widened when a beautiful—it was the only way she could describe it—jade green and silver dragon with glowing gold eyes moved a step toward her. She was captivated by its beauty. For several timeless moments she couldn't see anything else. The regal head and blazing eyes, the huge body encased in gold, the long curve of its claws, and the graceful whip-like tail with silver and gold spikes on the end. Trisha cataloged each magnificent part of the dragon's body, unable to break the hold it held over her. She felt like it was calling to her, demanding she surrender to it. Trisha's whole body shook as she fought for control. She felt like she was drowning. It was Ariel's soft cry for help that finally penetrated the daze that clouded her mind and forced her out of her reverie. Trisha shook her head at the dragon, breaking the hold it had on her before she hurried over to Ariel.

"How is she?" Trisha asked quietly as she knelt down next to Ariel. She made sure she kept her senses tuned to what was going on around her. It could turn ugly real fast, and she wanted to be prepared in case it did.

"There's so much blood," Ariel said frantically as she tried to use the cap Carmen had been wearing to stem some of the blood flow from the wounds to her chest. "Her pulse is getting erratic. I think one of the wounds may have hit her lung."

Ariel turned to the huge green, red, and gold dragon. "Please, help me. She's my sister. Please…" Ariel's voice faded as tears filled her eyes.

Trisha heard the dragon growl out something to the two standing next to them. She had a sense of forewarning that something was about to happen, and she didn't think she was going to like it. She stood quickly and went to turn toward the truck. Her legs, still stiff from the long flight and torturous truck ride, gave out on her. She gasped and reached out trying to keep her balance. Her hands encountered a silky smooth wall. Trisha's eyes jerked up as she realized the jade green and silver dragon had stepped in front of her when she started to fall. Long, curved claws gently held her elbows while her hands were splayed across a wide chest covered in some type of gold armor. Trisha's eyes widened as thin threads of gold began weaving out from the armor and up through her fingers and along her wrists where they formed delicate bracelets. She felt a sudden warmth invade her, almost as if the gold bands were trying to reassure her she was safe, protected. Trisha's head snapped back when she felt vibrations under the palms of her hands as the dragon purred at her. She was staring into a pair of flaming gold eyes when a bright light suddenly surrounded her.

* * *

Trisha blinked several times to adjust her vision as the bright light blinded her. She realized two things immediately—she was no longer on a dark road outside of Shelby, California, and the dragon who had been holding her was now a very tall man. Trisha tried to jerk her hands back, but the huge male holding her by her elbows pulled her closer with a low growl, as if warning her not to move away from him. She turned her head as a group of men rushed toward Ariel and Carmen. When she struggled to free herself to go to them, the huge male simply tightened his grip and snarled something at the men.

Trisha watched as Carmen was carefully lifted onto some type of gurney with tubular sides that closed around her body. Two other men restrained Ariel by her arms when she started to fight the men who were taking Carmen away from her. Trisha couldn't understand what any of them were saying, but she felt like they were trying to help Carmen, not hurt her.

"Let me go!" Trisha said as she struggled against the man holding her. "I need to go with them. They are my sisters. I have to be with them."

Trisha could feel the man's indecisiveness before he grunted and slowly released her. As soon as she was free, she moved to follow Ariel and the other men who had Carmen. Subconsciously, she counted the number of men in the room and along the corridors. She knew she was on some type of spaceship—this was something a rational part of her said she would dissect later—but she needed to focus on making a mental map of where they were going for now. She would need the information if they were to get away and back home. The tall man who had been holding her followed them closely. Trisha shivered as she got the weirdest feeling he didn't want her out of his sight.

* * *

Kelan was in a daze. The female was his true mate. There was no other explanation for the way he felt when he'd first laid eyes on her standing so still by the foreign transport. His dragon's response the moment she walked around it was evidence enough he accepted her. It took every bit of self-discipline in him to not just sweep her up in his arms and fly to a secluded place where he could claim her. His dragon's roar filled his head as he followed her and the other two women to medical. *Mine! Mine! My mate!* It snarled at the men they passed. Kelan's eyes were glowing with gold flames daring any other male to even look at her. The message must have been clear because the warriors they passed in the corridors on the way to medical gave him a wide berth.

His eyes moved lower to the gold bands wrapped around the female's wrists. His symbiot had changed into the shape of a large creature resembling the dog that stayed with Abby. It was trotting next to the female, making sure its head or another part of its large body brushed against hers as she walked. Kelan's lips curved when the female absently reached out and ran her fingers along its big head. His eyes drooped in pleasure, and a low rumble broke from his throat before he could contain it. Kelan felt the touch as if she had run her fingers along his skin. The warmth of it was transmitted through the bands around his upper arms. He loved the way her hair swung back and forth as she walked. His eyes followed the path down her back, to her slim waist and full hips. She was slightly taller than the other two females. He liked that. He really liked her long legs. His body heated up, and his groin filled and pulsed at the idea of them being wrapped tightly around him as pumped deep inside her. He wanted to mark her so badly he could practically taste her on his lips. His dragon was moving in circles inside him, panting and pacing as it fought back its own desire. There was no doubt his symbiot accepted her. His dragon was more than ready to bite her and initiate the dragon's fire mating into her, and Kelan had to admit as he clenched his fists in a desperate effort to not grab her and take her in the middle of the corridor, he wanted her just as bad.

* * *

Kelan let out a curse. It had been three days! Three long, hard, frustrating days! His cock turned hard as a stone whenever he thought about the female he'd brought aboard. The only time he had been able to hold her was in those few precious moments back on the primitive planet and on the transporter platform. Since then, one mishap after another had prevented him from having a chance to even speak with her.

After following her to medical to see how the injured female was doing, he pulled the healer aside. Kelan wanted the translator implanted in the females as soon as possible so he could talk to his true mate. Unfortunately, he was called away shortly afterward on an emergency. It seemed as if his younger brother Trelon had destroyed their transporter room. He later found out it was his brother in his dragon form and his symbiot. They attacked a warrior who had touched the female Trelon wanted to claim. Then, he received some messages from both of his brothers back on Valdier. They needed him home as soon as possible. He no sooner gave the command to take them home before he started getting reports from Jarak, his head of security. It appeared Trelon's mate, Cara, was reprogramming everything. He and Jarak spent hours trying to figure out what she was doing and how she was doing it. Every time they thought they finally figured out what she was doing, she would be into something else. Then, to top everything off, he received a report that the injured female was fine now, but she had almost killed one of their males. The man was in medical due to injuries he received in the transporter room brawl. The healer informed Kelan the man was given authorization for release back to his normal duties and thought to celebrate by offering to have sex with the female named Carmen before his next shift. The female obviously did not like that idea. It might not have been so bad, but the other two females, Ariel and Trisha, reacted badly when his security force tried to restrain Carmen who was attacking the warrior in question. He now needed to repair his medical unit. He finally ordered the females, Ariel and Carmen, removed to their own quarters where they were being guarded around the clock. It appeared their skills had drawn the interest of the unmated warriors on board who wanted a chance to court the warrior females. Kelan couldn't handle any more destruction of his warship; between Trelon, Cara, and the three females, he was pulling his hair out.

Kelan let out a deep breath as he tried to find his center again. He hadn't seen his symbiot since the female came on board. *Trisha,* Kelan breathed out her name. It was as lovely as she was, he thought. He ordered Jarak to escort Trisha to his living quarters last night after Carmen was given the all clear to be moved out of medical. His true mate refused to leave the medical unit until she knew Carmen was going to be all right. Jarak called to tell him she refused at first to leave the other two females until Jarak pointed out the living quarters were too small for the three of them. He assured her she would not be far from her two sisters and could see them at any time. It was only after he reassured her several times that she agreed to follow him.

Kelan could feel his dragon pouting. He wanted to go to her last night. He wanted to curl up with his mate. Kelan knew exactly what he was feeling. He was exhausted as well and could think of nothing more gratifying than to curl up in his bed with his cock buried deep inside Trisha. Just the thought of it had his body hardening again. He couldn't remember the last time he had so little control over his body and feelings. Kelan decided the *V'ager* could do without him for a little while. Snapping out an order he was not to be disturbed unless they were under attack from someone other than Trelon's mate, he left the bridge, striding with determination toward his living quarters. It was time to go claim his mate.

* * *

Trisha woke up feeling angry, frustrated, and worried. Three days had passed since their arrival aboard the warship. Her dad was probably frantic by now. Harry, the old airport air traffic controller she had met when she first flew in to pick Abby up would have found their bags by the jet and notified the local authorities about them. Her dad would have expected her phone call two days ago, as well. He knew if she said she was going to call, she would. She would never tell him that and not follow through. She had to get back to Earth. She couldn't imagine never seeing him again.

Trisha turned her head as she felt a movement on the bed next to her. The huge golden dog-looking creature who had been her constant companion for the last three days was lying curled up next to her. It was watching her with big, soulful golden eyes. Trisha smiled gently and ran her hand over its head and down its back. It had been her shadow since her arrival on board the ship, sleeping next to her in the medical wing and keeping any of the big males away from her. She didn't where it had come from or even what it was, but it seemed to have attached itself to her. She laughed softly as she felt the warmth spread through her fingers and up her arm. It didn't take long before the bed began to vibrate as it purred.

Shaking her head, Trisha climbed out of the huge bed. She was going to get cleaned up and go find her friends. They needed to get home as soon as possible. She didn't care if she had to tear the spaceship apart. She wanted to go home now!

Trisha padded barefoot into the bathroom. She figured out last night how to use the shower unit and toilet after a few trials and errors. It really wasn't that different from hers back home as far as how it looked, but how it worked was another matter. During her exploration of the cabin, she found some clothing in one of the panels in the wall and decided to use one of the shirts as a nightgown. It was plenty big enough. As she went through the clothing a shiver ran down her spine. She felt like she hadn't been given just any random room. She wasn't real sure who the room belonged to, but she suspected it might be the tall man who had grabbed her down on Earth. Another shiver went up her spine as she remembered the beauty of his body and the strength in his arms as he held her. Trisha wasn't a weakling. She had grown up always being physically active thanks to her dad, but since her accident, working out was a necessity. If she didn't work out, she didn't walk. It took her over a year of intensive physical therapy to learn how to walk again. She was never going to go back to a wheelchair if she could help it. Anyway, it didn't matter to her who the room belonged to—as far as she was concerned she was going home today, so he could have it back.

Trisha thought back to last night as she brushed her hair out and piled it up on top of her head. So much had happened. After Carmen creamed the guy in the medical unit, they were escorted out of it. Of course, she and Ariel helped a little with the creaming part. When the doctor called for security, all hell broke loose when two of the men tried to grab Carmen who was beating the shit out of the guy who propositioned her. Ariel jumped into the fray adding to the confusion. When one of the men grabbed her, Trisha couldn't stay out of it any longer. The three girls always stuck together. By the time they were done, the man was readmitted to medical for additional healing, and the medical unit was in shambles with broken chairs, overturned beds, and bent instrument trays. The bent trays were Trisha's doing.

They are going to need a team of carpenters to repair the damage, Trisha thought with a grin as she passed by a hole in the wall near the door. *The last time I had this much fun was in the bar fight down in New Mexico the weekend before Scott and Carmen took off for South America.*

Trisha was alarmed at first when she was told she was not going to be staying with Ariel and Carmen. They were shown to a much smaller cabin containing only a large bed, a bathroom, and a small table with two chairs. She was determined not to be separated from them, but the huge man who escorted them insisted she follow him. It was only when he promised she could return to see her "sisters" that she gave in. In truth, she was exhausted from staying up for the past two nights worrying about Carmen. She hadn't been able to sleep at all in the chair, and there were no free beds because not long after they arrived the medical room became swamped with injured men. All she was able to get out of it was bits and pieces. Something about a guy named Trelon, a dragon, his symbiot, and his mate. All she knew was there was barely even any room to sit down by the time the last guy was brought in.

Her first priority after she was left alone last night had been to find a weapon. She explored the room extensively trying to find anything she could use. She found a sharp curved blade in the bathroom that she kept with her, as well as a smaller knife next to some fruit on a small table in the other room.

Trisha sighed as she stepped into the shower, letting the warm flow of steam pour over her. She hated that she was always stiff in the morning. She almost wished she didn't need to sleep. If she kept moving she was fine; it was only when she stopped for any length of time that the pain came back.

She slowly stretched as the warm steam poured over her tight muscles. The showers were different. They consisted of a type of misting steam that jetted out on three sides from top to bottom. The jets were of a pale purple color that changed after just a few seconds. Trisha discovered the purple was a type of cleansing soap. The mist then changed to a rose color before becoming clear. When it was done, a light came out and seemed to surround her. She was not only clean, but mostly dry. She shook her and smiled. She definitely couldn't complain about the effiency aboard as far as showers went.

Saves on having to do a lot of laundry, Trisha thought with a humorous twist to her lips.

She sighed heavily. She needed to get with Ariel and Carmen. If Abby wanted to stay with her guy, that was one thing, but she, Ariel, and Carmen had nothing to hold them here and everything to get back to. Trisha frowned. She didn't know what happened to Cara. Had she gotten away? She had been over near Abby. If she was able to escape, then she would let Trisha's dad know what happened to them. There wasn't anything he could do to save her, but he had taught her how to save herself. He would know she would do whatever she could to get back to him. Trisha prayed Cara had gotten away. She hated the idea of her dad not knowing what happened to her, Ariel, and Carmen.

Trisha stepped out of the shower unit and out of habit reached for a towel to wrap around herself. She was glad that Carmen was alive and well. It had been touch and go for a while. She knew that Carmen would have never made it if it hadn't been for the advanced technology. It was beyond mind-boggling that she been healed so quickly! She would have been in intensive care for at least a week. That was if she'd even lived, which Trisha seriously doubted she would have considering the wounds she received. Then there was the translator that was imbedded in all of them. Trisha hadn't understood any of the words the men were saying until one older man came over to her and Ariel and indicated he wanted to check them out. Before she knew what was happening, he pressed a device up against her skull. Ariel started toward him when she saw what he was doing but stopped when Trisha told her she understood what the man was saying. The healer apologized as he explained he implanted a translator so they could communicate.

Trisha walked into the bedroom to retrieve her clothes when the low sound of a growl made her turn in surprise. Trisha spun around awkwardly, gripping the small knife in one hand and the larger curved knife in the other. Standing in the doorway was the tall man from the transporter room. His eyes glowed a brilliant gold as he stood staring at her.

Chapter 5

Kelan couldn't suppress the low growl that escaped him at the scent of his mate. It seemed to fill his living quarters with the essence of wild spices and something else. He didn't have a chance to discern the elusive fragrance before the female appeared from the cleansing unit wearing nothing more than a towel—and holding two very sharp knives. He frowned as he watched her move into a defensive stance. He did not want her to be afraid of him.

"I will not harm you," Kelan began as he took a step toward Trisha, his hands raised up. "You may give me the knives."

Trisha shook her head and took a slight step back and to the side. She didn't want to give him a chance to corner her. "You can leave, and I'll keep the knives," she replied calmly as her dad's training kicked in.

"These are my living quarters. Why would I leave?" Kelan said with a slight smile as he took another step toward Trisha.

Trisha studied the man in front of her carefully as he talked. She noticed he moved gracefully, quietly. He was taller than her by almost a foot and outweighed her by at least a hundred pounds or more. He was very handsome in a rough sort of way. His black hair was tied back and hung almost halfway down his back. He was lean but muscular, with a wide chest and narrow waist. His face and coloring reminded Trisha of some of the Native Americans she knew near her hometown. He had the same type of graceful movement and quiet strength she saw in them.

His eyes were what caught and held her attention the most. They were a deep dark-gold color with what looked like tiny flames burning inside them. His pupils were different too. They were elongated instead of round, Trisha observed with fascination. Trisha moved back another step as a wave of longing surged through her. She didn't understand why she felt such a need to go to him, to touch him. She cursed silently and forced her raving hormones back down where they belonged, buried deep inside her. The last thing she needed to do was get distracted by a hunk of alien male when she needed to find a way home. Trisha decided space was what she needed to win this particular battle. She wasn't far from the bathroom and her "safe space." Last night before she went to bed, she pulled the panel off the inside of the door controls so all she would need to do was slice through the wiring to seal it shut behind her in case she needed an escape route. From the look tall, dark, and dangerous was giving her, she felt like she was probably going to need it!

Trisha drew in a shaky breath. "Until I leave, it is mine," Trisha said waving the smaller knife toward him in an attempt to appear nonchalant. "And you can just stop right there. I'll have no problem gutting you if you come any closer."

Trisha blew a strand of hair away from her face as she continued to watch the man in front of her. No, gutting was not what she was really thinking of doing to him. She was thinking more like serving him on a platter laid out like her own personal all-you-can-eat buffet. *Damn, if I don't get out of here, I'm going to be the one doing the attacking!* Trisha thought in dismay. She never thought like this!

* .* .*

Kelan chuckled as his dragon practically squirmed at the thought of pouncing on his mate. He could smell her arousal, and it was igniting a matching flame in him and his dragon. Never in his lifetime had Kelan felt his dragon act so playful before. He wanted to chase, pounce, and devour his mate in only the most delicious way. Kelan was so distracted by his dragon's behavior and his own response to the idea of burying himself balls deep inside her that he missed the slight movement of his mate as she took another big step backward. The next thing he knew, the door to the cleansing room had closed.

Cursing under his breath at his dragon for distracting him, Kelan strode over to the door. *Enough of this,* he thought savagely. *It is time to claim her and be done with all the madness.* He was so used to the doors opening automatically for him as it was programmed to do, that he didn't even pause until he hit it face-first.

Kelan grabbed his aching nose. "What the...?" Kelan muttered darkly. He swiped his hand over the keypad. Nothing! What the hell was going on? Every door on the warship was programmed to open for him! He was the commanding officer; no room was off limits to him.

"Open this door!" Kelan said with a muffled growl. Damn, but his nose hurt.

"No. Go away," Trisha yelled through the door.

Trisha's hands were shaking so bad she was having trouble opening the panel for some of the clothes hidden inside. Once it opened, she quickly pulled the clothes out as fast as she could and slipped them on. She glanced at the door she rigged last night. It was supposed to prevent anyone from entering the bathroom long enough to give her time to slip up through the ventilation duct and over to the room next door. The other room appeared to be some type of storage unit. She completed a run through last night before bed. Her daddy always taught her to have an escape route. Hell, even back home they had at least four different ones!

Trisha chuckled as she reached up and pulled the cover off the ventilation duct. It was time to find Ariel and Carmen and figure out a way to get off this boat. It seemed the current resident of the cabin wanted it back and she was more than happy to give it to him. She didn't like the feelings he stirred up inside her when he was in the same room as she.

* * *

Kelan slammed his hand against the door to his cleansing room snarling in frustration. "Open this damn door!" he roared. He wanted his mate! His dragon didn't think this was fun anymore. Now it was clawing at him again. Kelan was not in the mood to deal with it. *Go lie down,* he snarled.

Kelan turned toward his symbiot. "Why the hell didn't you stop her?" He snapped at the huge golden creature lounging in his bed. "You could at least help! Don't you want us to claim her?"

Kelan's symbiot snickered at Kelan. It stretched slowly before jumping down off the bed and heading for the door leading out to the corridor. Kelan muttered a series of expletives under his breath before he walked to a panel in the side wall. Pushing it open, he removed a small pouch containing tools. He was seriously thinking about doing physical damage to his damn symbiot. No sooner had the thought slipped out of his mind than he realized his mistake. The damn thing could be pissy as hell when it was mad or felt insulted. Kelan felt his arm bands dissolve and slide down to his wrists. He closed his eyes and waited.

"*Shit!*" Kelan yelped as the twin bands shocked him before they turned into little dragons and headed for his mother symbiot.

"Damn, that hurt!" Kelan complained as he bent over, picking up the tool pouch he'd dropped when the shock hit him. "It's not like I really meant it," he muttered under his breath.

Kelan popped open the panel to the door and quickly bypassed the electrical panel so he could manually open the door. Dropping the tool pouch on the floor by the door, he splayed his palms against the door and pushed. With a yell of triumph, he stepped into the cleansing unit and found it—empty. Kelan's loud roar could be heard throughout the level.

* * *

Trisha squeezed through the narrow opening to the room next door and used the shelving to climb down. She carefully opened the door to the storage unit and peeked outside. *Perfect!* she thought. The door was around the corner from the man's cabin so the guards who were stationed in front of the doors couldn't see her. She opened the door farther and found herself face-to-face with the grinning golden puppy dog.

Trisha laughed softly at the expectant look on its face. "You cheater! You took the easy way, didn't you?" Trisha whispered affectionately.

The huge gold body shook as its large tail moved back and forth. A moment later, two tiny dragons appeared fluttering over to land on her shoulders. Trisha looked at first one dragon, then the other in surprise. She couldn't resist giving them a kiss when they snuggled up against her cheek.

"You are incorrigible—you know that, don't you? Let's go find my friends," Trisha whispered.

Trisha was about halfway down the corridor when she heard a loud snarl and what sounded like a loud curse. Trisha knew the sound must have come from the tall man she had left back in the room where she was staying. With a gasp, she took off running. Trisha hurried down a long corridor and took two additional corners before she saw the three guards standing outside of Carmen and Ariel's cabin.

Breathless, she said urgently, "I need to see my friends. Now!" Trisha kept looking over her shoulder. She had the awful feeling the man was going to come after her.

The guards looked at Trisha cautiously but moved aside to let her pass. Trisha gave them a breathless, "Thank you," and hurried through the doorway, her golden friend and the two little dragons following close behind her.

Ariel jumped up when she saw Trisha. "Thank God! I tried to get past the guards this morning to go find you, but they wouldn't let me leave."

Carmen was lounging against the wall near the doorway tossing a cup up and down in the air. "I don't know about you two, but I am ready to blow this joint. I have business in San Diego that can't wait." Carmen moved away from the wall silently, the cup now fisted in her palm.

Trisha nodded. "I just had a run-in with one of the males on board. I don't think he is too happy with me right now."

Ariel grinned as she picked up a piece of the chair she had dismantled. She tapped the leg of the chair against her palm. "Want me to have a talk with him? I'm sure we can help remodel another section of the ship if you want."

Trisha laughed. "No, I just want to get home. Daddy is probably tearing apart Shelby, California right about now." She sobered as she continued, "I don't want him to worry any more than he already has. It liked to have killed him when I had my accident. I can't imagine what this must be doing to him."

Carmen walked up to Trisha and put her arm around her in a brief, supportive hug. "I love your dad, too. We'll get back to him," Carmen pulled away and stood back a step. Her expression turned dark as she stared at Trisha and Ariel. "Let's go find that transporter room you told me about, Ariel, and get back home."

"Okay," Ariel said before she turned to Trisha. "We'll need you to distract our guards. They haven't let us out of here at all."

Trisha nodded. "Okay. There are three of them. Carmen, leave one for us, okay?"

Carmen shook her head in resignation. "You always did like to horn in on my fun."

Trisha chuckled as she went to take a step toward the door. Before she could get to it, the golden symbiot she had nicknamed Bio stepped in front of her blocking her from going any farther. Every time Trisha would try to take a step around it, it would push her backward, away from the door. Trisha tried several times before she threw her hands up in the air in aggravation.

"Come on, Bio. I need to get out of here," Trisha said impatiently.

"Maybe you should go to the bathroom before we go," Ariel said with an exaggerated wink. "You know how weak you are sometimes. I would hate for you to fall down and hurt yourself."

Trisha looked at Ariel puzzled for a moment before the lightbulb in her brain came on. "Oh, you're right. I would hate to get hurt again," Trisha responded with a wink.

Carmen just rolled her eyes as she shifted from one foot to the other. "Well, you better hurry, or we are never going to get out of here," she muttered under her breath.

Trisha hurried into the bathroom glancing over her shoulder as she went. Kelan's symbiot sat by the door blocking the exit to the corridor. The big golden head turned back and forth, looking first at Ariel and Carmen and then at the doorway where Trisha had gone. A moment later, Trisha cried out. Kelan's symbiot was up and through the doorway to the bathroom in a flash. As soon as it cleared the door, Trisha jumped down off the counter with a grunt and palmed the door close. Carmen came up behind her and drove the other chair leg into the control panel.

"That should hold it for a little while," Carmen said. Behind her, the symbiot was snarling and clawing at the door.

"Let's move! I don't think that door will hold it for long," Trisha said urgently as she rushed past Ariel who was standing by the door to the corridor.

As soon as the door opened, Trisha struck out a stunning blow to the guard closest to her, striking him in the throat while kicking out her leg at one of the other guards. She gritted her teeth at the impact as pain radiated up through her. Ariel and Carmen were right behind her. Ariel knocked out the guard Trisha had kicked with one swing of the chair leg, while Carmen kicked the third guard in the groin before taking him down in a sleeper hold. Trisha finished off the guard she had chopped in the throat the same way by pulling around him and taking him into the wrestling move her dad taught her. As soon as the three guards were incapacitated, the girls dragged them into the room where a very pissed-off symbiot was denting the door. Trisha shook her head as images began appearing of the tall man needing her, wanting her. Trisha pushed the images away, frightened by the intense need. As the women exited the room again, a loud roar, unlike anything they had ever heard before, filled the corridor.

"Let's go," Trisha said hoarsely. "He's going to come for me."

Ariel grew pale as she saw terror flicker through Trisha's eyes for a moment. "Come on."

Following Trisha, Ariel and Carmen took off down the corridor at a run. They knew if anyone could find their way back to the transporter room, it would be Trisha. Trisha mentally retrieved the map she had drawn in her head from the time of their arrival until they were escorted to their cabins: first the transporter room to medical, then from medical down to their rooms. She quickly reversed the path. They met a few men in the corridors, but none seemed willing to stop them. It could have either been the frantic pace they were keeping or the threatening glare Carmen was sending them; either way Trisha was thankful. She was trying hard not to show how much pain she was in. Before long, Trisha skidded to a stop outside a set of doors.

"This is it," Trisha gasped. She started to move forward, but Carmen put her hand out.

"Let me go first. I know you can handle it, but I saw how much it hurt you when you kicked that guard," Carmen said softly.

Trisha started to protest but stopped and nodded. Carmen was right. She was paying for that kick. Her entire leg was throbbing, and it felt like she was being seared with hot pins up and down it. Trisha took a step back and motioned for Carmen to go ahead of her. Ariel took up the rear.

"Thank you," Trisha said softly. "Let's do this. I want to go home."

Carmen squared her shoulders and rolled her head side to side before she moved toward the door. As it slid open, Trisha quickly scanned the room noting where every man stood. She gripped the larger knife in her hand but kept the smaller one tucked safely in the borrowed pants she was wearing. Several of the men glanced up with the door opened, popping to attention when they saw the three women silhouetted in the doorway. One of the men started forward. As soon as he was close, Carmen struck out, grabbing his arm, pulling him forward and off balance, and twisting at the same time until she had his arm pinned behind him and a knife held to his throat. When he started to struggle Ariel stepped forward and held the dismantled chair leg up under his chin, forcing him to raise it to an uncomfortable level.

Trisha held the larger knife out in front of her, encouraging the other men who had started forward to stand back.

"Just stay where you are," Trisha said quietly. She glanced at the man standing in front of the console to the transporter. "I want you to beam us back down to our planet. Do you understand? I'm not asking; I'm telling you."

Trisha counted five men in the transporter room. One by the console, two over by a panel near the platform, the one they held, and one on the far side of the room. She motioned for the two men near the platform to move back.

"Go to the back with the other man," Trisha said harshly. She needed to remain focused. She was a soldier now. She breathed in and out through her nose, pushing away the pain, the fear, until she found the calm center within the storm. "Ariel, make sure no one can get into the room."

Ariel gave a warning glance to the man she was holding the chair leg to and took a small step away from him. She never turned her back but moved in slow, cautious steps backward. Glancing behind herself briefly, she gripped the chair leg tightly and swung with all her might, driving it into the panel. Sparks flew as the damaged panel hissed.

"Done," Ariel said with a grin.

Carmen looked like she almost had a smile on her face. It was the closest to one Trisha remembered seeing in the past three years. "You know, I haven't had this much fun in years. We should get together more often. I know this great little bar down in Mexico…" Carmen was saying before a loud thump sounded on the outer door to the transporter room. "Uh-oh, I think we have company."

* * *

Kelan was beyond furious. His warship had never taken as much damage as it had in the last three days since they brought the females on board. After he finally got into his cleansing room and found it empty, he discovered that Trisha had destroyed the inside control panel. He didn't know how she was able to get out of his living quarters, but he was going to find out and prevent it from happening again. He then tracked her to the other females' living quarters only to discover his men just regaining consciousness. They did not have their symbiots with them, at the time thinking it wouldn't be necessary. His symbiot, in the meantime, was just finishing reshaping after it had flowed through the hole it created in the cleansing room door.

"Where is she?" Kelan growled out to his symbiot. It shook itself from the tip of its snout to the tip of its spiked tail. It was back into the shape of a werecat. Kelan stood aside as it moved swiftly toward the door.

Kelan glanced once at the three men who were just beginning to sit up and sighed. He barked out a command for medical assistance for them and for their symbiots to be called to the females' living quarters. He stormed out of the cabin, yelling for several of the warriors who were gathered outside the room to follow him. His fury became red hot as soon as he realized where the females were heading. He was almost to the transporter room when the alarms began sounding.

"What is it now?" Kelan bit out in response to the call from his chief of security.

"Trelon's mate has started a flood in docking bay 4," Jarak said in a weary voice.

"A *what*?" Kelan asked startled.

"A flood," Jarak replied. "From the looks of the programming in our environmental controls, it appears she was working on creating rain in space. It worked."

Kelan shook his head and wondered what he had ever done to deserve this. He always tried to live his life along the guidelines set forth as a Valdier warrior. So what if he strayed a time or two; it wasn't as if he deserved such punishment for a few slips.

"Clean it up and try to find out how she was able to get into the environmental system. I want her locked out of everything! And see if you can get Trelon to tie her down," Kelan added, thinking that wouldn't be such a bad idea for his Trisha.

Kelan paused outside of the transporter room doors when they didn't open automatically. He called out a series of command codes, but it still wouldn't open. Kelan slammed his fist against the solid door in frustration. Closing his eyes, he sought the cool, calm center that had kept him alive for so long and discovered it had been shot to hell. The only thing he could find deep inside him was his dragon laughing its ass off at its mate's shenanigans. *Fat lot of help you are!* Kelan muttered crossly. Kelan's dragon just rolled over, overcome by mirth.

Opening his eyes, he turned to one of the warriors standing near him. "Get me a tool kit immediately."

"Yes, Commander," the huge warrior said with a surprisingly stoic look to his face.

Unfortunately, his eyes gave away his true feelings. He was enjoying the surprising drama the females brought on board the warship way too much. Kelan sighed as he watched the warrior hurry down the corridor. Traveling for long periods in space could be very boring. Since the end of the Three Wars, they had little to worry about as far as threats. On occasion, a renegade pirate ship might attack when it accidently mistook the *V'ager* for something other than the power warship it was. It was a mistake it never made again as Kelan made sure it was destroyed. Kelan shook his head. He was ready for a nice pirate ship to come along right about now so he could blow it to pieces—since he couldn't do that to the aggravating females who were systematically destroying the *V'ager*.

The warrior returned quickly with the tools Kelan needed to remove the panel and engage the manual control. He really hoped the females hadn't destroyed the transporter room. Trelon had just finishing fixing it from the first time they were in there. He didn't think his brother would be too happy if he told him it had been destroyed again. Kelan dropped the cover to the floor of the corridor and went to work on the wiring. From the sparks he was getting, he had a feeling the females had destroyed the inside panel like they did in their living quarters. Kelan reached for the manual override bar and began pumping it open just far enough so he could get his hands into the crack that opened. Straining, he slowly pulled the doorway open far enough for one of the warriors to stick a metal bar into it to keep it opened. Kelan stepped through the opening and sighed heavily. *Yes,* he thought in resignation. *Tying them up is beginning to sound pretty damn good.*

Kelan just stood looking at the situation before him, wondering what in the hell to do next. His mate was brandishing his shaving knife at Tulex who was standing at the transporter console looking at her with a combination of amusement and lust. The crazy female who had a tendency to hurt all of his warriors was poking a knife into Burj's throat, and the other crazy one was swinging a piece of a broken chair at the other three warriors while begging them to "take a piece of me." Kelan ran his hands through his hair, threw back his head, and roared out his frustration.

"Enough!" Kelan growled out, staring at the three females.

Normally when Kelan growled, roared, glared, or showed any signs of losing his tightly controlled self-discipline, the warriors and more than a few of his enemies were smart enough to run in the opposite direction. Why he ever thought these females would react the same way was beyond him. They just looked at him like he was the one with the problem and raised their eyebrows before turning back and threatening his warriors again. He really needed to kill his older brother for landing on that stupid planet, or at the very least, beat the shit out of him. As he gazed at his mate, he grudgingly admitted she looked beautiful pointing that knife at Tulex. *Though,* Kelan admitted to himself, *if Tulex doesn't quit looking at Trisha with lust in his eyes, I might gladly gut the bastard for her.*

"What is going on?" Kelan asked with a resigned sigh.

"The females are demanding we transport them back down to their planet. I have tried to explain to them we left it three days ago and are not even near their galaxy anymore," Tulex said, wincing as Trisha jabbed him with the point of the shaving knife.

"And *I* told you to take us back!" Trisha said angrily. "I have to go home."

Kelan crossed his arms and looked sternly at Trisha, then the others. "There will be no going home for any of you. This is your home now."

Burj made a distressed noise when Carmen tightened the knife at his throat. "Commander, I don't think they like that answer," he choked out as a thin line of blood trickled from the small cut on his neck.

"Oh, quit being a big baby. I didn't mean to cut you," Carmen muttered under her breath. "If I had meant to, you would be dead."

Trisha looked at Kelan, really looked at him for the first time. "You are the commander of this ship?" she asked hesitantly.

"Yes, my name is Kelan Reykill. I am the commander of the *V'ager*. Now, will you please quit threatening my men and return to my living quarters? We can discuss this in a much less destructive way," Kelan said gently. She really was beautiful standing there biting her bottom lip and looking at him with a vexed expression on her face.

Trisha paused for a moment before replying. "No," Trisha said firmly, turning back to Tulex and poking him again. "I want to go home. Now! Since you are the commander, you can tell him to turn this thing around and take us home."

"We all want to go home right now," Carmen gritted out. "You had no right to take us away from our planet without our permission."

Kelan turned to look at Carmen before he addressed her coolly. "I do not require permission from anyone. All of you had seen too much. Might I remind you, you would have died had I not intervened on your behalf. All of you are now my guests aboard my warship. I would appreciate it if you would cease threatening my men and damaging it. It is beginning to make me very angry." Kelan no sooner finished that statement when the alarms sounded again. A moment later he heard Jarak's voice in his communicator.

"What now?" Kelan snapped out.

"Trelon's mate again," Jarak replied anxiously.

"What has the human female gotten into this time?" Kelan asked impatiently. He was trying to deal with the situation in front of him and did not have time to hunt for the other human female. Trelon needed to get her under control, immediately.

"She was running different tones in engineering. The good news is we are getting power levels never seen before from the crystals," Jarak said in surprise.

Kelan rubbed a hand across his eyes. His head was beginning to ache badly. If his symbiot hadn't abandoned him, it would be no problem. Unfortunately for him, it was currently lying on the floor next to Trisha, watching her carefully.

"What is the bad news?" Kelan muttered darkly.

"It appears all the symbiots currently assigned to help in engineering are drunk and wrecking it," Jarak responded hesitantly.

"Take care of it. I don't know and I don't care how, but take care of it," Kelan growled back before signing off.

"What other human female?" Ariel asked suddenly.

"The tiny one you call Cara. She is a pain in my…" Kelan began before Tulex interrupted him.

Trisha bit her lip as she listened to the conversation going on over the sound of the alarms. She was trying to not focus on the spasms of pain that were running up and down her leg and into her back. She wasn't sure how much longer she would be able to stand. It was taking everything inside her not to cry out as the needles became sharper and sharper. She tried to relieve the pressure by moving most of her weight to her other leg, but that just made her back worse. Small beads of sweat started breaking out on her forehead as the nausea started to build in her stomach. She wouldn't let her friends down. She couldn't. She was tough. Her dad taught her techniques on how to ignore pain. Trisha tried to remain focused on breathing through each spasm, but the pain was becoming unbearable. Trisha was in so much pain she was unaware of the two tiny symbiots on her wrists moving in agitation as they sensed her increasing discomfort.

"Commander," Tulex called out softly. His eyes grew wide with concern as he saw the pain darkening Trisha's already dark brown eyes to black. He was closer to her so he was able to see the sweat on her brow and how she turned from pale to almost sheet-white.

Kelan jerked his head around when he heard the thread of concern in Tulex's voice. "What?"

Tulex was about to reply when a particularly sharp pain swept through Trisha, clouding her vision. She was unable to hold back the cry of pain as her muscles tensed up into severe spasms. Trisha felt herself falling as her legs went out from under her.

Carmen muttered a curse and thrust Burj away from her, spinning and rushing for Trisha at the same time Ariel threw her chair leg at the three men and sprinted across the room. Both of them were still behind Kelan, who reached Trisha first and took her from Tulex's arms. Kelan slowly lowered Trisha to the floor. Trisha's eyes were closed, and her teeth gritted as the waves of pain radiated throughout her body. Her hands were clenched so tightly into fists, Kelan couldn't open them. His symbiot circled around him and was pressing close to Trisha, spreading fine threads of gold all over her body as it searched for the cause of her pain.

"Get away from her," Carmen said roughly to Tulex as she moved to kneel down next to Trisha's head. She was wiping her hand across her brow. "Breathe deep, sweetheart, and try to relax as much as you can," she kept repeating over and over softly.

Ariel moved down to Trisha's leg and began massaging it. "I should never have let you take on those men," Ariel said in remorse as she continued to massage Trisha's calf and thigh muscles. "You need to tell us when you are in pain before it gets too bad. You know what happens if you push too hard."

"What is wrong with her?" Kelan asked desperately. His eyes were focused on the pale, clammy face of his mate. Tiny white lines of pain were etched around her mouth, and she was trying to breathe deeply through her nose, but instead small quick gasps were slipping past her tightened lips.

His symbiot was moving over Trisha's entire body, pausing and shaking as she moved. He laid his hand on top of it so thick gold bands would form around his wrists and he could connect to what it was doing to his mate. His breath caught in his throat as wave after wave of intense pain flooded him.

"What is wrong with her?" Kelan demanded harshly, glaring first at Carmen, then at Ariel.

Carmen just shook her head and looked away. When Kelan realized he would get nothing out of her, he turned his gaze on Ariel, daring her to not tell him. His mate was obviously in excruciating pain, and he wanted to know why.

Chapter 6

Trisha rolled over frowning. She stared up at the ceiling, focusing on her body. She didn't hurt. She slowly moved her feet back and forth and up and down. *Nope, no pain.* She thought, confused. She pulled her knees up slightly, waiting for the pain in her lower back to warn her she had been lying still too long. *Nothing!* She lifted her arms up and stretched toward the ceiling rotating her wrists back and forth. Still nothing, nada, zip. Where was the pain through her shoulders and neck? A movement on the bed next to her made her smile. Turning her head, she let out a small yelp. Instead of the big golden dog she was used to seeing next to her there was a huge dark-haired man with golden eyes.

Trisha scooted over to the edge of the bed as fast as she could, taking the top cover with her. She could feel the soft cloth of the bedspread against her skin, so she knew she wasn't wearing her borrowed clothes anymore.

"What in the hell are you doing in my bed?" Trisha squeaked. She pushed her heavy mane of curly hair out of her face as she sat up.

"Actually, this is my bed, and you are the one in it with me," Kelan responded with a slight curve to his lips. His mate looked beautiful with her hair all tousled and curly around her. Kelan felt the low rumble of a purr as his dragon woke and responded to the presence of his mate so close and delectable.

Trisha frowned at Kelan in confusion. "You know what I mean. How did I get here, and where are my clothes? Where are Carmen and Ariel? Did you say you have Cara too? When are you taking us home? And why don't I hurt anymore?" she finished breathlessly. God, he was so cute! She was having a terrible time keeping her eyes and her thoughts above his chin.

Kelan folded his arms under his head as he leaned back against the pillows. The movement pulled the covers farther down his chest until they rested just above his hips. His lips twitched when he saw the color rise in his mate's cheeks, and she turned her head slightly to the side as if she was uncomfortable at seeing his body. She would have to get over those feelings very quickly if that were the case. He planned on being around her a lot without his—or her—clothes on.

"That is a lot of questions. I carried you here; I removed 'my' clothes from you; your two friends are locked up so they cannot do any more damage to my ship or my men; and yes, the one you call Cara is also on board although we are trying to find her again after her little experiment in engineering. As for you not hurting anymore…" Kelan began roughly as he remembered the amount of pain she endured. He sat up, twisting toward her. The movement caused the sheets to bunch around his waist and made him look even bigger and closer and definitely more dangerous to her libido. "…You should never have been allowed to have felt such pain. My symbiot and I both regret not seeing to your physical wounds sooner. If we had known, we could have healed you sooner."

Trisha frowned. "What do you mean you would have healed me sooner? There is nothing else that can be done. The doctors did everything they could to put me back together after the accident," Trisha said in bewilderment.

Kelan studied his mate's face, watching as emotions flickered across it: sadness, pain, and finally resignation. He wanted to chase all of those away and erase whatever caused it. He'd tried to get Carmen or Ariel to tell him what had happened to Trisha. Carmen merely shook her head and turned away from him. Ariel looked at him with tears in her eyes and said it was up to Trisha to tell him if she wanted him to know. Both refused to say anything else.

In the transporter room, his symbiot moved over and over Trisha's body, healing and mending. Kelan could not comprehend how a body could have so much metal inside it and be able to function. His symbiot moved carefully over each part of Trisha, absorbing the metal inside her into its own body while mending the bones, muscles, nerves, tendons, and tissue. It worked on Trisha for the better part of an hour before Kelan finally stopped it. Trisha had lapsed into semi-consciousness by then, before falling into a deep, exhausted sleep. Kelan carried her to his living quarters after instructing several of his security force to escort the now subdued females back to their own quarters. Once he, his symbiot, and Trisha reached his living quarters, he carefully undressed Trisha and placed her in his bed allowing his symbiot to finish the healing process. He sat watching over her until his symbiot finally moved away, satisfied she would be all right.

Kelan called Jarak before he joined Trisha to have someone go by and repair the damage to the other females' cleansing unit door and panel but cautioned him to maintain adequate security for the men doing the work in case the females decided to attack again. Jarak informed him all warriors assigned to guard them were now required to have their symbiot with them at all times, and he increased the number of guards from three to six. Satisfied his ship was safe from at least four out of the five women—Trelon's mate was still on the loose—he ordered Jarak not to disturb him unless it was an emergency. Kelan spent the next six hours with his arms wrapped around Trisha. It was only in the few minutes before she woke that he simply lay next to her watching her.

Trisha pushed her hair away from her face where it had fallen again. "What do you mean when you say you would have healed me sooner?" she repeated again softly, trying to understand what he meant.

Kelan couldn't resist leaning toward her and running the back of his hand down along her soft cheek. "My symbiot has the power to heal me and my mate. *You* are my mate, Trisha Grove," Kelan replied to her softly spoken question.

Trisha gasped and pulled away, catching herself before she almost fell off the bed. "I am *not* your mate," she replied as she swung her legs off the edge of the bed and stood up, wrapping part of the huge bedspread around her. "I don't have time to be a mate. If I did, I certainly wouldn't choose you! I have to go home. You never responded to that question. When are you taking us home?"

Kelan frowned at Trisha's withdrawal. His dragon growled a low warning. It would not let its mate go again. *Bite! Now!* it was demanding. *Mine! Now!*

I'm trying, Kelan replied, frustrated. He swung his legs over the other side of the bed and stood up.

"As I said before in the transporter room, you will not be returning to your home world. Your new home will be on Valdier," Kelan stated determinedly. He did not want Trisha to doubt he would not let her go.

Trisha kept her eyes focused on his face, refusing to look any lower or to be intimated. It wasn't like she had never seen a naked man before. She used to catch sight of plenty of guys growing up running through the woods, and she had been married for three years even if a year and a half really didn't count. She would not give him the satisfaction of making her uncomfortable. If he wanted to prance around in the buff, so be it.

Trisha was already shaking her head. "No, I have to return home. I have no other choice. If you do not return my friends and me as soon as possible, then I will consider this an act of war against my people," Trisha said determinedly. She would get home to her dad come hell or high water.

"War?" Kelan repeated in disbelief. How in the hell did they get from him lying in bed being horny as hell to her declaration that he was at war with her and her people?

"War," Trisha said desperately. Maybe she could be the one to intimidate him, she thought. "Under the conditions of the Geneva Convention, I expect the articles concerning the capture of prisoners of war to be upheld and respected. The articles include: Quarters, food, and clothing as stated in Articles 25–28, hygiene and medical attention as stated in Articles 29–32…" Trisha continued speaking in a rushed voice as Kelan stared at her in horror as she recited what she had learned in basic training.

What in the hell is she talking about? Kelan wondered in dismay. He just wanted to claim her; what in the hell did this Geneva have to do with that? "I am not at war with you or your people," Kelan broke in. He walked around the huge bed until he was standing in front of Trisha.

Trisha gripped the bedspread tightly and kept her eyes trained on his face, refusing to look anywhere else as he moved toward her. When he stopped in front of her, she tilted her head back to look into his eyes.

"I have to go home…please," Trisha pleaded softly. "It's very important I return as soon as possible."

Kelan gazed down into Trisha's deep, dark-brown eyes, drowning in them. He reached out to gently touch her cheek again, letting his fingers trail down along it to her jaw before he groaned and lowered his head until his lips were almost touching hers. He moved his other hand to her hip and pulled her against his hardened shaft. He wanted, no, needed her badly. His dragon was practically purring at having his mate so close to him. *A taste,* he thought. He would sample a taste before he responded to her plea. He knew deep down she was not going to be happy with his answer, but he also knew it was the only one he could give her. He would never let her go. She was the light to his dark. She filled the emptiness that had been eating away at him, his dragon, and his symbiot for so long. She was the rest of him, and he would do whatever it took to make her realize he was the same for her.

"I can't," Kelan said softly before he crushed his lips to hers and pulled her tightly against him.

Trisha recognized two things instantly. He said *can't*, not *won't*, and she had never been kissed like this before. She knew she should pull away. Instead, she took a step closer. *It's like stepping into the sun for the first time or feeling the rain on your face after a hot day,* she thought in awe. It held a sense of wonder about it that made her want more, even as she knew it was impossible. Reluctantly, she pulled away from the kiss and looked down to where her free hand was splayed across his bare chest. She let her fingers thread through the light coating of hair. Trisha shivered at the pleasure she felt deep down inside at the touch of his skin against her sensitive fingertips. She gently pushed away from Kelan, taking a step back to put a small space between them, so she could get herself back under control, at least a little bit.

Trisha drew in a shaky breath. Looking back up into Kelan's eyes, she said softly. "Then, I can't let you kiss me or touch me, again. I have to go home. It is not for me, but for my father. I can't let him go through what he did before. I...won't let him go through it. He thought he had lost me once, and it almost killed him. If he loses me again and never knows what happened to me..." Trisha's voice faltered as she thought of the pain her dad must be going through at that moment. "...To not know what happened to his only daughter, his only living family..." Trisha stared deeply into Kelan's eyes fighting back the tears of pain and sadness. "It would kill us both, him for not knowing and me for being unable to stop his pain."

* * *

Kelan was going out of his mind! He looked down at the reports but didn't see a thing. His mind replayed the scene from earlier over and over in his head. After Trisha pulled away from him, telling him about her father, he tried to explain to her why he could not take her back, but it had been fruitless. Every time he tried to touch her, she would move away from him. He tried to get her to see reason. He had a mission. He needed to return to Valdier and find out what was going on. His oldest brother needed to return home. He needed her! But it all fell on deaf ears. She refused to listen, just repeating over and over that she needed to return home immediately. When he still refused to take her she began reciting her name, rank, and a long series of numbers until he finally lost what little patience he had left.

Kelan ran his hands through his hair and rested his head against his palms as he leaned forward in his seat. He thought if he could kiss her into submission she would finally see things from his point of view. His dragon was more than ready to initiate the dragon's fire mating, but when he tried to grab her, she shrank away from him with a startled cry. His dragon had been too close to the surface, and she was not used to seeing him. His symbiot took offense to Kelan and his dragon scaring Trisha, shifting into a pytheon, a large six-limbed creature found in the deep forests of their planet. It attacked Kelan, wrapping large bands of gold around his waist and dumping him and his dragon naked in the corridor outside his living quarters. Then, the damn thing had the nerve to refuse to let him back in for some clothes. It was only Trisha's compassion that allowed him a pair of pants, which she threw out the door the minute his symbiot cracked it open, hitting him in the face with them. Before he could even pull the damn things down, the door closed again, sealing him out.

Kelan was simmering with anger and frustration. He was left with two choices: stand in the corridor and look like a fool or go and kill his older brother. The second choice sounded much, much better. After the looks of disbelief he kept receiving from the warriors who passed him by in the corridors, not to mention the two guards stationed outside his living quarters who were not even trying to contain their amusement, he could use the physical release of beating on someone, namely Zoran. Unfortunately, his older brother was occupied with his true mate at the moment. Since killing his brother was going to have to wait, he decided to head to the commander's quarters off the bridge where he stored some spare clothes for when he couldn't get back to his living quarters. He'd just stepped off the lift when Jarak caught up with him. It seemed Trelon's mate was at it again. This time their communications system was down due to an overload of requests for his younger brother's Personal Virtual Companion holovids. Jarak took one look at Kelan and shook his head. Kelan was standing barefoot in front of him wearing nothing more than a pair of pants and a pained expression. Jarak didn't even bother asking what he should do. He just threw his arms up in the air in resignation and said he would take care of it.

For the first time in his long life, Kelan didn't know what to do. Throwing his head back, he stared up at the ceiling wondering how his life had gotten so complicated. It used to be so simple before. Get laid when he felt the need, attack the bad guys, and kick some ass on occasion. *Is that too much to ask?* Kelan thought in frustration.

Don't want simple. Want my mate, no one else, his dragon grumbled bad-temperedly.

I want her too, but you heard and saw her. She is being stubborn. Kelan growled back in frustration.

Take her anyway. Claim her. I want to bite. NOW, his dragon responded, pacing back and forth impatiently under his skin.

Kelan growled out again as he looked down at the scales rippling up and down his arms. He fought for control. Even if he wanted to do what his dragon suggested, he couldn't. His damn symbiot wasn't letting either one of them near Trisha right now. The visions it was sending him was tearing him up inside. He wanted to go to her, to hold her. He could feel her emotional pain. The only consolation he had was that her physical pain was no longer an issue. With a muttered curse, Kelan stood up and headed for the door. Maybe there were some warriors working out in the training room. Since he couldn't beat either one of his brothers up right now, maybe he could beat up some of the new warriors on board.

* * *

Trisha stood looking at the closed door. She was in total confusion, and it was pissing her off. She was always in control. Her dad taught her that to lose control could mean the difference between life and death. Not that she was really in a life-or-death situation right now. She was more in a battle of wills, she thought with a grin. She would get home to her dad one way or another. It had been years, she thought distractedly as she moved toward the bathroom, since she had felt this alive. Not since before her accident. Trisha looked at Bio, who was back into the shape of the big, droopy-eyed puppy dog with an amused smile.

"Does he know just how evil you really are?" Trisha asked humorously. "Those images you are sending him are totally bogus." The symbiot, Bio, just snickered and wagged its enormous tail back and forth.

"I guess us girls really do need to stick together. You just make things up to your heart's content until he feels so bad we'll both have him eating out of our hands," Trisha giggled.

Trisha was trying not to laugh at the images the symbiot next to her was making up and sending to Kelan. *Kelan,* Trisha thought with a silly smile. *God, for an alien he sure could kiss and those muscles...just WOW.*

After Bio tossed Kelan out into the corridor naked as a jaybird, Trisha started planning her next strategy. He'd said can't, not won't. Well, she was a "can" kind of girl. Whenever anyone told her she couldn't do something, she made it her mission to do just the opposite. She laughed quietly as she remembered being told she would never make it in the space program because of her accident.

Well, poop on them! I'm so far into space I am a black hole in their you-know-what! Trisha thought with a contented sigh. Now all she needed to do was fulfill her promise to her dad to take him with her!

Trisha's thoughts were jerked back to the present when she caught sight of her reflection in the bathroom mirror. Her eyes widened in disbelief as she stared at her stomach. Her fingers lightly traced over the flat, smooth surface that had been covered in a scattering of scars. She let her eyes wander up to her shoulder where there was supposed to be another long ribbon of scars from where her collarbone had shattered. Trisha turned her arms looking for the incisions where the surgeons inserted the metal rods in her wrists and forearm. Trembling, she continued her scrutiny, looking at all the places where the surgeons worked on her battered and broken body. The pain was not the only thing gone—so were all the scars. In their place was soft, smooth, undamaged skin. Trisha looked at Bio, who was lying in the doorway of the bathroom silently watching her.

"You did this, didn't you? You were able to fix me when no one else could," Trisha asked softly in disbelief. Tears shimmered in her eyes when she felt warmth enfold her as Bio sent waves of comfort through her. *Oh, Daddy, I wish you could see me whole again,* Trisha thought as she continued to stare in disbelief at her image.

* * *

Kelan rubbed his shoulder where one of the warriors got in a lucky punch. He probably shouldn't have tackled six at one time, but he was feeling like a challenge. He was getting too old for this, he thought dismally as he stared into his near-empty cup. Kelan pulled another bottle toward him. He was on his fifth bottle of prized Curizan wine. He'd left the training room earlier under Jarak's disapproving eye, making his way up to the dining area. Before he left, Jarak informed him in no uncertain terms that he was tired of Kelan, Trelon, and those infuriating females. They were sending all of his men to medical, and he was running short of personnel. By the time Kelan made it up to the dining area, word had already spread about his head bashing down in the training room. After most of the men hurried out of the room when he came in, Kelan decided to pick a back table away from everyone. Now, he was slowly drinking himself into oblivion. He was just pouring himself another glass of wine when his brother Zoran came in.

"I do not know what to do, Kelan," Zoran began as he grabbed the bottle away from Kelan and poured himself a tall glass of wine. Kelan sort of heard what his brother was saying, something about fading away…blah, blah, blah. It was too much for his sodden brain to really absorb. Kelan frowned; wasn't he supposed to do something to his older brother? *Oh yeah, I'm supposed to kill him,* Kelan thought with a wobbly smirk. Kelan reached for another bottle since Zoran had taken his. He would kill him later. It took to much energy to do it right now. Kelan poured some more wine into his cup and a little on the table. Shrugging his shoulders, he focused on trying to connect his cup with his mouth.

"I am ready to take them all back!" Kelan slurred out slowly.

He frowned. *No, I'm not ready to take them all back. I want to keep the one called Trisha. She is mine. I just need to show her. Now, the other ones I would take back in a heartbeat, especially Trelon's mate. No,* he frowned again, *not Trelon's mate. Trelon needs her. I would take the other two back. But if I do that, then my mate and Trelon's mate would want to go back, so I can't take them back either.* Kelan felt a groan escape him. *Damn, I'm going to have to keep them too,* he thought in despair. *My warship and my men will never make it home in one piece.* Kelan raised a blurry-eyed glare at Zoran. It was all Zoran's fault!

"I have had it with her…them. They are bossy, opinionated, stubborn…" Kelan hiccupped in the middle of his accusation, "…beautiful, and too damn sexy."

Zoran frowned down at Kelan. He had never seen his brother lose control like this in all the years they were together. Before Zoran could think of a reply, Trelon came in growling and muttering under his breath.

"I need a drink," Trelon said, casting a look that sent daggers at Zoran. Trelon grabbed the bottle of wine Kelan had just pulled toward himself and drank deeply from it before he pointed a finger at Zoran and let loose all his pent-up hostilities toward him.

Wiping a hand across his mouth, he growled, "I'm going to kill me a tiny human female with red and purple hair. I'm going to rip her apart, burn her to ash, and then put her back together again, so I can do it over and over until she begs for mercy."

It took everything inside Kelan not to join Trelon when Zoran had the nerve to ask, "What is wrong?" He could have given Zoran a list that would have lasted to the next century. What was wrong was he was hornier than hell and except for using his own hand, he wasn't getting any! His dragon was ready to take him over and destroy the ship if that was what it took to get to his mate, his symbiot was sending him erotic images of Trisha in the cleansing room bathing, and he was stuck beating the shit out of the greenhorns on board the ship since his own older brother was too tied up with his mate to take the beating he deserved! Then, to top it off, he was too damn drunk to beat the shit out of Zoran when he finally had the nerve to make an appearance. Life was not fair, and it was beginning to piss him off royally, self-discipline be damned. He wanted his mate!

"Wrong? Wrong, he asks," Trelon growled pointing the bottle at Zoran. "I'll tell you what is wrong. You landed on a damn planet of females who would drive any male to distraction, then act like it is the male's fault! No, you *couldn't* land on a planet where our symbiots would want to kill the females and our dragons would find them repulsive. No, you *had* to land on a planet where my symbiot is so infatuated with the female it does every damn thing she asks regardless of what I say, and my dragon is so horny it is about ready to disembowel me if I don't claim her before another male does, only I can't catch her long enough to do so."

"You too?" Kelan slurred before giving Trelon a blurry-eyed frown. There was two of him. *When did Trelon clone himself?* Kelan thought in confusion. "My female refuses to even acknowledge me as a male. All she does is quote her name, rank, and some awful number I can't remember. She insists I take her home. My symbiot is sleeping with her like it is her new pet and sends me images of her stroking and scratching it and talking nonsense while me and my dragon get to suffer." Kelan grunted as his head fell forward. He probably shouldn't have drunk that last bottle of wine. "She even said if I wanted to stay in my dragon form she would scratch my belly, but she wouldn't touch me with a ten-foot pole." Kelan's dragon liked that idea a lot at the time and was still mad at Kelan for refusing to shift.

Kelan wondered distractedly if all human females were this annoying. If so, the men of that planet could have them. Well, not all of them. At least, not Zoran's, Trelon's, and his own mates, but they could have the rest. He was of the mind to ban any knowledge of their planet in case some other poor unsuspecting male should find it; although, he might could send the Curizans there. That would serve them right. *No,* Kelan thought dismally again. *Creon liked Ha'ven who was the leader of the Curizans. Dammit, life was so unfair!*

Kelan listened as Trelon told Zoran about the other two females he had under guard. Kelan was in no mood to deal with any more of their shenanigans. They caused enough damage to last him a century or more. He was quite happy leaving them locked up in their living quarters until they reached Valdier. Then, he would turn them over to Zoran and let him deal with them.

"Why are your females not under guard?" Zoran asked as he finished off his drink and reached for another bottle of wine.

"The one named Trisha is under guard, in my cabin," Kelan slurred. "Unfortunately, I can't get in because she has my symbiot attack me and drag me out every time I try to enter. Wait until I get her home. I am going to send my symbiot to play, and as soon as it is gone...*bam*, she is mine!" Kelan giggled at the thought of finally having the female defenseless. Okay, he was done. Commanders of a Valdier warship did not giggle. It was time to call a quiet retreat to the commander's conference room which was his current residence. He was going to have one hell of a hangover when they reached the planet tomorrow since he didn't have his symbiot to help him, and he was too damn proud to ask the healer for medication. No, life wasn't just unfair; it was downright shitty at times. That thought was confirmed when Zoran announced he was going to have Mandra set up a dinner to introduce all the women to their world.

"Oh joy, we get to be humiliated in front of everyone," Kelan said sourly before he hauled his drunken ass out of the chair while he could still walk and made his way to his lonely new living quarters off the bridge. He was getting awfully tired of sleeping on the couch.

Chapter 7

Trisha looked on in stony silence as Kelan ordered the men to prepare the transporter for the next group to beam down to the planet. She had seen only brief glimpses of him over the past two weeks during the travel from Earth to Valdier. She didn't understand how they could have traveled such great distances. She got vague impressions from Bio about the symbiots and crystals bending and displacing space at intervals. She would need a lot longer to completely understand what it was trying to show her. Trisha spent most of the time alone trying to figure out how to get back home and how to get a certain irritating alien out of her mind.

It didn't help that she was now having very erotic dreams of him. Trisha glanced down to see Bio looking up at her in innocence. *Innocence, my ass,* Trisha thought with a raised eyebrow. *More like sabotage.* She suspected Bio was not only playing with Kelan's mind but her own. Bio snickered and looked back at Kelan with a large yawn, showing teeth that looked like daggers. Kelan was doing a good job of sending looks like daggers at Bio. It was the looks he was sending to Trisha that worried her. He looked like he was ready to pounce on her again, only this time she didn't think he was planning on stopping. Trisha was slightly embarrassed about how she reacted to him when he tried to grab her. She was used to seeing the shape of his pupils change as his dragon; she finally accepted he could shift after the numerous images Bio sent her in her dreams, but was startled when she saw the rippling of scales and the slight change to his face. It was probably for the best, she kept telling herself. She didn't want to develop feelings for Kelan. It would make it harder to stay focused on going home. *Home*, Trisha thought, looking around at all the men, symbiots, and equipment. It was beginning to seem more like a dream than the reality of who she was.

Trisha glanced over at where Ariel and Carmen were standing under guard. Ariel glanced back and rolled her eyes. Carmen just bared her teeth at any of the men who looked at her. Trelon—she was finally able to put a face with a name—was trying to catch Cara. Good luck with that one; Trisha couldn't help but smirk as she watched Cara flit out of Trelon's reach time and time again. Trisha looked up when the door opened again, and Abby and her guy, Zoran, came into the room. Abby looked shocked to see them. Trisha watched as she turned to Zoran and spoke to him rapidly. Whatever he said didn't seem to make her very happy. Welcome to the club, Trisha thought sarcastically. *That isn't nice,* Trisha chided herself. *Look at all the good things that have come from being kidnapped!* She was as good as new; she had traveled to the stars; she now knew the answer to whether they were alone in the universe. The only thing missing from making this perfect was having her dad with her. Then she could enjoy everything that was happening without feeling guilty about what her dad must be going through since her disappearance.

Trisha started when Kelan called out to her. He motioned for her to step up onto the platform. Trisha's hand went to her stomach to calm the horde of butterflies that were fluttering inside her. Bio seemed to sense Trisha's unease as she stood up and rubbed against Trisha's leg. Trisha smiled down at Bio and gently ran her hand over the large, golden head. She looked back up and stared into Kelan's eyes. She saw his lips curve in a gentle, understanding smile. It was like he knew she was scared but didn't want to show it. Her own lips curved in an answering smile. When he reached out his hand in support, Trisha couldn't deny him. She placed her much smaller palm against his and let him draw her up onto the platform.

* * *

It took a while, but Kelan thought he finally understood what he needed to do with Trisha. Zoran explained about some of the issues he was having with his own mate's fear of being abandoned in a new world where everything was so different. Kelan also listened to what Abby said about the differences between human mating and Valdier mating. Kelan went back over the information they archived about the human females' planet, as well. He spent hour upon lonely hour reviewing, studying, and absorbing everything he could about Earth and its cultures. Kelan discovered the females liked to be courted. It was a foreign concept to him as Valdier warriors saw their mate and claimed her. That was it. If the female fought, it just meant a more exciting mating. Valdier warriors never took a female against her will, if a female was not interested than the warrior and his dragon would know through her scent. True mates gave out a scent that aroused the male and the female, as well as the dragon counterparts of themselves. Kelan could smell Trisha's arousal every time he was near her. That was one of the reasons he stayed away from her. He knew she wanted him physically, but mentally she still fought against their mating. *Take her!* Kelan's dragon roared out furiously. *Claim my mate.*

Soon, my friend. You remember our agreement. We must court our mate according to the customs she is used to. We must convince her that this is where she belongs, Kelan replied calmly. He refused to be distracted from his plans. This was a war he was determined to win. He couldn't afford to lose it. To lose would mean to die, and he did not plan for that to happen for a long, long time.

* * *

Trisha held on tight to Kelan's hand as he guided her through huge gleaming corridors of polished stone. Huge plants in large planters dotted the corridors giving it a lush feeling. The floors and walls were an off-white with threads of what looked like gold and black weaving throughout. Trisha tilted her head back and looked at the high arched ceilings. Carvings of warriors, dragons, and a wide variety of plants and animals adorned them. She gasped when it looked like some of them were actually moving. She tried to focus on mapping the way they were going in case she needed to reverse it, but she was having a hard time focusing when all she wanted to do was absorb all the wonders around her. It was only when she felt the warmth of Kelan's arm around her back and waist that she realized he had drawn her closer as they walked. It didn't help that Bio was pressing against her other side pushing her against Kelan's tall, muscular length.

Trisha blushed as she realized Kelan was watching her more than he was watching where they were going. "It's very beautiful," Trisha said shyly. *God, I feel like a schoolgirl again. Who wants to go through that twice?* she thought in disgust.

"Yes," Kelan replied with a smile.

That was all he said, but Trisha knew he wasn't talking about the palace they were in; he was looking at her with those little flames in his eyes again. *Oh, boy,* Trisha thought as she started heating up again. *I'm in trouble.* Trisha smiled hesitantly at one of the warriors they passed. She started when she heard a low growl.

"Did you just growl at that man?" Trisha asked, looking up in surprise. She started to turn to look at the man they had passed, but Kelan tightened his hold on her.

"I'm afraid my dragon and I do not like you smiling at other men at the moment," Kelan smiled tightly down at Trisha.

He was having a hard enough time holding his dragon back. If she smiled at another male, he wouldn't be responsible for the consequences. He had been harder than hell for the past two weeks and was barely holding on to the little self-control that remained inside him and his dragon. If he didn't claim Trisha very soon, he was afraid of what could happen. He was fearful enough of her surviving the dragon's fire mating. The last thing he wanted to do was endanger her by being too rough with her. He kept telling himself she was more fragile than their females, but he was too far gone to care anymore. He pictured the amount of damage his symbiot had healed, in the hope it would help remind him of how delicate she really was. Kelan frowned when he remembered all the damage to her body. What had happened to her?

"What happened to your body?" Kelan blurted out suddenly. "What caused so much damage to you?"

Trisha started and would have pulled away from Kelan but he kept his tight grip around her waist. They began walking at a slower pace as Kelan waited for Trisha to answer his questions. She bit her lip, hesitating to tell him, but then decided it really didn't matter anymore. She was healed, and Peter was in the past. Neither one could hurt her any longer.

"I was in the military, the Air Force. I wanted to be an astronaut and had been accepted into the space program training program." Trisha paused before adding, "I used to dream of touching the stars." Trisha glanced up at Kelan with a slight smile.

Seeing his intense look, she continued softly. "I guess I should start at the very beginning so you can understand everything. My mom and dad married; that's our way of mating, at a very young age. My mom died of a brain aneurysm when I was a year old. My dad raised me by himself. He is the most amazing man! He is smart, gentle, and the best dad a girl could ever wish for. He owns a business called Grove Wilderness Guides in a state called Wyoming." Trisha paused and looked up doubtfully at

Kelan. Surely, he didn't really want to hear about her life history.

..*

Kelan wanted to know everything there was to know about his true mate. He knew deep down what she was about to tell him was very important. He looked around the corridor and noticed they were not far from his living quarters but far enough he wanted her to finish what she was saying before she changed her mind. Spying an alcove to the right beside one of the huge planters that graced the palace, he stopped and slowly backed Trisha into it. He pressed her up against the wall while his symbiot lay down in front of it, preventing them from being disturbed. Kelan brushed a loose strand of Trisha's hair away from her face, letting the long curl wrap around his fingers. He drew it up to his nose and sniffed at the delicate fragrance. Keeping it between his fingers, he touched the soft strands to Trisha's cheek.

"Go on," Kelan said softly.

Trisha looked up at Kelan in a daze. She wanted him so badly at that moment she wouldn't have protested if he were to take her right then and there. She had never felt this strongly about anyone before, not even Peter.

"Kelan?" Trisha asked in an uncertain voice. "Will you kiss me?"

Kelan felt his dragon snap to attention at Trisha's softly spoken request. His dragon wasn't the only thing snapping. His blood heated and flowed south to pool in his cock, stiffening it with need until the pain of it throbbed against the front of his pants.

He answered her request the only way he could, by sealing his lips to hers in a desperate kiss filled with longing and need. He wanted her so badly it was an addiction coursing through his veins. He had never craved anything in his life like he craved the taste of her. Kelan deepened the kiss when Trisha parted her lips, slipping his tongue inside and drinking deeply. He couldn't suppress the moan of hunger that escaped him as Trisha's sweet taste washed over him.

Kelan wrapped his arms around Trisha's slim waist, pulling her up against him at the same time as he pushed her farther back against the wall. Trisha lifted up onto her toes to get a little higher. Kelan seemed to understand Trisha's need to get closer and lifted her up so she could wrap her long legs around his waist. The position aligned Trisha's hot, feminine core with Kelan's hard shaft. He rocked his hips against her, needing to feel, touch, and taste every part of her.

He pulled away and began running passionate kisses down along Trisha's jaw, moving toward her neck, his teeth beginning to elongate as his control slipped and his dragon began taking over. Kelan could feel the dragon's fire building inside him, but he was beyond trying to control it. He wanted to claim Trisha, then and there. It took a couple of moments for the sound of a feminine throat clearing to penetrate his and Trisha's passionate hunger.

"Kelan," an amused feminine voice said from behind him.

Kelan leaned his head against Trisha's shoulder with a shuddering sigh. *The gods and goddesses are against me. That's all there is to it. I am never going to get a chance to claim my mate,* he thought despondently. *I must have done something really, really horrendous to deserve to be kept in such constant agony.* His dragon groaned in agreement. It knew better than to argue with the female trying to get their attention.

"Who is that?" Trisha whispered, looking wide-eyed at the beautiful woman standing behind Kelan with an amused expression on her face.

"My mother," Kelan whispered back with a groan.

Trisha turned a bright red and slowly released her legs from around Kelan's waist. Once she was standing on her own two feet again, she resisted the temptation to bury her face in Kelan's chest in embarrassment. This was not the way she would have liked to have met his mother. Kelan's mom probably thought she was a harlot for making out with her son in the middle of the corridor in broad daylight. This was definitely a new experience for Trisha. Her only other experience in dealing with mothers came from Ariel and Carmen's mom and her former mother-in-law.

"Hello, *Dola*," Kelan said with resignation. He could feel his dragon curling up in a pout. His mother was going to really enjoy this. It must be payback for all the mischief

he and his brothers did when he was younger, he thought
with regret.

* * *

Trisha's fears of meeting Kelan's mom, Morian, were
quickly alleviated. Instead of being upset at finding one of
her sons in a compromising position in a public place, she
turned out to be delighted. That was more than Trisha could
say for Kelan. He growled, moaned, and groaned to no
avail. Morian would not be turned away from meeting
Trisha. She accompanied them to Kelan's living quarters
where, Kelan informed Trisha in no uncertain terms, she
would be staying. If Trisha understood him correctly, he
also made a veiled promise to finish what had been started
in the corridor.

Kelan finally excused himself to deal with some urgent
business but not before sending his mother a furious glare.
Morian simply ignored her son and waved him away with a
mischievous smile. Trisha decided then and there she loved
the woman.

"There is a dinner tonight to welcome you and the other
women to our world. I can't begin to express my joy at
finding that not just one of my sons has been gifted with a
true mate but three! For them to find them from another
species brings promise to our world," Morian was saying as
she poured a hot beverage that smelled a lot like a type of
tea. Handing one cup to Trisha, she leaned back against the
cushions of the couch with a contented smile. "Hopefully, I
will be gifted with children of my children soon," she
added with a sparkle to her eye.

Trisha blushed and took a sip of the drink. It tasted like a mint-flavored tea. She hoped it would help calm her stomach the way mint tea back home used to. Thinking about home brought sudden tears to Trisha's eyes. She needed to get home, the sooner, the better. Her dad must be devastated by her disappearance. Maybe Kelan's mom could help her.

"I have to return home to my planet as soon as possible. It is imperative that I return," Trisha said fiercely.

Morian's hand paused in the act of raising the delicate cup to her lips. She frowned as she looked into Trisha's eyes and lowered her cup back to her lap. "Did you not want to come with my son?" she asked softly.

"I…We…" Trisha tried to answer her question without upsetting Morian. "It's complicated. Our friend, Abby, had been kidnapped by a really bad man. We were chasing after them to rescue her. We didn't know there were any such things as aliens or dragons or whatever they are called. We just wanted to save our friend," Trisha explained disjointedly.

Morian gazed into Trisha's eyes, like she was trying to see deep into her soul. "Why is it so important for you to return?" She asked carefully.

Trisha's eyes filled with tears and pain as she thought of what her dad must be going through. Disjointedly at first, Trisha explained what she had tried to explain to Kelan earlier in the corridor about her dad and why it was so important for her to return to him. She told Morian about the accident, her failed marriage, and the pain and grief her father endured during the year and a half it took for Trisha to learn how to be whole again. Trisha left nothing out, not her pain, not her grief, not even her fight to live again.

"Does my son know all this?" Morian asked softly when Trisha's voice faded to silence.

Trisha shook her head. "I was just starting to explain it to him when we got distracted," she said with a rosy color highlighting her cheeks.

Morian sat back against the cushions of the couch and studied Trisha for a few moments before she replied. "Then you must return for your father. It is the only way." She held up her hand when she saw Trisha's look of hope. "But understand this, you are my son's true mate whether you want to believe this or not. You have been accepted by his symbiot which adorns your wrists. You have been accepted by his dragon who wants you just as desperately as my son does. You must understand that to leave him now would be to condemn him to death. Now that he knows you exist, he cannot survive without you." Morian paused to let what she was saying sink in before she continued.

"But if I return to my dad…" Trisha began only to stop when Morian shook her head.

"I said you must return for your father. You said you promised if you went to the stars you would take him, is that correct?" Morian looked expectantly at Trisha. At Trisha's nod, she continued. "Then my son must take you back so you can bring him with you here. It is the only way for all of you to be happy."

Trisha looked at Morian in disbelief. She made something that seemed so impossible, sound so easy. "Do you think Kelan will do that? For me? For my father?" Trisha asked hesitantly.

Morian laughed softly. "My dear, my son would give you the entire universe if he could. Don't you know? You are the most important thing in his life. You are the very breath he breathes."

* * *

Trisha was laughing at some of the stories Ariel was telling her. She almost felt sorry for Kelan's other brothers, Mandra and Creon. Ariel and Carmen were giving both men a run for their money.

Trisha was in a much better mood after spending time with Morian. She seemed to make life appear so much simpler. After hashing out what Trisha needed to do to convince Kelan to take her back to Earth for her father, they spent the better part of the afternoon with the dressmaker. Morian ordered one of the guards to bring Ariel, Carmen, and Cara to Trisha's new living quarters for fittings for the dinner that night. Unfortunately, Carmen refused to come, and Cara couldn't be found. The last anyone saw of her, she was off flying on the back of a giant bird of some type. Morian was determined not to be denied though and gave the dressmaker measurements for both of the absent women so they could have clothing made. Ariel and Trisha loved the fashion show the dressmaker put on for them using different women from the palace to model for them. After some haggling, Trisha was able to pick out some outfits. Trisha was not much of a dress kind of girl so it took both Ariel and Morian to finally make her give in. Ariel on the other hand, loved wearing dresses. She even made suggestions for altering the designs of a few to match some of the styles found back on Earth with a grin that promised the men on Valdier would love the changes. They were just finishing up when a servant came to ask them to join Abby for refreshments.

"Why didn't you ask Abby to join us?" Trisha asked politely as she placed a bolt of material back on the cart for the dressmaker.

"The dressmaker has already prepared several outfits for Abby. Zoran was concerned she was exhausted and wanted her to rest for a while. I am afraid I have other pressing issues so I will not be able to join you. I look forward to meeting my new daughter later this evening. If you will excuse me, I will take my leave for now," Morian said with a soft smile. She gave both Trisha and Ariel a hug and a kiss before she parted ways with them in the hall outside of Trisha's living quarters.

"I really like her," Ariel said with a grin. "And don't tell Carmen, but I think this place is pretty hot."

Trisha laughed. She agreed. She wouldn't tell Carmen, and she was thinking this place was pretty "hot" too, especially when she thought of Kelan in it.

They were following the servant down a series of corridors. Trisha and Ariel were almost there when Kelan's and Mandra's symbiots came trotting up to them. Bio was back into the shape of a dog and Mandra's, well, Trisha wasn't quite sure what it was in the shape of but Ariel didn't seem to mind. Trisha didn't say anything when she saw additional gold bands swirl up Ariel's arms forming delicate bands on her forearms when Ariel reached down to hug the golden creature.

Trisha was just responding to a comment Ariel made when the door to Abby's living quarters opened. "Did you see the material and some of the outfits those women brought in?" Trisha was saying. She absentmindedly ran her fingers over Bio's huge golden head.

"I know I'm going to look good tonight in that green creation. The men won't know what hit them!" Ariel replied.

"Hey, Abby," Trisha and Ariel called out together with a huge grin when they saw Abby looking at them with a dazed smile on her face. Trisha looked around the extravagantly decorated room curiously and gave a low whistle.

"Wow, can you get over the size of this place?" Ariel asked as she moved aside to let a young female servant by with a tray of refreshments.

Trisha watched Abby move over to the low table and made room for the tray, quietly thanking the young girl, who quickly bowed and left, closing the door behind her.

She couldn't help but feel Abby fit this place perfectly. Abby seemed to have that quiet elegance that fit perfectly into a palace setting.

"Hi. Come sit and have some refreshments," Abby said as she poured three cups of tea, then settled into a plush, cushioned chair near the window. "Isn't Carmen with you?"

Ariel let out a heavy sigh before shaking her head, "No. Carmen…is being Carmen."

Abby's long hair draped over her shoulder and down one side as she pulled her long legs up under her. "What does that mean?"

Trisha took another chair as Ariel sat down heavily on the couch across from Abby. "Carmen has issues," Trisha said as she kicked off her shoes and curled her legs under her.

God, it felt so good to be able to do it without any pain. Trisha still couldn't believe she was as good as new. She really needed to ask Kelan how Bio was able to heal her. She needed to talk to Kelan about a lot of things, Trisha thought with a sigh. She didn't understand all this true mate stuff, but she knew something was going on inside her and wanted to find out what it was and where it was going. All she could think about anymore was Kelan this and Kelan that. Trisha's lips curved into a small smile when she felt Bio come and lie as close to her chair as possible, propping her huge head on the armrest. Trisha gently stroked the smooth golden head, letting her fingers twirl into the gold.

It should have felt weird, but it didn't. A calming warmth seemed to fill her. Bio must have felt it too as her eyes seemed to droop, and she let out a little puff of air before they closed all the way. Trisha returned her focus to the conversation at hand. She not only heard the sad tone in Ariel's voice as she talked about her sister, but saw it etched across her face as well.

"Not issues so much as just so much pain," Ariel was saying. "She lost her husband three years ago and has never recovered from it."

"Do you think being here is making it harder on her?" Abby asked softly.

Trisha could see the concern and guilt in Abby's eyes as she asked the question. Trisha personally thought this might have been the best thing to have happened to all of them. She knew once her dad was here with her, she would be perfectly happy to stay. She wanted to explore the feelings she had for Kelan and knew there was only one place she could do that, on Valdier. Kelan would never be safe on Earth. She just needed to convince the two most important men in her life that she needed both of them.

Both Trisha and Ariel shook their heads at the same time. Ariel gave Abby a small smile, "I think being here was the best thing that ever happened to Carmen. She can't run away here, at least not like she has been doing. She was looking for a way to die to be with Scott again. She can't do that here."

Trisha couldn't resist adding with a mischievous smile. "I don't think Creon is going to let her get away with running anymore."

"Who's Creon?" Abby asked, looking back and forth as Ariel frowned at Trisha.

"Creon is a scary son-of-a-bitch…" Ariel began.

"…Who has the hots for Carmen and is probably the only one who can break through the wall she has built," Trisha finished stubbornly. It was true; she'd heard about what happened in the transporter room after she and Kelan transported down. It seemed when Creon first met Carmen there was one hell of a fight. What surprised Trisha was it sounded like this Creon guy wouldn't let any of the other warriors near Carmen, and it hadn't been because she would have hurt them. From the little she heard, he was roaring *Mine!* at anyone who went near her.

Ariel glared at Trisha before she gave a delicate sniff and replied softly. "You're right, of course. Carmen would never have let go as long as she was back on Earth. I don't know if this Creon guy will be the one, but I have to agree he looked mighty interested when he first saw her." Trisha almost laughed at that understatement.

"So…" Trisha asked looking at Abby. She could tell Ariel wanted to change the subject. "Do you know what this dinner tonight is about? And has anyone seen Cara?"

Abby laughed as she explained what had happened earlier with Cara. It seemed, as of fifteen minutes ago, Trelon was still trying to catch their nimble little dragonfly.

"As for the dinner tonight, I don't know. Zoran has been very hush-hush about it."

Trisha shook her head as she listened to Cara's new mischief. It was just like her to keep things fun. After visiting for another hour, Trisha decided if she was going to knock Kelan's socks off she better head back to their living quarters. A small smile curved her lips as she thought of the word "their." She never thought she would meet another man. Hell, she never thought another man would ever want her after her accident, what with her being so broken and scarred. Peter used her injuries as an excuse as to why he wouldn't touch her anymore. Later, he blamed her being confined to a wheelchair on why he was having affairs. What he neglected to tell Trisha was the affairs actually started before her accident. She found out that wonderful little news when she went through some papers he forgot to take with him. Trisha shook her head in self-disgust. She needed to open that black hole again—Peter, damn his hide, had snuck out.

* * *

Kelan growled at his brother, Creon, in frustration. Couldn't he read the damn report any faster? Or better yet, just let them read it themselves when they could focus on it better! Between his symbiot, his mother, and now his brothers, he was still in the same position he had been in for the past two weeks—hard and horny. His focus on the topic of Zoran's capture and the Curizan military base Creon found abandoned was limited to nil. His brother was safe, and they didn't have anything to blow up or anyone to kill. As far as he was concerned everything else could wait until after he claimed his mate. Looking at the position of the sun, he sighed in aggravation. By the time he left here he would need to get ready for the damn dinner Mandra and his mother set up for the human females. He couldn't help but think darkly perhaps Trelon's mate would sabotage it, and it would be cancelled. He glanced over to where Trelon was sitting across the table from him. He seemed to be paying about as much attention to the discussion as he was. At the rate they were going, Valdier could be under attack and not one of the brothers would give a damn. So much for the royal family protecting their people! Every single one of them, Creon included if the dark scowl on his face was any indication of his mood, was being turned upside down and inside out by a bunch of delicate, infuriating females from another world. Kelan practically yelled out in relief when Zoran finally said there was nothing else they could do for the evening. Kelan suspected Zoran just wanted to get back to his true mate, lucky bastard. *If, no, not if,* Kelan thought with grim determination. *When I get Trisha alone tonight I am not leaving our living quarters until I claim her as my true mate.*

Kelan headed for the door. He was halfway down the corridor when he heard his name called out. The only reason he slowed down was because it was his mother. Kelan looked at her as she walked quickly toward him. He knew the look on her face, and it did not bode well for his peace of mind. She was on a mission, and Kelan somehow suspected it involved his mate.

"Hello again, *Dola*," Kelan said, giving Morian a light kiss on her cheek. "I would have thought you would be making sure all the preparations for the dinner were completed."

Morian gave Kelan a reproving look. "Of course, I made sure everything was prepared. I need to talk to you about your true mate," Morian said as she threaded her arm through Kelan's and began walking toward his living quarters with him.

Kelan frowned. "What of her?" he asked suspiciously.

"You must return her to her home world as soon as possible," Morian began.

"*Never!*" The word exploded out of Kelan before he could even think to hold it back. His dragon came to life in a sudden fury. It would never let its mate go. *Mine! She is mine!* it snarled possessively. *Calm, my friend, I will never let our mate go.* Kelan reached inward to calm the swirling fire threatening to escape him. How could his mother even suggest he return his true mate? She knew that was impossible.

Morian stopped in the middle of the corridor and turned to stand in front of Kelan. She continued gently but firmly. "You must return her to her home so she can bring her father back. There is much you do not know about your mate. She loves her father very much, and he is her only living family. She is slowly tearing herself apart knowing the type of pain he is feeling at losing her." Morian paused when she saw the stubborn set to Kelan's jaw. "Kelan."

Morian waited until Kelan looked down into her eyes. "…remember the pain of your own father's loss. Now, imagine what it would have been like if you could have prevented it, or worse, never knew what happened to him. For a parent, it is even worse. When Zoran was taken, and I did not know where he was or what was happening to him…" Morian's eyes filled with tears as she remembered the pain and despair she felt at the loss of her oldest son. "…it is unbearable. You cannot leave Trisha's father to spend the rest of his existence not knowing. You cannot sentence Trisha to live the rest of hers with the pain and regret of not being able to let him know she is safe and happy."

Kelan's jaw worked back and forth. "*Dola*, I cannot let her go," Kelan said in a strained voice. He and his dragon were terrified. Was he meant to lose his true mate before he ever had a chance to claim her? he wondered.

"Take her back but return with both of them. Only then will your true mate know peace," Morian said softly.

Chapter 8

Kelan nodded distractedly to the guards stationed outside of his rooms. He entered quietly, not sure of the reception he would receive after talking with his mother. His mind was buzzing with all the possible outcomes. Ever since he met the human female his life was no longer his own. He could not believe how much it had changed in such a short time. He knew he would have to take Trisha back to Earth. He only hoped she would return with him, with or without her father.

He was beginning to discover the human females did not feel the same compulsion to mate as a Valdier female. A Valdier female would not care what happened to anyone other than her mate. The human females cared about others, often times above themselves.

He often wondered what made his own mother different from the average Valdier female. Was it because of her royal blood that was said to come directly from the gods and goddesses? Was it because she never met her true mate? He knew she loved his father passionately, but there was never the binding of souls with his father's dragon or his father's symbiot. When his father was killed in the hunting accident that took the life of his uncle as well, his father's symbiot, which his father foolishly sent off on its own, returned to the hive. The location of the hive was known only by his older brother Zoran and Zoran's symbiot. Should something happen to him, then the next royal blood's symbiot would guide the new king to it. Some thought the symbiots were actually the blood of the gods and goddesses sent to protect the Valdier warriors. Those who did not live by the code of the Valdier warrior lost the right to the symbiots' protection and healing powers, and normally did not survive long.

Kelan walked through the living area into his sleeping quarters. He was in the process of removing his shirt when he heard a soft gasp. Jerking the shirt the rest of the way over his head, he looked in stunned disbelief at the vision before him. All thoughts and doubts, as well as all of his blood flow, went south. Kelan let his shirt drop to the floor. He took a small step forward before he stopped, clenching his fists tightly and praying he could remain in control.

* * *

Trisha looked at Kelan and wondered if she had made a tactical error. She should never, ever have let Ariel pick out and modify the design for a dress. She knew what Ariel was like. She liked to wear daring outfits that showed off all the curves. Ariel insisted on coming in and helping her get ready for the dinner tonight. Trisha sat through two hours of agonizing torture as Ariel braided and twisted Trisha's hair up into an elaborate hairdo any movie star would envy. Then she brought out the dress the dressmaker had altered. It was a stunning gold and black sleeveless halter gown with a scooped neckline and no back to speak of. There was a slit running from her hip all the way down to the floor. Black sandals with glittering gold gems peeked out from under the hem. Bio made sure Trisha had plenty of jewels. There were delicate wraps of gold threading through her hair. Thin ribbons of gold hung from her ears and a delicate chain with a tiny dragon in the shape and color of Kelan hung from her neck. Bio decided to finish off the accessories with twin gold armbands around Trisha's forearms. Each one was of a dragon, one of Kelan and one of a female intertwined. Ariel only applied a small amount of makeup to Trisha's face. She said all Trisha really needed to do was enhance her already dark eyes. The outlining Ariel did around Trisha's eyes gave her an exotic look and brought out the dark chocolate-brown in them.

Trisha ran her hands down over her stomach and along her hips. She gave Kelan an uncertain smile. "Do you like?"

Trisha knew she liked what she was seeing, lots of bare chest and muscles. She hoped he didn't cover up any time soon. She wouldn't mind doing a little exploring before they left for the dinner. Hell, at this point in time she wouldn't mind if they ended up missing the dinner.

Kelan stood there devouring Trisha with his eyes. His hands clenched and unclenched as he fought for control. His dragon was panting and drooling at his mate. *Beautiful. My mate is beautiful. Bite now!*

Kelan nodded his head silently. He didn't know if he was telling Trisha he liked what he was seeing or agreeing with his dragon about biting her now. He drew in a deep breath. *Oh, gods and goddesses,* Kelan thought with despair. *She smells good enough to eat!*

Trisha watched as Kelan seemed to start to pant. A wicked smile curved her lips. Maybe she hadn't made a bad choice after all. If he liked the front, she wondered what kind of reaction she would get when he saw the back—or lack of it. Feeling incredibly beautiful and more than a little bit horny and daring, Trisha decided she wanted to find out just how much control he really had.

"What do you think of the back? Ariel modified the design. She thought the guys here might like to see what Earth women wear," Trisha said with an innocent smile just before she turned her back to Kelan and looked over her bare shoulder.

A low, deep growl burst from Kelan's throat. His dragon refused to be denied any longer. The idea of other males seeing his mate like this almost drove Kelan insane. Normally, Valdier men and women were not shy about their bodies or their desires, but for some reason, the thought of other males gazing upon his mate in something so sexy, so arousing, was more than he could stand. He did not want to share Trisha with any other males. Kelan's golden eyes darkened as the need to claim her poured through him. He would not be denied any longer. With a low growl, he moved on silent feet toward Trisha. He heard her swift intake of breath and smelled her arousal at his approach.

He stopped directly behind her, daring her to resist him. "You are mine, Trisha Grove. I claim you as my true mate. No other may have you. I will live to protect you. You are mine, *mi elila*…forever," Kelan whispered against the sensitive skin behind her ear.

Kelan let the tips of his fingers run up the length of Trisha's bare back. A deep groan escaped him at the feel of her silky skin. Leaning forward, Kelan ran his lips lightly across the top of Trisha's shoulder, enjoying how she leaned back against him. Trisha didn't even try to contain the moan that escaped her at the feel of Kelan's lips against her overheated skin. She tilted her head to the side to give him better access, thankful that she had let Ariel talk her into putting it up. She wanted, needed, to feel his lips all over her.

"No dinner tonight?" Trisha panted out the plea for agreement.

Kelan ran his hands down over the front of Trisha's dress gripping her hips and pulling her back against his hard shaft. "No dinner. The only thing I am going to be eating is you," Kelan replied hoarsely.

Kelan drew Trisha back against his bare chest. The feel of her skin against his ignited a raging fire deep inside of him. They would be lucky if they made it to the bed tonight, Kelan thought. Kelan leaned forward so he could stroke his tongue along the curve of Trisha's neck once, then twice. He felt his teeth elongate as his dragon came to the surface partway. *Now, my friend, now we claim our mate.* On the third pass over the delicate curve between Trisha's neck and shoulder, Kelan bit down hard, locking Trisha to him. He wrapped his arms tightly around her when she would have jerked away, trapping her against his hard length. When he felt her shudder of surrender, he began breathing the dragon's fire into her bloodstream. He not only felt his dragon's roar of triumph but felt its possessive claim on its mate. Tonight, if the gods and goddesses willed it, a new dragon would be born. Kelan let the dragon's fire pour from him in wave after wave of hot need. He was afraid of the intensity of the fire pouring out of him and into Trisha. He was afraid he had waited too long to claim her. He wanted to draw back, but it seemed to continue to build until he heard Trisha's soft moans turn to whimpers of pain as the fire swept through her body.

"Kelan!" Trisha wailed as her body reacted to the surge of dragon fire sweeping through it.

She tried to clamp her thighs shut as a flood of hot desire swept down to her feminine core soaking her panties with need. The pain from Kelan biting down on her was nothing compared to the pain of need she felt rolling through her body. Her nipples swelled to tight round pebbles, throbbing and aching. Kelan continued to hold her still against his body. He pressed one of his legs against the back of hers forcing her to open for him. The slit in her dress fell to one side leaving a long length of pale skin open for Kelan's hand to slide down and around until he pressed up against the throbbing ache between her legs. Trisha threw her head back and screamed as she came hard and fast.

Trisha's body was on fire. Never in her life could she remember being this aroused. It was almost like her body belonged to someone else. She needed Kelan fiercely. Trisha moved against Kelan, rubbing her body against his and arching her back so her ass was pressed against his hard shaft. She had been startled when she felt him clamp down onto her neck. The pain that flashed through her at the first bite was nothing compared to the pain of arousal she was experiencing now. She could actually feel her pussy pulsing, begging for relief. Whatever Kelan was doing to her was unlike anything she had ever experienced before. As his grip around her waist tightened, drawing her closer, she whimpered. The feel of his bare skin against her bare back made her crave even more. It was so bad, even her clothes were beginning to hurt where they touched her swollen breasts. Kelan must have understood the need and her growing discomfort because he pushed aside the long length of fabric where the slit was exposing her bare leg to his touch. Trisha could feel the pressure building as he slowly worked his way under the fabric to her overheated core. The moment his fingers slipped between the material covering her mound and her pulsing pussy she felt a hot wave wash over her center, and she came hard and fast just as he sank his fingers deep inside her. Trisha couldn't contain the scream that broke from her. Her vaginal walls clamped down tightly on Kelan's fingers as she pulsed around him. Trisha threw her head back as the wave of the climax crested, falling into the furious tide of heat washing through her. As she started to come down from the heaven of release, she became aware of Kelan gently lapping at her neck. She moaned as he turned her toward him. The feel of his broad chest brushing against the fabric of her dress caused her nipples to tighten to aching peaks.

Trisha leaned her head against Kelan's chest as he pulled her close. He was running one of his hands up and down the heated surface of her bare back while the other forced her impossibly closer to his hard rod. He continued to lap at her neck. The feel of his rough tongue was beginning to arouse her again. She closed her eyes as a sweet, but fierce shaft of pain swelled up from her pussy and radiated outward. Trisha couldn't help the restless movement of her body against his.

"Kelan, what have you done to me?" Trisha moaned softly as the restlessness grew.

Kelan reluctantly pulled away from the dragon's mark on Trisha's neck. Both he and his dragon agreed they had never seen a more beautiful sight. Kelan shuddered as he felt the stirring of the dragon's fire in his mate. The next few hours would be the most exhilarating and the most terrifying of his life. If Trisha was not strong enough… *No*, Kelan thought. He would not think of the danger to her. He would only focus on the joy of watching his true mate being born. He refused to believe anything else could happen.

"It is the dragon's fire mating. It has begun," Kelan whispered against Trisha's hair.

He began to gently undo the long, curly strands. He wanted to be able to wrap his fists around it as he took her. He wanted to see it spread out around her as he drove into her over and over. The gold threads of the symbiot dissolved pouring down around Trisha's neck. His symbiot would monitor Trisha and heal her if he accidentally hurt her during the mating. He could already feel the pressure building inside his body as the first waves of heat and the heady scent of his and his dragon's mate began the process of the transformation. Kelan finished undoing Trisha's hair and watched as it fell like a fragrant curtain down her back almost to her hips. He let one finger lengthen and change until a long, razor sharp claw protruded from the end.

Bending down to seal his lips over Trisha's, Kelan sliced through the top of the halter holding Trisha's gown on. It fell in a glittering wave around her ankles leaving her in nothing but a pair of black panties and her black and gold high-heeled sandals. Kelan groaned when he pulled back to look at the hard pebbles that were pressing against his chest. The pain of his erection reminded him he was still partially dressed. He smiled when he heard Trisha's whimper of protest as he pulled farther away so he could remove his boots and pants.

* * *

Trisha stood still as she watched Kelan step away from her. She wasn't in the least bit shy or embarrassed about standing naked in front of him. She was beyond that. Trisha closed her eyes and let her head fall back as a burning wave of need exploded over her suddenly. It was so strong she could feel the liquid of her arousal as it coated her already damp panties. What did Kelan say? Something about a dragon's fire mating. If it was anything like a real fire she would have to admit it was doing a great job at working her toward self-combustion. A whimper escaped her as another shaft of painful need swept through her. Trisha opened eyes so dark with desire they appeared black.

"Kelan," Trisha panted out through clenched teeth. "Kelan…I…need you," she struggled to get the words out as another wave built, stronger this time.

Kelan quickly kicked off his boots and sliced through the ties holding his pants when they became tangled. He stepped out of them as soon as they hit the floor. Moving quickly, he swept Trisha up in his arms and carried her over to the bed, placing her on her back. He let a claw extend briefly so he could slice through the sides of her panties. Trisha lifted her hips just far enough so he could pull them out from under her and toss them onto the floor near his pants. Kelan gripped Trisha's hips tightly in his hands keeping her slightly raised off the bed and looked down into her passion-filled face. His face tightened with need as he aligned his throbbing cock with her moist entrance. Never again would he and his dragon feel the gnawing, never-ending hunger. Never again would they be eaten alive with loneliness.

"You are mine forever, Trisha," Kelan growled in a deep voice as he and his dragon surged forward, claiming their mate for eternity.

Trisha gasped as she felt the thick length of Kelan stretch her tight canal, filling her until she didn't know where she ended and he began. She cried out at the fullness. It was only the fact she was drenched that allowed his thick, long length a smooth entrance to her hot core. The farther Kelan filled her, the hotter the wave of desire built until Trisha was frantically gripping Kelan's forearms, panting.

"Please!" Trisha begged. She didn't know for sure what she was begging him for; all she knew was if the pressure building inside her wasn't released soon she would explode into a million little pieces.

Kelan moaned as he seated himself fully inside Trisha. He held still for a moment, trying to get a better hold on his control. He was very close to losing it, and he was afraid of what would happen to Trisha if he did. Kelan closed his eyes and gritted his teeth at the pain of holding back. His dragon was growling and pacing furiously. It could feel its fire burning inside of Trisha. It wanted to see its mate born. Kelan was fighting for control with his dragon when a sharp pain on his neck jerked him back to awareness. A deafening roar erupted from Kelan as Trisha sank her teeth into his neck. Kelan's fragile control disintegrated as his and his dragon's hold on their need to claim their mate overwhelmed them. Kelan's eyes popped open, and he gazed down at the top of Trisha's head. She was sucking on his neck and biting it in a desperate attempt to find relief from the building waves of heat coursing through her. Kelan wrapped one arm around her waist, splaying his hand over her back to pull her closer while his other hand held both of them up. Trisha's legs were wrapped around Kelan's upper thighs, forcing him deeper into her as she tried to rock against him. Kelan pulled almost all the way out before slamming back into Trisha's heat. He held her tightly against him so each thrust would go deeper and deeper. He wanted to bury his scent so far into her essence there would never be any doubt as to who she belonged to.

Trisha released Kelan's neck and began peppering his jaw with frantic little kisses. Her arms wound themselves around his shoulders, clawing for purchase as Kelan's powerful strokes rocked her body. Trisha felt the wave of dragon fire burst up to meet Kelan's fiery claim on her. Her head fell back, and a silent scream tore from her throat as her body stiffened in a powerful climax. Kelan leaned his head down, rubbing his nose against Trisha's exposed throat. He thrust again and again until the swollen walls of Trisha's core swallowed him, holding him deep inside her as she came around him. Kelan's cry of fulfillment echoed around the room as he surged into Trisha, spilling his hot seed against her womb and filling her with his and his dragon's essence.

Trisha fell back against the soft covers of the bed, trembling. She gazed up at Kelan in wonder as he continued to pulse deep inside her. Kelan lowered himself down until he rested on his elbows, caging Trisha's body within his protective arms. He smiled down at her. The dragon's fire mating was only just beginning. They would make love over and over again, each time becoming more intense over the next several hours. Kelan was at a loss of words to describe how he felt at that moment. Because even though his body still craved more of his true mate, for once, the terrible, gnawing hunger that was never satisfied no longer clawed at his insides. Instead, a fire of warmth and contentment, of satisfaction filled him. He watched carefully as Trisha began moving again under him with a restless need. The next wave of dragon fire was building. There was no need to tell her it would only get hotter and more intense. He could tell by the widening of her eyes that she could feel the heat and intensity. Her lips parted in a pant as she tried to grip him again.

"No, *mi elila*. Put your arms up and hold onto the headboard. I want to see your beautiful face as I make love to you," Kelan said softly.

"Ah, *mi elila*, you are so very beautiful. Watch me as I claim you over and over," Kelan whispered passionately.

Kelan began rocking back and forth inside Trisha slowly at first. He changed his pace to match the building waves as they began breaking over Trisha, gentle at first, then with increasing intensity as if the outer edges of a hurricane were approaching the desolate shore that used to be her soul. Kelan watched as Trisha reached both arms up over her head and gripped the headboard of their bed. The move pushed her firm breasts up, the roses of her nipples taut with arousal. As Kelan increased the power of his thrust, he watched as her breasts swayed back and forth, teasing and tempting him at the same time. Trisha pulled her legs up higher so Kelan could thrust deeper, the flames inside her moving through her blood and calling for him and his dragon.

"Harder!" Trisha cried out as one wave flowed into the next. "Please! I need you so badly."

Kelan reached down and pinched Trisha's taut, plump nipples between his fingers, twisting and pulling on them until they were a dark rose. Trisha exploded upward with a husky cry as her body locked around Kelan's in another climax. Her arms strained behind her in an effort to hold onto what little sanity she had as one climax flowed into another. Kelan's hoarse yell followed shortly after Trisha's as her body milked his over and over. Kelan watched as the beginning shades of color rippled over Trisha's arms, chest, and neck. Bronze, gold, and black scales danced just under her skin, tantalizing him and his dragon with what their mate would look like. Kelan's dragon growled out encouragement to his mate. Tempting her to come forward and be born so they could be together. Trisha's head jerked around at the sound of the dragon's call, her eyes gazing deeply into her mate's. Kelan's eyes widened as he watched Trisha's eyes change slightly. The dark brown became even richer, darker, more succulent, with drops of gold sprinkled throughout them. Her pupils elongated into narrow slits as she searched for her mate. Kelan's dragon refused to be denied a chance to welcome his new mate into their world. Kelan released some of his tightly held control and allowed his dragon a chance to taste his mate.

Trisha's eyes grew wider as she watched the scales ripple along Kelan's chest, arms, and neck. His eyes changed to the narrow slits of black surrounded by gold that Trisha was used to seeing. She let go of the headboard and raised both arms up to touch the scales rippling across his broad chest. As she ran her fingertips lightly over him, she noticed the scales on her own arms. Trisha gasped and would have pulled away, but Kelan reached down and gripped her hands tightly against him.

"Don't," he said huskily. "Don't be afraid. You are beautiful."

Trisha watched as Kelan gently raised her arms up to his mouth. A shiver passed through her as his rough tongue moved over the scales on her palms. He moved slowly down, licking and kissing her wrists before moving back to her hands where he ran his tongue between each of her fingers. Trisha followed each move of his tongue in fascination. She could feel something moving deep inside her, answering the tender touch. Trisha opened her mouth to ask Kelan what was happening to her, but the next wave of dragon fire struck before she could utter anything more than a cry as a flash of intense pleasure/pain swept ruthlessly through her.

Kelan knew the worst, and most dangerous, part of the dragon's fire mating was just beginning. The transformation had begun. There was no going back for either of them. Kelan pulled out of Trisha and turned her over. When she would have curled up into a small ball, he growled out at her. Trisha turned and snarled back, showing her teeth. When Kelan snapped his teeth at her, she drew back—frightened by the intense burning inside her.

"What's happening?" Trisha asked. "What's wrong with me?"

Kelan brushed Trisha's long, curly hair to one side, letting it fall over her left shoulder. He pulled her up onto her hands and knees, thrusting one of his legs between hers to prevent her from closing them. He could see the effects of the dragon's fire on her body. Her mound was flushed and swollen from both their previous lovemaking and from the effects of the mating fire. The curly mix of light and dark brown hair glistened with moisture, begging him to take her. Kelan's mouth watered at the sight. He wanted, needed, to taste her desperately. Placing a palm in the center of Trisha's back, Kelan forced her forward and down until her ass was high in the air. He ran his hand gently over it before smacking it. Trisha's head jerked around, and she growled at him, but she didn't move. *Good*, Kelan thought with satisfaction. *She knows to submit to me even if she isn't happy about it.*

"You are going through the transformation," Kelan replied softly never taking his eyes off of her hot mound.

Before Trisha could ask Kelan what he meant by transformation, her world tilted as Kelan leaned back and buried his face in her throbbing cunt. Trisha leaned down and bit the covers of the bed, screaming as waves of pleasure unlike anything she had ever experienced washed over her. Kelan nipped the tight bud of Trisha's clit, moaning with pleasure as he was rewarded by another flood of her essence over his tongue. He spread the swollen lips so he could bury his tongue deep inside her, moving in and out as if his cock was riding her. Over and over, he drank from her, making her come time and time again until she begged him for mercy. Whenever Trisha would start to collapse down onto the bed, Kelan would nip her and slap her ass in warning. He and his dragon had been denied for far too long. He gave Trisha the time she needed on his warship; now was his and his dragon's turn. Trisha snapped back at Kelan when he nipped her again. Moving with a swiftness that took Kelan and his dragon by surprise, Trisha swung one of her legs back and around Kelan's neck and flipped him over. The move caused her own body to roll with them, giving her the advantage to continue the momentum until she was off the bed. Trisha threw the heavy weight of her hair over her shoulder and crouched down to give her a better center of gravity as she backed away.

"I was not finished," Kelan growled as he rolled onto his knees on the bed. "Come back here."

"No," Trisha snapped back.

Kelan's eyes narrowed and darkened as he recognized Trisha and her dragon were testing him. They wanted to know if he was the type of mate who could be easily controlled. He moved off the bed to stand. He flexed his shoulders, standing straight as he growled back a warning.

"I said...I was not finished," Kelan growled out again, taking a menacing step toward Trisha. "Come here."

Trisha stood up straight suddenly and looked Kelan in the eye. Tilting her head to the side, she let a small smile curve her lips before replying. "No."

Kelan moved with lightning speed toward his mate. He would make her submit to him. He was the warrior, the male, the protector. She was small and delicate. It was his and his dragon's responsibility to protect their mate. Kelan reached out to grab Trisha only to find she wasn't there. He spun in disbelief to find his mate sliding off the other side of the bed behind him.

Trisha felt invigorated at having the agility of her old body back. She didn't know why she wanted to challenge Kelan. It wasn't like she wanted to beat him or anything. She was just feeling playful, as if teasing Kelan to catch her was part of the mating rite. If he could not catch her, then he did not deserve her. Trisha watched as Kelan's eyes flared at her resistance. She felt an answering flame ignite inside her causing her to squirm as a flood of hot juice seeped down the inside of her leg. Kelan must have noticed. Trisha watched as his nostrils flared and his eyes darkened even further. He crouched down, and a low rumble sounded in the room. Trisha watched him warily.

She took a slight step away from the bed toward the back wall. Glancing around, she realized she didn't have a lot of options. There was a wall behind her with a bank of windows. There was the balcony overlooking the gardens and the city, but it was four stories below them. Access to the living area was out since Kelan was between her and the door. Her eyes flitted to the bathroom. It was the only other place she could possibly get to, if she could distract him long enough to reach it. Trisha took a step to the side, moving toward the living quarters in the hope of throwing Kelan off what she planned to do. He surprised her, though, when instead of coming around the bed like she thought he would, he leaped up onto it. Trisha let loose a squeal and dove for the bed again. Only this time, she rolled underneath it. Kelan let out a roar and jumped down just as she was out of his reach. Trisha continued rolling with a laugh and popped out on the other side. Kelan was still on his hands and knees before he realized what she was doing. His head popped up over the top of the bed, and he grinned at her in surprise. His little mate was not only frisky, she was smart, agile, and fast. Kelan could feel his dragon's rumble of approval. Trisha laughed as she twirled away toward the bathroom. Kelan was determined not to be outdone. He leaped up, rolling across the bed, and came after Trisha, capturing her just as she made it to the doorway of the cleansing room.

"Caught you, little one. Now, you are mine to ravish," Kelan teased as he wrapped his arms around Trisha's waist and lifted her against him. "I told you I wasn't done yet," Kelan whispered in her ear.

Trisha groaned as a heated wave answered his statement. "Kelan, what are you doing to me? I need you again. I don't understand this," she moaned out as she pushed back against him.

The heat was building inside her again, this time hotter than before. Sweat beaded on her forehead as the waves came faster and closer together. She felt something moving under her skin but couldn't concentrate on anything but the burning need to come. A particularly fierce wave hit her hard, almost making her double over from the intensity of it.

Trisha moaned again, trembling. "Please, make it stop," she whispered as the trembling increased.

"I can't, *mi elila*. Not yet," Kelan softly replied as he picked her up and took her back to the bed. "Don't fight it," Kelan murmured as he pressed soothing kisses against her forehead.

Trisha rolled over onto her stomach as soon as Kelan laid her down on the soft covers. She didn't understand any of this. The craving, the need, the fire inside her was like a riptide pulling her away from the safety of the shore. It didn't matter how hard she fought against it, it continued to sweep through her, pulling her under until she didn't know which way was up.

Kelan lay over Trisha, watching and waiting for the moment when he and his dragon would take her hard and fast. Kelan knew the dragon's fire in her blood was changing each of her organs—the very makeup of her blood—to match his. They would be as one, her light to his dark. Kelan's eyes darkened as he saw the thin veins dance across Trisha's back. She shuddered and moaned, kneading the covers of the bedspread between her fingers as she moved restlessly. It was time. Kelan gently lifted Trisha up until she was on her hands and knees again. This time, he aligned his swollen cock with her hot core. She was so swollen both of them moaned as he slowly pushed into her. Kelan gritted his teeth as he felt Trisha's hot channel close around his cock. When Trisha mewed in distress as the heat increased, he knew she was ready.

"Faster, Kelan. I need you to go faster," Trisha panted out as she rocked her hips backward, trying to impale herself farther on his hard shaft.

Kelan closed his eyes briefly as he fought for control, waiting for the tidal wave to strike. He moved slowly back and forth as it moved through her, building higher and hotter. As it reached its peak, Kelan slammed home burying himself balls-deep into Trisha. Trisha's moans turned to screams as the pressure built to a crescendo, engulfing her completely. Kelan and his dragon roared out in triumph as they watched the thin veins appearing along her back spread in the shape of delicate wings. He slammed into her over and over, pushing into her deeper and deeper as the heat built to a point he wondered if they would both be scorched by its burning intensity. Kelan leaned over, wrapping Trisha's long curly hair around one hand, forcing her head back and to the side while his other hand slid around her waist pulling her up against him. Kelan cried out as his body exploded in a powerful orgasm. Bending over, he bit down on Trisha's shoulder marking her a second time as his.

..*

Kelan's powerful orgasm burst through the fortress of heat and pressure inside of Trisha releasing it in a tidal wave of pleasure as her orgasm flooded her with intense pleasure. Trisha was beyond screaming. Her throat was raspy as she gasped for breath. She could feel Kelan's hard shaft pulsing in heavy waves inside her, filling her, possessing her in a way she never knew was possible. Trisha sobbed as the waves passed through her in an endless surge. How was it possible to experience so much pleasure and still be alive, she wondered. It was only as the final wave washed over her that she realized the heat and the aching, painful throb of need seemed to have subsided some. Trisha, unable to support herself any longer, slowly melted against Kelan's chest. Her eyes closed as the relief from the pressure swept away what little strength she had left. She was only vaguely aware of Kelan lowering her gently onto the bed without ever pulling out of her.

Kelan let Trisha's hair slide through his fingers, enjoying the silky curls as they resisted being let go. He held as still as possible, simply enjoying the feel of Trisha's hot core as tiny spasms continued to milk his seed from him. Never in his existence had he felt such a sense of contentment, of satisfaction, of completion. Pulling her closer against his body, he held her for a few more precious minutes. He would get up in a moment and bathe her. She would be sore, but his symbiot would take care of that discomfort. The dragon's fire mating was almost complete, they would make love at a slower, gentler pace over the next couple of hours until the fire burning in his mate's blood was finally put out. He would let her rest some. Her body would be exhausted from all the changes.

Kelan closed his eyes as the empty gulf that had been his soul was filled with an emotion so intense it frightened him. He held his life in his arms. Trisha was now the center of his universe and would always come first, even before his own needs. She was headstrong and stubborn and would make his life so much richer. Opening his eyes, he marveled at all the colors dancing in her curly hair. It reminded him of the scales that danced across her arms, chest, and neck earlier. His dragon stirred at the memory. *My mate is beautiful,* his dragon rumbled softly. *Our mate is beautiful,* corrected Kelan. Kelan slowly pulled out of Trisha, regretting the necessity of it. If he had his way, he would remain buried deep inside her forever. He shifted enough to gently roll her sleeping form into his arms and stood up. He would bathe her and let her sleep for a little while. He would also have his symbiot check her over to make sure she was okay. Carrying her to the cleansing room, Kelan quietly whispered the words binding Trisha to him as his true mate again before pressing a kiss to the dragon's mark on her neck.

Chapter 9

Kelan looked down at the sleeping form of his mate. One of Trisha's arms was thrown up above her head and the other lay across her stomach. Her long curly hair was all over the place, spread out in abandon across the pillows of his bed. Kelan felt a shaft of desire rock him making him hard again. Shaking his head, he wondered if it would always be like this when he looked at his mate. They made love on and off until the pale light of dawn began to lighten the sky. Kelan gave an order to his symbiot to check Trisha over again and protect her while he was gone.

He couldn't suppress the grin at the memory of her squeals last night when he commanded his symbiot to check her the first time. Kelan carried Trisha into the cleansing room to bathe her. She was so exhausted that she was barely awake when he lowered her into the bathing pool. Kelan was concerned about all the changes that were occurring inside her, especially after knowing the damage she had sustained previously. When his symbiot moved over her body, especially between her legs, she woke up with a squeal and started fighting him. That led to another round of lovemaking in the bathing pool. Kelan made a note to do that more often. It was the first time he'd ever made love in one but it would definitely not be the last, he thought with a satisfied grin.

As Kelan thought back to his symbiot's care of Trisha, he let out a curse. He still did not know what happened to her. It would be the first thing he found out when he returned. He was already doing a poor job of caring for his mate, he thought in disgust. Shaking his head, he forced himself to leave their sleeping area. He needed to check in with his brothers. The report of Trelon's mate being harmed at the dinner he and Trisha missed last night needed to be dealt with. If whoever took Zoran was now targeting their mates, he needed to know everything. He would do whatever was necessary to protect his mate. Kelan's dragon snarled in agreement. *Our mate, protect our mate always.* It growled fiercely.

..*

Kelan nodded to the guards stationed outside of his rooms. Between them and his symbiot, Trisha would be safe. He moved quickly through the corridors to the conference room. Opening the door, he saw Creon, Zoran, and Mandra already there. He nodded to them as he walked over to a small table set up with beverages and food.

"Do you know anything about what happened last night?" Kelan asked as he filled up a plate of food and poured himself a drink. Mating was hard work, he thought with a hidden grin; he would need to keep his energy up if he was to satisfy his mate.

Mandra looked at Kelan with a raised eyebrow. "Talking about last night, where were you? I did not see you or the female named Trisha there."

Kelan grinned as he moved to sit down in a chair near the windows. "We were detained."

Creon looked at Kelan with a scowl. "I'm glad someone was entertained."

Kelan laughed as he took a bite out of a piece of fruit before responding. "I take it the female named Carmen did not attend either? If she had, most of our male guests would have ended up in medical. I would have returned her and the one named Ariel to their planet if I could have."

Both Mandra and Creon surged to their feet in aggravation. Zoran, realizing Kelan was about to get his ass kicked by not one, but two of his older brothers, decided it was time to get back to business. He was just about to begin when Trelon slammed into the conference room.

"How is she?" Zoran asked quietly, looking with concern at Trelon's haggard face.

Trelon ran his hands through his hair in aggravation. "She is still sleeping. The healer has said she should heal completely. I can feel her dragon, but she is very weak. There was enough poison in Cara to kill a full grown warrior. Cara is less than half our size. Why? Why would anyone want to harm someone so beautiful?" Trelon asked, sinking down into a chair next to Mandra. He leaned forward, resting his elbows on his knees as he stared at the floor.

Kelan felt for his brother. He shuddered at the thought of anything happening to Trisha. As his true mate, he would do anything to protect and care for her. He would not stop until the person who harmed her was dead and no longer a threat.

"Do we know for sure she was the target? Could it be related to the Curizans' attack?" Zoran asked impatiently as he moved back around the table to sit down.

Trelon shook his head, responding in a tired voice. "She is the only one who was poisoned. We cannot even be sure how she was poisoned until she wakes so we can ask her what happened. Why was she so far away from the dining area? What did she eat or drink? Could she have been poisoned some other way?"

"Creon, what have you found out so far?" Zoran asked.

Kelan knew Creon was upset that the mate of one of his brothers was harmed. He knew Creon enough to know he would take an attack on one of their females personally since it happened in the sanctuary of their home. Creon was the darkest out of all five brothers, having seen and done things during the Three Wars none of the others knew about until it was over. He risked his life over and over on many occasions for the Valdier people. It was because of those risks the wars had finally ended. Still, if there was information out there, Creon would know about anything and everything that went on around the palace since last night. He probably even knew about Kelan's claim on Trisha as it was happening. That thought brought up his mate. He wanted to know if she could be in danger.

Creon responded to Zoran in a tightly controlled voice. "There appears to be more behind your capture than we suspected. I don't have enough information yet to give you the answers you are seeking. I am looking into some new intel I've received from some of my sources. Once I have confirmed they are valid, I can give you more information."

"Well, that was a great way to tell us absolutely nothing. Thanks, Creon," Kelan growled out sarcastically as his own frustration came to a head. Creon could be a tight-lipped son of a bitch when one tried to get information out of him. He wanted to know if Trisha could be in the same danger as Trelon's mate.

"Anytime, brother," Creon said giving Kelan a rude flick of his middle finger.

Mandra chuckled. "Creative, brother. Where did you learn that symbol?"

Creon grinned in amusement. "The human female Carmen seems to have a passionate use for it around me. Abby explained what it meant," Creon turned to Kelan with a twisted grin on his face. "It is not meant as a compliment."

Kelan growled. "I know exactly what it means. Trisha has used it more than once on me."

During the first few days on board the *V'ager,* Trisha would use the symbol whenever he refused to take her back to her home planet and then tried to order her to let him into his living quarters. He finally asked Trisha what the gesture meant. He was livid at first but soon began to see the humor of it. He began to think of creative ways she could "fuck him." Kelan bit back a curse as a wave of desire flooded through him, causing his cock to harden again. Just the thought of her was enough to fill him with need.

Kelan forced his mind back on what his brothers were discussing. Zoran went over areas of concern, plans for tightening security in the palace, and some of the day-to-day running that fell on the shoulders of the royal house before calling the meeting to an end.

* * *

Trisha came awake slowly, her body relaxed from a sound sleep. She blinked the sleep out of her eyes before rolling over onto her side and looking out the windows. The sun was high in the sky, telling her it was late morning. She curled an arm under her head and just lay there looking at the clouds as they danced across the bright sky. She shivered as she thought back to last night. What was she thinking? Trisha grimaced. *Obviously, I wasn't*, she thought in disgust. Tremors rocked her as she thought of all the ways and the number of times they had made love. Trisha rolled onto her back and closed her eyes as a sweet ripple of desire went through her at the memories. *Damn! I'm getting wet again just thinking about it.*

Trisha groaned out loud as she forced herself to get up. She needed a shower, some food, and a new strategy for getting home, because the saying "Resistance is futile" was definitely in full force whenever she was around Kelan. She had absolutely no willpower around him, she thought in disgust.

Trisha glanced at the end of the bed where Bio was lounging in a shaft of sunlight. "You were absolutely no help last night, do you know that? What happened to helping keep him away from me?" Trisha asked sternly. Of course, she blew the effect when she bent over and gave the big golden lump a hug and kiss on its snout.

Bio ran a silky, gold tongue over Trisha's cheek in affection. "Oh, and by the way, I didn't appreciate some of the moves you made on me last night! The thing between the legs..." Trisha wiggled her nose in distaste. "...Not happening again, is that clear?"

Bio just snickered and laid its huge golden head back down ignoring Trisha's complaint. It would do anything to make sure she was cared for, whether she liked it or not. It was bound to her essence as much as it was to Kelan's. Bio watched as Trisha walked into the cleansing room, a shimmer of color rippled over it as it sent warmth through the bands around Trisha's arms and neck to let her know its feelings about her. Trisha peeked back out of the doorway and blew Bio a kiss.

Trisha smiled affectionately and whispered, "I love you too."

* * *

Kelan returned to his living quarters as quickly as he could. He was concerned they did not know anything about what happened to Trelon's mate except the type of poison used on her. It was a type commonly found on their planet, so it was impossible to trace where it may have come from.

Kelan opened the door to his living quarters eager to see Trisha. He moved through the living area when he didn't see her, striding toward their sleeping area, concerned. Glancing around, he saw his symbiot on the rumpled bed lying contently in the sunlight. Turning toward the cleansing area where he heard water, Kelan grinned and quickly began removing his clothing. Wicked thoughts of what they did in the bathing pool last night filled his mind. He wondered how creative they could get in the shower unit. By the time he reached the doorway, a long line of clothing lay on the floor.

Kelan paused at the door to the shower unit, gazing with appreciation at his true mate. Her long, curly hair lay in heavy, wet strands down her back as she tilted her head back to raise it. Her eyes were closed, and a tiny smile curved her luscious lips. Kelan shivered as he imagined what those lips would feel like wrapped around his hard length. He silently opened the door and stepped in.

"I know you're there," Trisha said softly without opening her eyes.

Kelan reached out and pulled Trisha's wet body against his, lowering his head to brush a kiss against the dragon's mark. He loved how responsive her body was to his. He let his lips trail up her jaw while his hands trailed down over her hips to the rounded curve of her ass. Her moan filled the cleansing unit.

"Kelan…" Trisha breathed out on another moan.

"You are well rested?" Kelan asked between the light kisses he was peppering along her jaw and throat.

Trisha answered him by reaching out and grabbing his throbbing cock in her hand and stroking it from the base to the tip and back again. She opened her eyes and smiled as she felt his surprised jerk and answering groan. She cupped his balls with her other hand, massaging them gently while she let one finger stroke the underside of them behind his legs.

"What do you think?" she whispered, gazing into his blazing eyes.

Kelan sealed his lips over hers in a hungry kiss. He pushed her up against the wall of the cleansing unit, lifting her so she was forced to wrap her long legs around his waist. He kissed her with a hunger that shook both of them. Trisha curled her arms around his neck, tangling her fingers in his hair as she lifted up high enough to align his cock with her hot core. She locked her ankles tightly together forcing Kelan's ass forward. When they were aligned, she slowly lowered herself down onto his hard shaft.

"Oh, God!" Trisha groaned out loud as Kelan stretched her. "That feels so good."

Kelan's answering groan filled the cleansing unit as he began moving his hips back and forth. This position forced Trisha to open wide for him and gave him the advantage of impaling her deeply with each thrust. Kelan gasped as he felt her silky canal stroking the length of his cock. Burying his head in her shoulder, he tightened his arms and thrust upward faster and faster as the intense need to feel her come around him grew.

"Trisha, mine," Kelan muttered over and over as he thrust as deeply as he could go. Suddenly, he froze as his climax hit him. A groan left him, and he began to shake as his hot seed poured out of him in intense waves.

The feel of Kelan's cock pulsing, combined with the stimulation against her clit from where his cock stroked her again and again with each thrust, was enough to throw Trisha into her own orgasm. She gasped out Kelan's name as she felt her pussy answer his claim on her. As she started to come down from the explosive feelings rippling through her, she let her arms lie loosely around Kelan's neck while she rested her head against his shoulder.

"I think I love you," Trisha whispered against his skin.

A shaft of fear went through her as soon as the words escaped her lips. She wanted to withdraw them but it was too late. She could tell from Kelan's sudden stiffening that he heard her husky whisper. It terrified her because the last man she'd said that to didn't return it. Trisha turned her head farther into Kelan's throat, pressing her burning eyes against him in an effort to hold back her tears.

Kelan closed his eyes as he absorbed Trisha's softly spoken words. He could sense the fear behind them, as if she was afraid he would throw her declaration back in her face. He did not know what happened to her before on her planet, but he was going to find out. He would not let her fear telling him how she felt. He loved her with every fiber of his being.

We love her. Our mate. Our beautiful mate. Love our mate. Protect her, his dragon growled out softly.

Kelan leaned back and waved his hand to stop the cleansing unit. He kept his arms around Trisha, even as she tried to slide down his body. He simply curled one arm around her waist tightly and the other one under her luscious ass, preventing her from moving away from him. He stepped out of the shower and reached for the two towels stacked neatly on the counter. He gently set Trisha down on the counter, stepping just far enough away so he could tilt her chin up until she was forced to look at him.

Kelan smiled tenderly as he looked into Trisha's dark chocolate eyes. "I love you too, *mi elila.* You are my heart, my life, the true mate of my dragon and myself," Kelan said each word slowly, carefully, tenderly as he gently used one of the towels to dry the water from her hair and face. "Never doubt you mean everything to me."

Trisha gazed into Kelan's eyes. What she saw took her breath away. The depth of love, of longing in his eyes was clearly on display. Unlike Peter who swore he loved her but never really did, Kelan spoke words that she knew came from his heart. He was a warrior who was strong enough to admit how he felt.

"Tell me why you fear your love for me. Tell me who hurt you so badly," Kelan asked quietly as he continued to dry Trisha's soft skin.

Trisha nodded, biting her lower lip. Kelan's mom, Morian, told her she should tell Kelan everything. Trisha looked down as she thought of everything that had happened in her life. Perhaps, this was fate's way of preparing her for the odd twist it had taken. Trisha slid off the counter and looked up at Kelan before responding.

"Let's get dressed, and I'll tell you everything," Trisha said in a calm, quiet voice.

Chapter 10

Kelan watched Trisha as she dressed in a pair of loose-fitting black trousers and a silky white blouse that tied in the front. She quickly braided her hair, tying it off with a black ribbon on the end. She didn't bother with putting shoes on. He could tell she was lost in thought as he dressed just as quickly. He picked up his discarded clothes, tossing them into the cleansing unit in the wall before following Trisha out into the living area. Trisha poured herself a cup of tea, ignoring the food that one of the servants had laid out on the buffet along the wall. He waited until she was seated in the chair near the window before he poured himself a hot drink and came to sit down in the chair across from her.

"I told you about my mom and dad," Trisha began softly looking out the window instead of at him. She seemed to have sensed Kelan's nod because she continued. "My dad is the coolest guy I've ever met. He has this quiet strength about him that is just awesome," Trisha said with a small smile curving her lips as she spoke of the man who meant so much to her. "By the time I was three or four he had me out in the woods with him. He was really patient showing me how to look for tracks, what plants were good to eat and which ones to avoid. He showed me all kinds of really cool things most people never learn about. He started his own business, Grove Wilderness Guides, so he could stay home with me." Trisha paused to look at Kelan. She wanted him to understand how much her dad meant to her. She wanted him to understand why she needed to go home.

"I met Ariel when I was in kindergarten. That is the first year we start school. We became really close friends. Carmen started the next year, and she just kind of got stuck with having two older sisters." Trisha laughed softly as she thought of all the time and fun the three of them had over the years. "Mr. and Mrs. Hamm, Ariel and Carmen's parents, became my home-away-from-home parents. Mrs. Hamm tried to teach me how to be a lady which wasn't an easy task. They were killed in an automobile accident when Carmen was a senior in high school. Ariel and I were in college at the time and had decided to go into the Air Force after graduation in the hopes of making it into the space program. Ariel didn't make the cut, but I did. I was always more physically active than Ariel and a little more on the adventuresome side. Ariel is the homebody of us three girls," Trisha added before taking a drink of her cooling tea.

Kelan bit back a response to that comment. From some of the things he was hearing from Mandra, Ariel was more of a pain in the butt. He didn't say anything for two reasons. First, he didn't want to interrupt Trisha in case she stopped talking, and second, he didn't think she would appreciate his opinion of the females she considered to be her sisters.

"Anyway, by the time I was twenty-two, life was good. I was a test pilot in the Air Force. I had just been accepted into the space training program and was finishing up on my master's degree in aerospace engineering. My dad and I used to lie out every night under the stars. He would point one out and tell me my mom was on it. I was determined to go find her," Trisha laughed at how naïve she used to be. "I promised my dad if I ever went to the stars I would take him with me." Trisha sniffed back tears as she thought of the pain her dad must be in with her disappearance. It was probably killing him not knowing what happened to her.

Kelan was about to tell her he would be taking her back to her world as soon as he could to see her father when Trisha shook her head as if dispelling an unpleasant thought. He watched her take a deep, calming breath before she began talking again.

"I met Peter when I was finishing up my degree. Ariel, Carmen, Scott, and I had gone out to celebrate Ariel's and my graduation. There was this little club where the service men and women liked to hang out. They served good food and great beer. Peter was there with a couple of guys. I used to see him coming and going on occasion on the base but never spoke to him before. He was tall, blond, and cute in a surfer-boy kind of way." Trisha grimaced as she set her cup on the small side table and wrapped her arms around her middle. Kelan and his dragon bit back the growl of jealousy at the mention of another man meaning something to Trisha.

Calm, Kelan whispered softly to his dragon. *He is no longer important to her. We are.*

Trisha continued, unaware of Kelan's and his dragon's displeasure at the mention of another male. "He swept me off my feet. We married a month after we met. I had the fairy-tale life, a great career, a wonderful, loving husband, and the support of my dad and two best friends. Life couldn't get any better. We were married for a year and half before the accident." Trisha's voice faded away as the remembered emotional and physical pain flooded over her.

Kelan waited several moments before he said anything. "What accident?" he asked quietly.

Trisha looked at him for the first time since sitting down and beginning her story. "The one that changed everything," she responded quietly. "I was coming back to base with four other guys. We were returning from a training mission. A freak storm blew in unexpectedly. Mark, the pilot of the helicopter we were in, tried to go around it. We were flying over some pretty rugged mountains heading back to California where we were stationed. They think a microburst hit us. It took out the electrical system, and we crashed into the side of a mountain. For some reason, it wasn't my time, I guess. Mark, Aaron, and John were killed instantly. Tim and I were in the back and survived the initial impact. We were both in really bad shape. I had a shattered collarbone, both of my legs were broken, my right hip was shattered, one of my arms was broken in five places, and I had some internal injuries. Tim was in even worse shape. His back was broken, and he was bleeding heavily from a cut to his thigh. He lived for about an hour after the crash. I watched over him as he died," Trisha murmured, silent tears coursing down her cheeks as she relived the last moments of Tim's life and her feelings of helplessness at not being able to save him.

"How long before someone found you?" Kelan asked. It ate at him that his mate would have to suffer so much.

Never again, Kelan promised silently, never again would she endure something like that if he could prevent it.

"Two days," Trisha answered. "Two days of lying there with my dead friends just inches from me. Two days of pain unlike anything I ever knew a human body could handle. Thankfully, I lost consciousness on and off during the time between the crash until my rescue so it all kind of blurred together. Because of the terrain, they brought my dad in to help. I survived on the rainwater that dripped from the holes in the wreckage and the knowledge I couldn't let my dad and Peter down by dying. I don't remember much after they found me. I was more dead than alive by then. I spent six weeks in the hospital and had so many surgeries I quit counting. The doctors told me I was lucky to be alive. I probably would never walk again due to the damage to my legs, back, and hip, but I was lucky. It was six months later they also told me I would probably never have children either. The damage and the surgeries created a lot of scar tissue, and because of the damage to my pelvic bones I wouldn't be able to carry a child safely without endangering both of us." Trisha got up and walked over to stand near the window looking out over the gardens and the city far below. She didn't want to see the pity or disgust on Kelan's face as he found out she would never be able to give him a child. She remembered Peter's face only too well when the doctors told her and Peter during one of her many visits.

Trisha took another deep breath. God, she hated reliving the shitty parts of her life. "Peter acted like he was supportive, but I could tell the difference in him after the first couple of months. I was no longer the wife he could brag about to his friends. I was the wife who needed help going to the bathroom. I was in a wheelchair, and due to the damage to my shoulder and arm, was unable to do even some of the basic necessities of caring for myself. Six months after the accident one of Peter's girlfriends came by to see me. I was home alone for the first time in months. Dad had installed a remote speaker system throughout our house for me in case I needed something. I found out Peter was anything but the devoted husband he wanted my father and me to believe. His first affair began about four months after our marriage," Trisha said quietly. "I didn't understand why. I loved him so much and gave everything there was of me to him. She was still there when Peter came home." Trisha glanced at Kelan briefly. "He didn't even bother to deny it. He said he wanted an open marriage, especially now that I was no longer useful. He didn't think it was necessary to hide it any longer. I should understand, after all, he was still young and shouldn't be penalized because of my accident. When I disagreed and stated I wanted a divorce, that I would never remain married to a man who was unfaithful to me, he refused. He said it would hurt his career if I divorced him. My accident caused a lot of sympathy around the base, and he was on the receiving end of it. If it came out he was having affairs while his poor wife was recovering from a serious crash it could ruin his chances for promotion. Like I really gave a damn about his career after everything I was learning." Trisha laughed bitterly.

"What did you do?" Kelan asked, coming up behind Trisha and wrapping his arms over hers. She resisted by stiffening at first but relaxed back against him when his hold on her tightened, pulling her closer against his broad chest.

"I kicked his sorry ass out," Trisha replied with a smile. "News of his infidelity spread throughout the base, not by me but by another disgruntled girlfriend, and he was reprimanded and demoted. It took me another year and a half before he finally agreed to the divorce. He wanted a substantial payoff before he would agree to sign the papers. My dad, though he would deny it to this day, paid Peter a visit during the night and told him what would happen if he didn't sign the papers right then and there. It almost killed him when he thought I was dead, and he was furious Peter would do this to me after everything that happened. I love my dad so much, and he has always been there for me. I can't let him ever go through thinking I might be dead again. After the accident, it took me almost a year and a half to learn how to walk again, and it was my dad and Ariel who were there for me. My dad helped me with strengthening my muscles, but he also gave me the courage to live again," Trisha said in a husky voice filled with emotion.

"By the time I could walk again, I was almost twenty-five, divorced, and looking for a new career. Ariel told me about a friend of a friend who worked for Boswell International. They were looking for a good pilot. She was waiting for the last year of her commission to finish and planned to go to work for them. She made a call and before I knew it, I was hired. That was about the time Carmen was injured down in South America. Ariel took a hardship leave to take care of her and help me through the depression I was fighting. I owe her a lot. She has been there for me through everything. The night you took me from my planet was the night I told Ariel I'd quit my job with Boswell and was returning home to work with my dad. I was supposed to see him two days later." Trisha turned in Kelan's arms until she was facing him. She gazed into his eyes before saying, "Now, you know everything."

Kelan looked deeply into Trisha's eyes. She was the bravest woman he'd ever known. Her quiet strength, her determination, and her capacity to love deeply were all things he admired. He leaned forward, running his hand along her cheek as he kissed her gently on the lips.

"I will return you to your father. But know this, if he refuses to come with us I will not let you stay. We are one now, *mi elila.* We cannot be apart," Kelan said quietly but firmly.

He wanted her to know he would do what he could, but she was a different person than she was before they met. Her body was no longer just human. It would be too dangerous for her to live back in her world from all the information he had read. Besides, he, his dragon, and his symbiot needed her. Her dragon, which he was hesitant to tell her about as yet, would not allow her to be separated from his either. Her dragon was still young, not quite ready for the transformation. *Yes, she is,* his dragon growled out impatiently. *Want my mate.* Kelan ignored his dragon's impatience. *She is not yet ready. She is just accepting our mating. If we try to force too much on her right now, then she might rebel. You saw how she was on board the V'ager.*

Kelan's dragon gave an angry snort before he curled up to pout.

Chapter 11

Trisha couldn't believe how time was flying by. It was almost a week since the missed dinner. After she told him about her life back on Earth, he told her about his on Valdier. He also told her about what happened to Cara. Trisha wanted to go to Cara immediately, but Kelan assured her Trelon was taking care of her and that she would be fine. He also explained why it would take him a little longer before he could fulfill his promise to take her home. Trisha knew he regretted the pain her dad was going through but understood his responsibility as a member of the royal family to protect his people.

Trisha spent most of her day learning how to speak the Valdier language without the use of a translator and studying its history and customs. She often felt restless, wanting to explore the world outside of the palace. Kelan took her to the village several times, and she fell in love with the markets there. They also spent a large amount of time making love. Trisha laughed silently. If they were alone, they couldn't keep their hands off each other. It usually began with a look or a light touch and ended in heavy breathing and their bodies entwined. There wasn't a place in Kelan's living quarters they hadn't made love in or on. Trisha blushed when she thought of the dining table. She was setting out some plates this morning. When she bent over to set his across from where she was going to sit Kelan came up behind her with a low growl. The next thing she knew she was screaming out her orgasm. They didn't even take the time to remove their clothing. Kelan had reached around her, pulling the ties on her trousers until they slid down to pool around her ankles. When she started to protest, he snarled fiercely at her and pushed her until she was lying across the small table with her ass in the air. He had taken her hard and fast from behind. Damn, even the memory of it was enough to arouse her again. A knock on the door drew her out of her reverie.

Trisha opened the door to see Cara standing on the other side. "What are you doing here?" Trisha asked in surprise. "I thought you were still under house arrest or something."

Cara grinned. "I dismantled all of Trelon's stuff. He finally broke. I wanted to go see how Abby was doing. Zoran brought her back last night."

"What happened to Abby?" Trisha asked confused.

"Didn't Kelan tell you? Someone kidnapped her, but they got her back," Cara said in surprise.

"No, Kelan seems to have forgotten that little bit of information," Trisha growled out in aggravation. So that was the important business that kept him away for the past couple of days. No, wonder he was so damn horny this morning. He should have told her what was going on. She needed to have a talk with him about keeping things from her.

"I'm meeting up with Ariel and Carmen to go see her. You want to come?" Cara asked as she bounced up and down. Trisha looked at Cara closely. She was on a major caffeine high.

"Of course I do. You haven't been drinking any coffee or anything with caffeine in it lately, have you?" Trisha asked curiously as she pulled the door closed behind her.

Cara was bouncing up and down excitedly. "Oh yeah! I spent the last two nights working on the replicator. I figured out how to do all the really cool coffees, including lattes and cappuccinos. Of course, I had to taste test them all, so I've drunk, like, five or six pots of the stuff and have a really good buzz going. I probably won't sleep for a week. I can't wait until I tell Trelon about it."

Trisha held back the laugh as she thought of Kelan's poor brother. He wasn't going to know what hit him. If he was smart, he would find another job to take him away until Cara came down off her high; otherwise, he wasn't going to be getting any sleep either.

They met up with Ariel and Carmen in the corridor leading to Abby's living quarters. Trisha frowned when she saw all the guards surrounding them, especially Carmen. Several of the men looked like they would rather be eating nails than standing near her. Their symbiots didn't look like they were too concerned, though. Most of them were lying down or playing with each other.

"Hey, guys," Trisha called out, hurrying forward. She missed them so much. "How are you doing?" she asked quietly.

"I'm okay, but I would be better if I could get these guys to take a long hike off a short pier," Ariel said with a roll of her eyes. "I'm lucky if they let me go to the bathroom without following me," she added sarcastically glaring at the two guards assigned to her.

Carmen just shrugged her shoulders. "I'm ready to blow this joint. These losers are getting on my nerves." She looked at each of the guards assigned to her with a cool, assessing eye. Several of them shifted uncomfortably and watched her with an uneasy look.

"How many do they have assigned to you now?" Trish whispered softly. If she wasn't mistaken there were at least six guards behind her.

"Eight," Carmen murmured under her breath. "Two are in medical right now."

"Oh," Trisha replied with a sympathetic look at the remaining guards. She decided it was best to just find Abby before any more ended up in medical which, judging by the calculating look in Carmen's eyes, could be any moment.

"I am so glad Abby is okay," Trisha said as she began walking down the corridor toward Abby and Zoran's living quarters.

"What's with all the guards?" Cara asked curiously as she walked backward staring at the guards. "I noticed them outside of Carmen's room that day, but isn't this a little bit ridiculous? How many guards do we need to protect us, especially with our gold BFF's with us?"

Ariel snickered. "They're not here to protect us. They're here to prevent us from escaping again."

Cara's eyes brightened at the idea of getting into more mischief. "Again? Do you need help with anything?"

Trisha almost felt sorry for the men when a low groan filled the corridor behind them. It would serve them right if the four women were to plan and execute an escape from the planet. They could probably do it, but just the thought of leaving Kelan caused a tremor of pain to flash through Trisha. She frowned. It was almost like something inside of her whimpered at the idea of leaving him. Trisha shook her head. She was feeling a little weird lately, like there was something under her skin itching to get out. She briefly thought of how her skin seemed to change colors when she and Kelan were making love and the odd noises that kept escaping out of her. It was almost like she was either growling or purring depending on what they were doing. It was beginning to drive her nuts. She wanted to desperately ask someone about it but didn't know how to broach the subject. What was she supposed to say? "Sorry, but I think there is something inside me trying to get out?" That was a little too science fiction alien movie for her.

Trisha watched as Cara skipped up to the door bouncing with the aftereffects of the caffeine she had consumed. She smiled innocently up at the guards as she knocked loudly on the door. Abby opened the door wearing a silk robe and a surprised expression. Cara pushed the cart full of food and what suspiciously smelled like pots of coffee in the room before Abby could say anything. Trisha, Carmen, and Ariel with their new symbiot pets trotted in behind her.

"Good morning!" Cara said brightly as she laid a tray full of food on a low table. "We thought you'd be hungry."

"No, you wanted an excuse to find out what happened!" Trisha said with a grin as she picked up a piece of fruit from the tray and bit into it. "Damn, they have some good fruit here."

She really hoped Abby wouldn't get too upset with them invading her. Trisha thought with a sense of satisfaction that it was good to get out for a little while. What with everything going on, Cara's poisoning and now Abby's kidnapping, Kelan barely let her go anywhere.

"So, tell us all the good juicy details? I heard you fried Ben'qumain? How'd you do that?" Ariel said as she laid another tray with cups and a large pot of coffee down on another small table.

Trisha gave Abby a sympathetic smile as she accepted a cup of coffee from Ariel and the plate of food from Cara. Everyone seemed to wait until Abby sank down onto the soft cushions of the sofa and pulled her bare feet up under her before they helped themselves to the food and beverages.

Abby took a sip of coffee and waited a moment before she responded to the question. "I turned, can turn, into a dragon."

Trisha's mouth dropped open at Abby's declaration. Her brain seemed to explode as it reviewed all the changes going through her lately: her skin changing colors, the sounds she was making, the feeling of something crawling under her skin. Was it possible she was going through some type of change as well? Was it possible she would be able to turn into a dragon like Abby? Trisha sat in numb silence as she absorbed all the facts and possible reasons. She stared at Abby closely, trying to see if there was anything different about her. If it was possible, why hadn't Kelan said anything to her about it? Why did he not mention their being together could change her into something else? Something not quite human? Trisha laid a hand over her stomach as it rolled at the idea of something else living inside her body. What could she do to stop it? How did she get rid of it? A small whimper seemed to fill her at the thought of rejecting the new life deep inside her. Trisha forced herself to listen to what was going on around her. She would deal with this new information once she was alone again.

"That. Is. So. Cool!" Cara said excitedly, her voice rising as her excitement grew. "How did you do it? Can I do it? Oh. My. God. I have to be able to do it. I could totally drive Trelon out of his everloving fucking mind! Oh Abby, you have got to teach me how. Please! Please! Please!" Cara's eyes were wild with the idea of being able to change into a dragon. Trisha could see the barely concealed excitement in Cara's eyes.

Suddenly a small chuckle filled the air, followed by uncontrollable giggling. All eyes whipped around, unable to believe where the giggling was coming from. Carmen wiped her eyes trying to stop from giggling.

"Oh Abby, please teach us. I would love to be able to give someone else hell, and I'm sure I could think of a hundred different ways to do it in the form of a dragon."

Trisha stared in wonder at Carmen. It was the first time in three years that she'd heard her laugh. A quick glance at Ariel showed tears forming in her eyes as she smiled softly at her younger sister. Trisha smiled hesitantly and joined in the fun. Soon, all them were giggling and making up ways they could drive the men insane by switching between human and dragon and using the symbiot. While Cara's was the most creative, Carmen came up with the most devious and had all of them in hysterics. When Zoran walked into the room a couple of hours later and found all five women laughing uncontrollably, he had a bad, bad feeling he and his brothers were in for trouble.

Trisha walked slowly back to her and Kelan's living quarters. Bio kept brushing up against her as if trying to calm the flurry of thoughts and doubts running through Trisha's mind. She enjoyed spending time with the other women, but now all she could think about was what they had been joking about. She needed more information, time, and a quiet place by herself to process everything. Was it really possible for her to turn into a dragon? If so, would it hurt during the changing? She had only seen Kelan in his dragon form once, the night they met. Even though she knew he could shift into another creature, it just never seemed real since everything that happened the night Abby was kidnapped back on Earth seemed sort of surreal anyway. Trisha wasn't sure she was as enthusiastic as the other women were about the idea of being able to turn into another creature. Trisha felt a stirring deep inside her and a low cry.

Want my mate, a soft voice whispered. *Need my mate.*

Trisha stopped in the middle of the corridor as the soft voice washed through her. It was almost as if there was someone else inside her whispering. Trisha wondered if this is what people who suffered from schizophrenia or multiple personality disorders felt. Maybe none of this was really real. Maybe she was just in a coma, or worse, in some government experiment to test the human mind's ability to determine reality from fantasy. Trisha started when she felt a hand on her shoulder.

"You are well, my lady?" one of the guards asked Trisha with concern.

"What?" Trisha asked confused. "Where am I? I mean, really?"

The guard turned to the warrior standing next to him and said something softly to him. The man gave a brief nod, looking at Trisha with concern, before he hurried down the corridor and disappeared. Trisha watched him go with a sense of panic building. What if they were drugging her? What if it was wearing off, and they were going to go get more? She needed to get away. She needed to hide. Trisha thought of the thick forest surrounding the city. She could get lost there, and no one would ever find her. She could disappear forever and be safe. The low moan inside her started up again as if disagreeing with her logic. *No, stay with my mate. Mate protect us. Care for us. Want my mate,* the voice said a little louder as it became more agitated.

Shut up, Trisha growled as she moved slightly closer to the man guarding her. *I don't want to hear you. You are just my imagination. Something the drugs have created.* Trisha wondered if Ariel, Carmen, Cara, and Abby were real or just actors made up to look like her friends. Since her abduction from Earth, she had been allowed only small amounts of time with them. Trisha looked down where Bio was nudging her hand. She looked at the huge golden creature closely as if seeing it for the first time. She jerked her hand away, suddenly afraid. Bio tried to send waves of warmth through the bands around her arms and neck. As soon as Trisha felt the warmth she started pulling at the bands, first the ones on her wrists, then the one around her neck.

"Please, get off of me," Trisha whispered hoarsely as an irrational fear began to spread throughout her body, leaving her shaken. "Please."

The little gold bands dissolved slowly, as if reluctant to leave her. Trisha began breathing a little better once they were no longer touching her. Bio shook and lowered its head, almost as if hurt by Trisha's rejection of it. It turned and moved down the corridor heading toward their living quarters. Trisha watched as it rounded a corner and disappeared from sight. She was so focused on wondering why she was feeling guilty she didn't hear what the man next to her was saying at first.

"My lady, would you like to sit down and rest for a moment? I have sent the other guard for Lord Kelan," the warrior was saying softly.

Trisha reacted without thinking the moment he touched her arm. Bringing her hand palm up in an arc, she slammed it into the warrior's nose. Tightly gripping the arm that touched her, she rounded at the same time bringing her knee up into his stomach. The moment he bent over, she doubled her fists, bringing them down over the back of his neck and knocking him unconscious. Trisha drew in a deep breath. She grabbed the man by his arms, pulling him into a nearby alcove in the corridor. Using his shirt, she ripped strips from it and quickly tied his hands and feet. Patting him down, she removed the weapons he was carrying, tucking them under her shirt so they wouldn't be seen. She mentally retrieved the map of the palace she drew on her many trips through it. Deciding on a seldom-used entrance on the side near the kitchens, she moved quickly and quietly. She would seek cover in the forests. Once she felt safe, she would think about everything she had learned and hope to God if she was under the influence of any medication it would wear off. She refused to believe her friends were real. If they were, she would revisit her offensive strategy if necessary.

..*

Kelan was in a heavy discussion with Creon when the knock at the door interrupted them. Creon wanted the *V'ager* ready to go at a moment's notice in case there were problems. Kelan was updating Creon about where most of the Valdier fleet was at the moment and making some additional changes to repositioning some of the warships closer to the Sarafin and Curizan space borders.

"Come in," Creon called out without looking up from the holoscreen in front of them.

"I'm sorry to disturb you, my lord, but I need to speak with Lord Kelan for a moment," the warrior said quietly. He stood near the door at attention waiting for permission to speak.

Kelan turned with a frown. The frown deepened with he recognized the warrior as one of the guards assigned to protect Trisha. Had something happened to her? She was supposed to be visiting with Zoran's mate and the other females. At the thought of the other females, namely Ariel and Carmen, Kelan gave a silent groan. Had they talked her into helping them escape? He could care less if the other two females did, may the gods and goddesses of the universe help anyone they encountered, but he refused to let them take Trisha with them.

"What is it?" Kelan asked impatiently. So help him, if those other two females tried to influence Trisha, he would ban them from ever leaving their living quarters again. He didn't care what Mandra and Creon had to say about it.

The warrior stepped forward quickly. Once he was near enough to speak quietly, he explained the purpose of his visit. "My lord, your mate does not seem well. We were escorting her back to your living quarters after her visit with the other human females when she appeared to become very confused and frightened. She was unaware of where she was and was very, very pale." The warrior paused before adding, "We could smell her fear. Something has frightened her badly."

Kelan looked at the warrior carefully and saw the concern in his eyes. "Were any food or beverages served? Do you think she could have been poisoned?" Kelan's first thought was about what happened to Trelon's mate, Cara. Could some type of poison or drug have been slipped into the refreshments the females consumed?

The warrior shook his head. "No, sir. All of the food and beverages were carefully monitored and tested before being served. I stopped on my way here to see if any of the other females were having difficulties, and all appear fine, except for the one called Cara. She said she was 'okay,' that she was on a 'caffeine' high and the way she was acting was not abnormal for her. Lady Abby was very polite and said she was feeling fine. The one named Ariel did her usual eye roll, and the other one tried to attack me. Both behaviors were normal for them."

Kelan nodded. He closed his eyes briefly and stroked the gold band on his wrist trying to communicate with his symbiot. He frowned when he received an impression of his symbiot feeling overwhelming sadness. Had something terrible happened to Trisha and his symbiot couldn't help her?

With a muttered oath, Kelan threw a glance at Creon who was watching him closely. "My mate needs me. Something is wrong."

Creon gave a brisk nod. "I will check in with Zoran and with the guards protecting the other females. Let me know if you need additional protection or help for her."

Kelan stormed out of the room followed closely by the warrior. A shiver of apprehension went through Kelan as if something bad were about to happen. All he knew was he hoped the gods and goddesses had mercy on anyone who wanted to harm his mate because he wouldn't.

Chapter 12

Trisha wiped a hand across her forehead. She looked around at the huge trees surrounding her and forced herself to push forward. Today marked the third day since she escaped from the palace walls. She was steadily moving farther and farther into the deep forests. The first night she pushed for distance, not worrying about leaving tracks. Once she felt she covered a fair distance from the city, she slowed and began a more methodical path through deeper forest cover. At one point during the second day, she used a large river to cover several miles, letting it pull her along with the current. It was the sight of several dragons soaring above the river that finally drove her back to shore. She was using natural floating debris as a cover and sank as far under the water as she could when they flew over her. She watched them through the tangled limbs as they swept up and down before turning farther north. She didn't know if they were real dragons, just some type of aircraft designed to look like one, or if it was a drug causing her to hallucinate. She knew she couldn't be discovered. All of her dad's training was kicking in. She traveled throughout the last two nights stopping only once an hour to rest for fifteen minutes. Several times, she sensed she was being followed by a larger predator, and she moved up into the trees, waiting and watching as they passed under her. She continued to do the same each day after that until she figured she was more than a hundred miles away from the palace.

Trisha began focusing on the clues her surrounding environment provided her. She discovered the limbs of the massive trees were much larger than any she ever saw before in the mountains around her home. The third morning dawned bright and clear, and she was able to see quite a ways from the perch she was currently in. The logical part of her said if she had been drugged, the drugs would be out of her system by now, and all of this was as real as she was. Trisha drew in a deep breath. She would have to be careful. She wasn't ready to be found yet, not until she came to terms with what was happening to her. Trisha stood up and began moving again.

She decided to take advantage of the huge trees and their interwoven limbs to help get her farther away. She used them as a type of above-ground highway, much like the squirrels did back home. It slowed her progress but increased the difficulty of being able to track her. In addition, she used some of the mud, moss, leaves, and small branches as camouflage. She carefully applied a thick coating to any visible skin. She would need to stop and repair it, but, unless she needed to retreat back into the water again, she should be less visible. She wove thin twigs through her long hair, braiding them in and out and letting them stick out at an angle to resemble some of the nearby bushes.

Once she was satisfied she had done her best to blend her person with the surrounding forest, she looked at the weapons she took from the man in the corridor again. She studied each piece carefully. She had a long, curved knife about two feet in length, some type of gun, and a smaller knife. She shoved the smaller knife in her boot. Looking around, she saw several branches that would make a good bow. Balancing along the limb almost forty feet in the air, Trisha cut a branch, making sure it was not one that would be instantly noticeable. She carefully laid down several long, thick leaves to catch the shavings as she worked on shaping the bow. It would take her several days to get it just right and to cure it but she could work on it when she took her breaks. She didn't want to stay in any one place for more than an hour. Once she felt confident she was safe, she would stop to hunt. She would need protein to help keep her muscles from deteriorating.

Once the initial shape was done, Trisha carefully rolled the shavings up in the leaves and tucked them inside her shirt. She would use the shavings, as well as some dry moss, to build a small fire once she found shelter for the night. She stood up, listening carefully to the forest around her. It was her early warning system. She paid close attention to the changes as several dragons flew over earlier. She noticed the birds let out a long, sharp whistle of warning as they approached and a series of small, chirps when they were gone. She also noticed several plants tended to close up as they came by. She suspected it was a defense to protect their seeds which the dragons more than likely ate. She would have to check it out. Food and shelter were important if she was to remain strong. She spent the next six hours moving as rapidly as she could. She used the trees as much as possible. When it became too difficult or dangerous, she moved back down to the forest floor. She stopped frequently to rest. She could feel the drain on her body from the stress, intense physical activity, and lack of food and sleep. The last thing she wanted to do was make a stupid mistake that could get her hurt or killed. She would need to find food and shelter tonight. She needed both desperately. She would push on for at least another hour before she started to look for both, she decided.

It was closer to two hours later before Trisha glanced up at the sky. Dark, angry clouds were rolling in. She could smell rain in the air. She would need to seek shelter soon. She didn't want to take the chance of getting caught out in a bad storm. Trisha used the trees to cover about a mile of terrain before she climbed down. From her perch up high, she was able to see some of the plants that reacted to the dragons. She moved slowly, staying in the shadows until she was close enough to jump the remaining distance to the moist forest floor. Working her way carefully so she left as few broken leaves or impressions in the soft soil as possible, she came up to one of the huge flowering pods. In the center of the pod was a type of seed similar to a sunflower seed, only about the size of a cantaloupe. Trisha used the long knife to work two of the seeds free. As she drew them close, she felt the thing inside her moving again. Trisha held still and focused on the feeling.

Who are you? Trisha asked silently. *What are you?*

I am a part of you, your dragon, it whispered softly. *Please, I want my mate. We need our mates.*

Trisha slammed down on the creature when it tried to make a soft coughing sound. She could feel the sound building in her chest and throat. She clenched her jaw tight and closed her eyes, focusing on pushing the creature into a large metal cage. She could feel it struggle to resist her, but Trisha was determined. She'd learned at an early age how to create large, solid, strong places in her to put unpleasant things she didn't want to deal with. At this moment, the creature, or dragon, inside her was one of those unpleasant things. She needed to make sure she was safe before she let it out enough to examine it. Trisha opened her eyes and began moving again with a focused determination. She thought she saw a cave up ahead where she could seek shelter from the storm. Trisha couldn't help but wonder as she made her way through the thick undergrowth if she would ever find a shelter strong enough to help protect her from the storm of need brewing deep inside her, begging her to return to Kelan.

* * *

Kelan let out a roar of helpless rage. They lost her tracks again. If they didn't find something before the storm hit, it might be impossible to determine which way she went. When he found the body of the semi-conscious guard tied up in the alcove three days before, he feared the worse. He quickly called for his symbiot to come to him, wondering why it had not protected her or warned him of the attack on his mate. He was shocked to find out it was Trisha who was responsible for the guard's condition. Fear turned to fury as he tried to understand why she would do such a thing. After searching the palace, Kelan questioned each of the other women Trisha had been with in an attempt to try to understand why Trisha would run away from him. It was Abby who gave him his first insight. She said she noticed a change in Trisha after Abby had mentioned her ability to change into a dragon. She said it was more of a feeling than anything else. Abby said while the others joked about it and teased each other, Trisha only participated when she noticed someone watching her. She seemed distracted, maybe even upset. His visit with Ariel gave him the direction he needed to know where to start looking for Trisha. Ariel was worried when she heard Trisha had disappeared. She said Trisha always disappeared for a while when she was upset about something or needed to think things over. Kelan's mind drifted back to what she told him right after he discovered his mate was missing.

"Trisha would disappear for days, sometimes weeks into the mountains by herself. Her dad used to track her to make sure she was okay, but Trisha wised up to it one time when she was about fourteen. Some of the girls in town were giving her a hard time about being such a tomboy, calling her names and putting her down. When some of the guys started in calling her things and pushing her around, Trisha just got up and walked out of the class. She was gone for almost three weeks before she came back to school. Her dad found her living up near Bear Creek. There were some caves up there. Whatever happened up there she never told me, but she came back quieter, more reserved. She focused on making good grades and didn't hang out with anyone but Carmen and me after that." Ariel paused as she looked out the window. "If she is gone, she would have headed for the forests and mountains. It's where she feels the most at home." Ariel turned to look at Kelan. "You won't find her unless she wants to be found. She's good—really good—at disappearing. I honestly don't think even her dad could find her if she didn't want him to."

Kelan frowned as he stared over Ariel's shoulder into the distance where the forest rose up to surround three sides of the city. "Why? Why would she run from me?"

Ariel smiled sadly at Kelan before softly replying. "You were changing her without giving her a choice. Trisha seems tough on the outside, but inside all she has ever wanted was to be accepted for who she is. She's tried to be the perfect son for her father, the perfect daughter for her mother, the perfect friend, the perfect wife but it never seemed to be enough. Now, she isn't even just Trisha anymore if what Abby told us is true. We are doing the best we can to adjust to everything that's happened to us. Some of us are just better at it than others. Trisha needs time to accept what is happening and accept who she is becoming."

Kelan looked at Ariel, and for the first time understood why she was so important to Trisha. She accepted Trisha for who she was and loved her unconditionally. He was wrong to have judged her so harshly. Ariel's quiet strength and support helped his mate survive many painful events in her life.

Kelan walked over to Ariel and gave her a soft kiss on her cheek. "Thank you for all you have done for my mate. She is very fortunate to count you as her sister."

Ariel's eyes filled with tears as she smiled up at Kelan. "Just bring her home to us. Bring her home, accept her, and love her. That is all she ever wanted."

"You have my promise," Kelan vowed softly before taking his leave. He had a forest to scour and a mate to find. Calling to his symbiot, Kelan shifted as soon as he was out of the palace. Four of his brother's best trackers followed him.

"Lord Kelan," Jaguin—one of the trackers Creon had recommended—called out from high up in one of the trees.

Kelan jerked back to the present. He quickly shifted and lunged up to where the warrior was kneeling on a large branch forty feet in the air. Kelan landed lightly, shifting at the same time. He carefully worked his way over to where the man was kneeling.

"What have you found?" Kelan asked. He looked down at the ground far below and couldn't help the thought that his mate needed her ass spanked for taking so many risks with her life. If she were to fall from this height she would be killed.

"Here, there is an impression and some slight scraping of the moss covering the limb. I also found what looks like wood shavings," Jaguin replied.

Jaguin frowned as he held the tiny specs of wood in the palm of his large hand. He couldn't make sense of it. If the female were cutting on a branch, there should be more shavings. He looked around, studying each branch along the limb carefully. It didn't make sense for the female to carry a branch up the tree. He was still shocked by all he was learning about the human female Creon asked him to help find. Never in his life had he tracked anything this difficult. At first, he and the other three trackers thought the female was just lost. If that were the case, it would only take them an hour or two to find her. It soon became evident the female knew what she was doing. The first day she moved at a fast pace. She was careful about not leaving obvious tracks but did not try to hide them. It was as if she was putting distance between her and those who might follow her. Palto, Gunner, Kor, and himself all thought by the end of the first night, when they still didn't catch up with her, she would make a camp for the night, and it would be easy to find her. After all, the night could be the most dangerous. The werecats were nocturnal and so were the bear beasts. It would make sense for the female to hide until first light. Instead, they discovered she kept moving deeper into the forests. They lost her trail dozens of times. The first time it became clearer that she was now covering her tracks was when they came across a set of werecat tracks. Kor discovered the barest impression of her boot before it seemed to vanish. Two steps later, the huge paw prints of the werecat were found. Lord Kelan, Palto, and Gunner quickly shifted to dragon form to see if they could scent any blood, the werecat would have sliced through the female's stomach and eaten her right there. None of them could detect any trace of blood. Palto finally found a small section missing on the mossy bark of a nearby tree where it looked like something knocked it loose while climbing. Lord Kelan shifted back at the finding and slowly climbed up the tree until he came to the limb where it appeared something had lain down, crushing a few of the ferns growing along it. The marking of a boot heel was outlined on one of the large leaves. That was their first clue the female was using the tree limbs as a way of moving. Now, three men covered the ground looking for tracks while two others were in the trees at all times. Their tracking slowed to a crawl as it became more difficult to find any tracks.

"She was here," Kelan said quietly looking around. "Look at the impressions in the moss. They are several hours old."

Kelan stood up and looked around. What was she doing? Kelan moved over to several branches hanging down. He moved several aside before he found what he was looking for, the fresh bark of a cut branch. Kelan touched it and felt the still sticky sap. He looked into the distance trying to figure out what she was doing.

"She continued along the branches. I can see where the moss is smudged from her boots," Kor said. "She is very good. I don't think I have ever hunted a more worthy adversary."

"She is not an adversary," Kelan responded quietly. "She is my mate."

"I'm sorry, Lord Kelan, I meant no disrespect," Kor said. "You should be very proud of her. I do not know many warriors who could have made it this far, not with the five of us following."

Kelan nodded in agreement. "We don't have much time. The storm is moving in rapidly, and it looks to be a bad one. Can you tell which way she went?"

Jaquin nodded toward the northwest. "She changed direction again. She is headed that way."

Gunner growled out low. "The forests thicken and become more dangerous the closer you get to the mountains. My home is not far from the valley leading between the two highest peaks. Only the experienced warriors go there to hunt the bear beasts."

Kelan looked grimly at the darkening skies and then at the mountains in the distance. "Gunner, you lead the way. You are familiar with the area. Where do you think she would seek shelter?"

Gunner was silent for a few moments as he thought about the terrain they were about to enter. "If she continues toward the mountains, there are many caves lining it. There are at least six big enough for your human female to seek shelter safely. If the female was able to reach the beginning of the mountains and if she was able to find one of the caves, then that is where I would look first."

A flash of lightning streaked across the sky followed by a loud rumble of thunder. "I suggest we find shelter in one of those caves, as well. The storm will be here soon and from the way my dragon is acting, it is going to be a nasty one," Palto said as he joined the others.

Kelan looked at the men with him and knew they were right. As much as he would prefer to continue searching, doing so in one of the fierce electrical storms that were common in their world was suicidal. Kelan looked at Gunner who was studying him and gave a sharp nod.

Gunner didn't say anything, merely shifted to his dragon and lifted up into the air. Kelan followed last. He let the sharp eyesight of his dragon look for signs as they moved in and out of the trees. He could see the path she followed through the trees. When the trail vanished, three of them moved closer to the ground while the other two continued to search the branches in an unspoken pattern of teamwork.

A bright streak of lightning flashed close by just as Gunner landed on the ground, shifting. "We need to take cover. It is too dangerous for us to be out in this," he shouted above the rising winds.

Kelan landed beside him and nodded. Gunner led them a short distance until Kelan saw the odd rock formation jutting up from the side of a rock mass. Gunner drew his gun and approached slowly. He let his eyes shift to his dragon's to search the inside for other creatures who may have taken refuge from the storm.

"It's clear," Gunner yelled moving into the darkened space.

Kelan nodded to the other men to enter before he did. He took one last look around the darkening forest, letting out a snarl of frustration. He knew they were getting closer. He could feel it. *Yes, find my mate. I need my mate*, his dragon coughed out softly. *Soon, my friend, soon we will have them both with us,* Kelan said soothingly.

* * *

Trisha pulled in the last of the larger branches and stacked it near the pile of moss she had gathered earlier. The storm was now raging fiercely outside, and she was shivering from the combination of being drenched to the skin, the coolness of the cave she found, and the wind whipping through the narrow opening. First things first, get a fire going. Trisha pulled the leaves containing the shavings of wood closer to her and grabbed a small mound of dry moss she gathered before the storm hit. It took her almost an hour to get enough wood, moss, and leaves gathered once she found the small cave. She worked quickly clearing out an area big enough for her to create a small hideaway. The cave, if you could call it one, was probably no bigger than a ten-by-ten bedroom, but it was relatively clean and dry. She almost missed the entrance to it. The one rock area she thought was a cave turned out to be an oversized trunk of a tree hollowed out against the side of a rock face. It was as she was turning away that she caught a glimpse of the small, dark cut in the rock face about twenty feet higher. Once she explored it, she discovered it was perfect. It was on high ground with little chance of a rock slide; the opening was barely big enough for her to fit through giving her protection from the larger creatures she noticed during her nightly travels, and unless you stood just right, you wouldn't be able to see it. The storm was moving in faster than she liked, and she didn't know how long storms could last on this planet. She didn't want to get stuck with no heat or food on the off chance it lasted more than a night, so Trisha made a judgment call— get what fuel and food she could and hope the storm covered her tracks. She was able to get enough wood to last her a couple of days if she only used a small fire and several more seed pods, as well as some of the fruit growing wild that she recognized from eating at the palace.

She made a ring of some of the loose stones and carefully piled some moss in the center. Taking one of the leaves, she opened it and piled some of the shaved wood on top of that. Trisha reached over for two of the rocks and began striking them against each other. After a few minutes she saw a small amount of smoke. She gently blew on it until the dried moss caught fire. She slowly added slightly larger sticks until the fire was going well enough she could add some of the bigger ones, making a small teepee.

Trisha stared at the flames for a moment, holding her hands over the heat to defrost her frozen fingers. Once she was satisfied it wasn't going to go out, she picked up several of the larger branches and carefully used them to create a door over the crack leading into the cave. She cut strips of bark off and used it as roping to hold the pieces in place against the wind. She could already feel a difference as the small area began to warm up. Using the light of the fire, Trisha glanced around. There was water seeping in from a tangle of roots through the ceiling of the cave and dripping into a shallow bowl-shaped rock formation. She would have plenty of drinking and bathing water.

As the cave grew warmer, Trisha removed her wet clothing, just keeping her bra and panties on for the time being. She used several long sticks to make a lean-to near the fire and draped her clothes over it so they could dry. Next, she used some of her precious moss and formed a thin padding for a bed. She covered it with several large leaves. She took one of the seed pods and gently laid it in the fire over some of the hot coals. She would let it roast while she wove a blanket out of the other leaves she had.

Trisha sat for the next two hours carefully cutting the leaves into long strips, then weaving them back and forth like the old-time yarn pot holders Ariel used to make for her mom. She stopped several times to add more wood to the fire, to turn the seed pod, and to rinse some of the fruit in the water. She didn't need to worry about washing away her mud and leaf camouflage. The rain did an excellent job before she got into the cave. She checked her clothes and was pleased to find they were almost dry. The sharp crack of lightning followed by a loud rumble of thunder filled the air and shook the ground. It sounded like the demons of hell were having a party outside, Trisha thought with a small smile. She was glad she wasn't invited.

Trisha was soon dressed again in her warm, dry clothes. Her belly was full from the roasted seed and fresh fruit, and she could barely keep her eyes open. She banked the fire, adding just a couple of pieces of greener wood to keep it burning a little longer before she curled up on her makeshift bed, the knives and gun within easy reach. She was lying watching the shadows dance across the ceiling of the cave when she felt the now familiar stirring deep inside her.

Trisha closed her eyes and focused inward. *Tell me who you are,* she whispered softly.

The creature deep inside her moved slightly. It lay curled up in a ball, shivering. *I am you. You know me,* it whispered back faintly.

Trisha frowned. She looked closely at the small, shivering creature. It was so beautiful. Bronze, gold, and black scales covered its delicate body. It slowly raised its head to look back at Trisha. Trisha bit back a cry at the despair she saw in its eyes.

Why are you so sad? Trisha asked in a quiet voice.

Because you don't want me...you don't want our mate. I cannot live without my mate. I need him. We are one. We will all die without each other. Why do you not want him? He is so strong, so beautiful. He will protect us, it whispered back.

You are just a figment of my imagination, Trisha said angrily. *You don't really exist. I am human. I can't change into a dragon. I have to go home. I have to find my dad. I didn't ask for any of this.*

The creature inside her seemed to shrink at the anger in Trisha's voice. *I do exist. I want out. I want to touch my mate just as you have touched yours. Why? Why do you keep me inside?* it whimpered.

Trisha could feel the pain radiating out from the creature. It spread through her body, reminding her how it felt to be trapped in a body that didn't work anymore. To be hopelessly trapped with no way out.

Trisha felt something inside her crack, as if a dam that held too much water behind it and could no longer contain it finally reached its breaking point. She was flooded with memories. Memories of her dad's gentle teachings and loving support, of always having Ariel and Carmen to hang with, to tell her dreams and wishes to, of Ariel's mom and dad and the love they always had for her. She remembered the bad, as well, but it didn't seem to have the power to hurt her like it did before. She recognized the girls were just jealous of her ability to do things they couldn't. She knew the guys were just flirting with her in their adolescent way. And Peter was just Peter. She saw what she wanted to see, not what was real. But, most of all, she remembered Kelan's gentle touch. She remembered the crooked little smiles he gave her and how patient he was on board the warship that brought her here. He didn't try to pressure her, he accepted her—hang-ups and all.

Trisha imagined reaching out to the shivering creature inside her and recognized it was a part of her. The part that was scared, unsure, young, and vulnerable. It was a younger version of herself and just as new to this world as she was.

Shh, it's okay. I'm here, Trisha murmured softly as she gently stroked the small delicate dragon. *I'm here. I just need a little time. That's all I'm asking for. Please be patient for just a little longer, and I promise we will go find our mates.*

Our mates are beautiful, it whispered shyly.

Trisha couldn't contain the small chuckle that escaped her. *Word to the wise—guys like to be called handsome. They get offended if you call them beautiful. It just isn't masculine enough for them, I guess.*

The delicate dragon inside her snorted before replying, *I still think my mate is beautiful. If he doesn't like it, he can get over it.*

Trisha giggled. Yup, the little dragon inside her was definitely a part of her. Trisha let the warmth of the fire outside and the warmth of the love inside wash over her until she fell into a deep, restful sleep.

Chapter 13

Kelan stared out at the raging storm through the narrow entrance to the cave. Palto talked to one of the men at the palace an hour ago during their regular check-ins and was informed the storm would be dissipating in the next few hours. The storm had raged for the past two days. Kelan thought about trying to go out in it to search for Trisha, worried she could be out in the raging fury, but all four men pressured him to use his head. Gone was the calm self-discipline, gone was his ability to remain in command in any situation, only his skill at handling any challenge remained. He would not stop until he found her.

Kelan leaned back against the hard stone wall listening with half an ear as the men talked quietly. He gently stroked his symbiot as it lay stretched out beside him. They were discussing all the new strategies they learned while tracking his mate. The new skills for evading capture needed to be explored more in depth and integrated into their training programs, Palto was insisting. It wasn't until one of the warriors turned and asked him a question that he forced his attention back to their conversation.

"Kelan, where did your mate learn such survival skills?" Kor asked again. Kelan told all four men to drop the "Lord" part the night the storm hit. It was getting on his nerves.

"Her father taught her," Kelan responded with a smile. "She told me of how he trained her since she was a little girl. He taught her how to hunt, track, and defend herself in the remote regions of her world."

Gunner looked grimly at the fire for a moment before he turned his intense gaze on Kelan. "Why would a male, especially the father of a female, teach his daughter such skills? He should be protecting her until she is mated."

"Their world is different from ours. It is not uncommon for the females to live alone, away from all males. My mate was in their military. Her father taught her to be strong. She loves him very much and wishes to return to her home world so she can bring him back with her. I have promised her I would do this," Kelan said calmly, understanding Gunner's initial resistance to teaching a female how to defend herself. It had always been the responsibility of a Valdier warrior to defend those who were weaker.

Gunner looked down again at the flames before he spoke quietly again. "Is it true she bears the mark of the dragon? That she is your true mate?"

Kelan nodded realizing all four men were intensely focused on his answer. "Yes…she bears the mark and is my true mate."

Jaguin finally spoke up from where he was sitting by the mouth of the cave watching the storm. "I wish to go with you when you go to her planet. I wish to see if I can find a true mate from among the females there," he said quietly, not looking at the other men but just staring out into the storm.

Kelan glanced at the other men and realized they were waiting for his answer. "For your help in finding my mate, I will take you. But you must understand. Her world is different from ours. None of the women were happy about being taken without their permission. In addition, the species of her world are unaware of life outside their planet. I can make no promises to you that you will find your true mate among her people," Kelan said.

Gunner stood up, throwing a stick into the fire and watching as hot sparks flew out in all directions. "You get us to her planet, and we will take care of finding our true mates."

The other men nodded silently in agreement. Kelan nodded in return. He could make no promises to them. His gaze turned inward as he felt his dragon stir. It lifted its head, listening carefully.

The storm is fading. Find my mate. It growled as it unfurled its massive length inside him. He could feel it claw at him, impatient to get back to the hunt. This time, it would not stop until its mate was under its wing. As if the other dragons sensed the same thing, all the men stood as one. Palto quickly put out the fire. Gunner was the first one out of the cave. He knew where the other caves were located. They would search every damn one until they found her.

* * *

Trisha giggled as she watched bronze, gold, and black scales dance along her arms. For the past two days, she and her dragon had taken the time to get to know each other. Trisha learned it would not hurt to transform into her other self. That it would actually be a wonderful experience.

While she didn't have the courage yet to change completely, she and her dragon had experimented with just letting the scales roll over her in rippling waves. Trisha began recognizing the faint tingling feeling that came over her right before they appeared. In addition, she understood her dragon's need for her mate. It was the same clawing need that was eating away at Trisha to be with Kelan.

Trisha no longer had any doubt that everything around her was real. There was no government experiment, no drugs, no mind meddling. She blushed at how stupid she was for becoming so scared and running off the way she did.

Not stupid, just scared—like me, her dragon said softly. *This is new. Too much, too soon. Kelan bad mate for pushing you without telling you,* it coughed out angrily.

No, he's not a bad mate. It is a learning experience for both of us, Trisha replied calmly. She was beginning to like having her dragon there all the time. She never felt alone.

Wait until we have our mates and his symbiot. Her dragon giggled. *It will be crowded then, yes?*

You haven't been talking to Bio have you? Kelan won't know what to do with three of us girls giving him fits. Trisha teased back.

Bio? her dragon asked curiously.

Kelan's symbiot. I nicknamed her Bio, Trisha explained.

Trisha's dragon rolled over in laughter. *All symbiots are male except for the queen which never leaves the hive.*

Well, shit, Trisha thought. No wonder the damn thing was playing her for a fool. It was just humoring her. Trisha blushed when she thought of how many times she got naked in front of the damn thing. Her blush turned even darker as her dragon let a long peal of laughter loose as she remembered the damn thing healing her after her and Kelan's intense lovemaking sessions. *Well, double shit.*

..*

Kelan's dragon stood on a branch high above the empty cave far below. It was the last one and still nothing. Kelan gritted back his roar of rage. His only thought was that Trisha never found shelter. She must have been out in the storm and there was no way she could have survived two and half days of the intense weather. Kelan felt his dragon's snarl of denial. It did not believe its mate would not have found some type of shelter. His symbiot sent a wave of warmth through him in agreement. It felt strongly their mate was too smart not to have found someplace safe to stay.

"Kelan," Gunner landed next to Kelan.

"What?" Kelan growled back in dragonspeak.

"There is one more. I didn't think it a possibility because it is small and is very difficult to see unless you know what you are looking for. I used to hide there when I was a boy," Gunner replied in a subdued voice. *"It is*

highly unlikely anyone else would find it, but your mate is very skilled. If anyone could find it, it would be her."

Kelan's sharp eyes studied the surrounding forests. Gunner was right. If anyone could find a hidden cave and seek refuge, it would be his mate. Kelan let his huge head turn toward Gunner and stared at him intently before nodding his reply.

* * *

Trisha watched as five dragons flew over her still form. She was lying under some branches about fifty feet in the air above the cave. She wanted to take a look around before she headed out. She decided that morning she would return to the palace and Kelan. She organized her little hideaway thinking it might be nice to bring Kelan back one day to visit. After she cleaned the cave, a habit left over from her father's lectures of always leaving an area cleaner than when you got there, she began the tedious task of camouflaging herself again. While she didn't care if Kelan found her now, she didn't want to run into any of the other large predators she saw during her earlier travels. She was probably only about a hundred yards or so from where they landed. Trisha hushed her dragon when it would have cried out with joy at seeing her mate. Trisha was curious as to how they found her.

Want my mate, her dragon whispered fiercely.

Hang onto your pantyhose. I want to see what they do, Trisha replied. It was always good to study those who were hunting you so you knew what to expect the next time.

Watch later, her dragon snarled impatiently.

Oh, come on. Just for a few minutes, Trisha said quietly, an idea forming in her head. She bit back a grin as she slowly reached down into her back pocket. A bow wasn't the only thing she had made during her time in the cave.

* * *

Kelan lowered his head as relief washed through him. She was here. He charged up the slope when he heard Gunner yell down to him that the cave had been used recently. Kelan's large frame could barely fit through the narrow opening but he squeezed until he was through. Inside he could see the neat circle of stones and the emptied moist ashes from the fire in a far corner. A small pallet with a woven leaf cover was lying near the fire pit. He saw the remains of several empty seed pods. It looked like she used the empty hulls as dishes.

"Look," Jaguin said, pointing to the wall.

Kelan looked at the wall and felt his breath leave him in such a rush he was almost dizzy. Trisha left him a message, written in his language. She said she was heading home to the palace. She missed her true mate. Kelan's fingers trembled slightly as he reached out to touch the words that went to his heart. She acknowledged him as her true mate. She accepted they were one.

Gunner, Jaguin, and Kelan turned as one toward the entrance of the small cave when Kor's surprised shout filled the air. Kor was yelling they were under attack while

Palto was cussing up a blue streak. Gunner moved out of the entrance in a blur of speed. He leaped down the twenty feet to the moist forest floor below. His feet no sooner hit the soft surface when a bright red stain soaked the front of his shirt right over where his heart was. He stared down in disbelief as the stains dripped down in a river of red.

Jaguin yelled for Kelan to stay back just as he was hit in the side of the head, throwing him back into Kelan. Bright red was splattered through his hair and ran down his neck in a stream of sticky ooze. He shook his head as he tried to clear his vision.

Kelan lowered him to the floor with a growl and burst out of the cave, shifting into his dragon. His symbiot quickly formed thick gold armor over his chest, arms, and legs. Long claws covered in gold glimmered from his front and back feet. A helmet of gold formed around his elongated head, protecting his forehead. He snarled as he landed in front of the other men who were busy trying to get the red, sticky pulp of the fruit they had been attacked with off their bodies. Kelan's eyes narrowed as he searched the dense forest for the slightest hint of where the threat might have come from. His dragon rose up on his hind legs and roared out a challenge. No sooner had the roar left his mouth than a piece of red fruit came at him, striking him in the throat. Luckily, his symbiot was able to deflect it.

Move to the left, Palto, Kelan snarled in rage. He was not about to let anything stop him from reaching his mate. *Kor, you go to the right. Gunner, Jaguin, go up.*

Trisha watched carefully as the men separated. It was a typical military maneuver. Trisha knew her scent was covered by the plants she used, and she was well camouflaged. The only way they would see her was if she moved too rapidly. She remembered her daddy's instructions. *"Wait them out, baby girl. Let them come to you. Take out the leader if you can. This way you cut the head off the snake. Remember to be patient. It could mean the difference between life and death. Always think about your opponents and study them. Everyone has a weakness, including you. Your job is to make sure they don't find it."*

Trisha sank back down under the dense growth, already moving away from where she fired last. She slowed her breathing until it seemed she only took a breath every couple of seconds. She gripped the slingshot tightly in her hand and carefully crawled on her belly, moving so slow a snail would win a race against her. She was looking to get to the rock outcropping about eight feet away from where she fired her last shot. She chose the spot for several reasons. It was thick enough to hide her, she was able to move without leaving any tracks, and once she moved a couple more feet she would be out of their line of sight, even from above. She would use the rock overhang to give her cover from above, and the rock surface she was now on covered her tracks. Her objective was clear—capture the leader, a.k.a. Kelan. Trisha wiggled and crawled until she was on top of a small ledge. She was now behind the men. If Kelan moved about six feet to the left, she would be able to drop down onto his back. From this view, she could see the symbiot covered him with armor in all but one vulnerable place, the junction between his wings. It left the dragons susceptible to an attack that could kill them. She would have to point that out to them. Her dad would love it here. He could train all the warriors in guerilla warfare, Trisha thought wistfully.

* * *

Kelan reached out with his senses trying to discover the scent of their attacker. His dragon growled in frustration. All it could smell was the natural forest around it. It did not scent anything out of the ordinary. Kelan's eyes narrowed as he watched the men with him spread out silently in the hope of surrounding whoever was attacking them. He crouched down onto all four of his powerful legs and moved slowly to his left, keeping the rocky slope to his back. He growled menacingly while swinging his head back and forth. Where was the bastard? Kelan thought in frustration. Since the last piece of jaka fruit was fired at them there was nothing. He let his gaze sweep over to where Kor and Palto were. Each gave a negative shake of his head as they moved silently through the dense undergrowth. He let his gaze turn to where Gunner was in one of the high trees above them. Gunner motioned with his hand that he saw nothing. He was just turning to check with Jaguin when he felt a flash of warning right before a wet river of jaka spilled down his side from between his wings.

Kelan let out a roar at the same time as a small figure leaped onto his back. It gripped him tightly with its legs, wrapping its arms around his neck. Kelan lowered his head twisting at the same time as he struck out at the figure with his spiked tail. The figure let go of his neck and did a flip over his shoulder, rolling across the ground. Before Kelan realized it, his dragon let loose a long stream of dragon fire at the creature that attacked him. Kelan's cry of horror was echoed by his dragon and his symbiot as they recognized the tiny figure of his mate a split second too late.

* * *

Trisha was expecting Kelan's defense. It only made sense. It wouldn't matter because if this were a real military situation, all of the men would be dead by now. Technically she ignored the others as she'd killed them with each of her first shots. She knew their symbiots could heal them in most cases, but a kill shot was a kill shot—hit the victim where the damage could not be healed fast enough to recover. With Kelan, he would have died the moment she drove the lance, or in this case the piece of fruit representing it, through his heart. If by chance he would have survived the initial blow, her second attack would have finished him off. She made a provision for his being able to throw her from his back and the knowledge he might use his dragon fire on her. By the time the flames were within reach, she was already disappearing into the undergrowth like a ghost. She sank down, becoming one with the native flora.

Two of the men with Kelan ran by her without even seeing her. The ones in the trees had shifted and landed heavily on the ground next to Kelan. She heard one of them growl out something in a deep voice.

"Who is that?" Gunner growled to Kelan in dragonspeak. His sharp eyes were sweeping back and forth as he tried to see where the figure disappeared.

Kelan stood stunned for a moment. How in the hell did she do it? One moment she was there, the next it was as if she vanished into thin air. When his dragon let loose the stream of dragon fire he was sure his mate was doomed. As the flames died down, he thought he would see nothing but her ashes. Instead, it was as if she had never stood in front of him.

His dragon rumbled in frustration. *Whip your mate's ass,* it snarled. *Your mate crazy. Scare me!*

Kelan laughed. *Yes, she scared me too.*

"It is my mate. I think she is playing a game with us. One she told me about. Her father would send her in after the warriors he was training. She called it tag. I believe we have all just been tagged. That is what the fruit was for. If you look at where she struck us, we would all be dead." Kelan chuckled proudly.

Jaguin swung his head to look at Kelan like he had lost his mind. *"Her father did what?"*

Kelan was about to reply when the small figure of his mate rose up out of the undergrowth not more than ten feet from them. She startled Kor and Palto, who took a step back as she emerged almost between them. He watched as she approached him slowly, a small knowing smile on her face, as if she knew what he was telling the other two dragons near him.

Kelan's eyes grew heavy as she reached out her hand, caressing the ridge of his left nostril. "Tag, you're it," she said tenderly.

Kelan was about to transform when he heard her soft request. "No, don't shift, not yet. I want to see you like this."

Trisha ignored the other two dragons and the two men standing behind her. She was focused only on the beautiful jade and silver dragon standing in front of her. She vaguely heard Kelan growl out something to the other men. Whatever it was, all four must have understood as the two dragons soon became four. All four nodded respectfully to her before leaping up and swiftly flying away, leaving her alone with her mate.

"You are so beautiful, just as my dragon said you were," Trisha murmured as she ran her hand down along Kelan's jaw.

Kelan lowered his head to give Trisha better access. He understood she needed to explore him in his dragon form. While he missed her dreadfully and wanted to claim her, he learned from his previous mistake about not giving her time to explore and accept who he was and what his world was. Kelan slowly lowered himself all the way to the ground so Trisha could walk around him. A shiver ran down the length of his dragon as he felt the soft, tentative touch of her hands as they moved over his head. His symbiot dissolved, reforming into the shape of a huge dog.

Trisha smiled at Bio. "I'm sorry I hurt you. I shouldn't have done that to you," Trisha said softly to the huge, golden beast as it came to rub against her side. She let one of her hands brush across its head. Trisha couldn't hold back the wobbly smile as thin bands of gold formed around her wrists. "I'm so sorry," she repeated softly.

Bio sent a wave of warmth through Trisha letting her know all was forgiven. She also caught the waves of relief at finding her safe and sound. It worried about her and would do anything to protect her.

"I know that now," Trisha said quietly as she bent over and gave it a kiss on the top of its huge head. Trisha watched as Bio trotted over and began exploring some of the trees around the area near the cave.

Trisha turned back to see Kelan studying her intently through flaming, golden eyes. "I'm sorry for scaring you, for running away. I shouldn't have. It's kind of a bad habit of mine when I need time to think." Trisha bit her bottom lip as she gazed up into the beautiful eyes of Kelan's dragon.

Trisha couldn't hold back the giggle as a long, rough tongue came out and swiped her face from her chin all the way up to her forehead. "Oh, gross!"

Kelan's dragon coughed out a laugh. He nudged Trisha gently with his head, encouraging her to continue exploring him. He liked the feel of her hands on his scales. He purred as she moved her hands up to trace around his eyes and ears.

"You are so soft," Trisha said in wonder as she traced the shape of the scales on his neck.

Trisha continued her exploration down Kelan's neck, moving toward his wings. He lifted them so she could run her palms along their thin membranes. He chuckled again when she squealed in surprise as she touched the claws at the tip of his wing, and he closed them around her hand. Her head swiveled to look at Kelan. He snorted a puff of smoke at her before releasing her hand. Trisha gave him a crooked smile. She let her fingers continue their slow exploration, moving closer to his body. Kelan's eyes drooped until they were almost closed, and he rolled onto his side, exposing his belly to Trisha's magic touch.

Trisha bit back a grin as the vibrations from his purrs increased until his whole body vibrated with the low rumbling sound. She moved until she was rubbing her hands over his belly, letting her nails scrape along the thick scales covering it. She couldn't control the soft chuckle that escaped as his head fell backward to rest on the ground, and his left leg began moving on its own as she scratched. It reminded her of the old hound dog she had when she was a kid—scratch the right spot and its leg would move a mile a minute. Somehow, she didn't think Kelan would appreciate that analogy. Her hand moved lower to the long slit in his lower region. The moment her hand touched it, Kelan's head jerked up with a growl, and she found herself wrapped in his tail. Trisha's gasp of surprise froze as she saw the flames blazing in Kelan's eyes. She felt herself being lifted off the ground and moved back up toward his front claws. Trisha couldn't break the hold Kelan's gaze had on her.

When he puffed out a heated breath, Trisha closed her eyes as the warmth flowed over her. When she opened them, she was staring at Kelan's dark, passion-filled face.

"You are mine, *mi elila*," Kelan said softly, dangerously.

His blood was heated to boiling as he stared down into his mate's face. He didn't care that she looked like the flora surrounding them. The fact that she could camouflage herself so well only heightened his desire as he recognized her as a fierce mate. Their children would be strong, like their mother.

"I need you, Trisha," Kelan whispered, gazing down into Trisha's eyes.

Trisha nodded, never looking away. She laced her fingers around Kelan's and took a step away, pulling him toward her hidden shelter. Kelan didn't say a word, just followed Trisha silently as she climbed up to the small cave. Trisha squeezed through the opening of the entrance. Kelan watched as she let go of his hand. His eyes flared as she began unwinding her long braid, pulling the small sticks, leaves, and flowers out of it until it fell like a curtain down her back. When she moved toward the shallow pool of water, he quickly stacked some of the leftover firewood back into the small stone circle and shifted just enough to breathe a small amount of dragon fire to start it. He didn't want his mate to get chilled.

Trisha quickly removed her clothing and knelt to use the chilly water to wash the camouflage off her face and arms. She shivered as the icy water ran down her neck onto her breasts, causing her nipples to bead up into hard pebbles. Trisha's breath caught in her throat as a pair of warm arms wrapped around her, cupping her suddenly heavy breasts.

"Kelan," Trisha breathed out in a soft, needy moan.

"*Mi elila.* My heart. You are the heart of my heart, the soul of my soul, the very breath I breathe. I love you, Trisha. *Suma mi mador.* I claim you as my true mate. No other may have you. I will live to protect you. You are mine," Kelan whispered in her ear as he gently pulled her up into his arms.

Trisha's eyes glowed with deep, dark chocolate-brown flames as she followed Kelan over to her makeshift bed. He lowered her down to the soft cushion following her with a groan as he pressed his lips into her neck. He was muttering in his own language too fast for the translator or her limited knowledge of their language to decipher. Trisha's legs parted as he pressed between them. Her breathing escalated until she was almost panting as Kelan pushed his hard length against her heated core, sliding slowly in until he couldn't go any farther. He held himself still for a moment, his lips pressing deep kisses against the throbbing pulse in her neck. It was almost like he didn't trust himself to move yet. Trisha heard him draw in a deep breath as a shudder ran through his long, muscular length. It was the only warning she got before he pulled almost all the way out before slamming into her even deeper. He continued to whisper rapidly under his breath as he moved faster and faster, pumping into her over and over as he tightened his hold on her. It wasn't until her body suddenly exploded at the heated friction of his hot, heavy length against her swollen core that she finally understood what he was saying. Trisha's loud cry echoed through the small cave followed by Kelan's louder roar of release.

Kelan shook at the intensity of his release. Subconsciously, he wanted to bind Trisha to him in every way. He fought against losing control. He knew she would want input as to when they would create a child. Trisha would be furious with him, but he couldn't hold back. No matter how much he tried, he couldn't hold back the desire to plant his seed deep inside her. Kelan let his head fall forward until it was buried in Trisha's curly strands. He was so screwed. She would never forgive him for this, he thought in despair.

Trisha lay in the warm cocoon of Kelan's arms in shock, his words flowing through her over and over. At first, she hadn't understood what he was saying. The words were muttered so softly and fast it didn't compute. As he jerked his head back during his release, the words were almost torn from him. *I give you my seed, my child...our child, our child*, he groaned over and over as he pulsed deep inside her.

Trisha closed her eyes and whispered to her dragon. *What did he mean?* she asked silently.

Trisha's dragon bounded inside of her, excited and happy. *Look!* her dragon cried out in excitement. *Our mates gave us their seed.*

Trisha focused deep inside her where her dragon was curling up into a ball around a small flicker of light. It was so faint she would have missed it if it hadn't been for her dragon.

She frowned. *What is it?*

Our baby, her dragon replied tenderly.

Trisha's eyes popped open to stare up at Kelan who was looking down at her with a worried expression. She searched his face trying to come to terms with the information her dragon just gave her. When she saw the truth of what her dragon said in Kelan's eyes, hers filled with tears.

"Shush, *mi elila*. It will be all right. I didn't mean to do it, but I have no regrets. You will be a strong mother for our children," Kelan said hoarsely.

"My injuries…" Trisha began in a small, scared voice.

Kelan was shaking his head. "…Healed. There is no danger to you or our child." Kelan hesitated before continuing, "Can you forgive me?"

A lone tear escaped from the corner of Trisha's eye and coursed down the side of her face at Kelan's quiet plea for forgiveness. How could he even ask when he gave her something she never thought she would have? Trisha's lips curved into a shaky smile as she thought of how excited her dad would be to discover he was going to be a grandpa.

"Of course I forgive you," Trisha replied softly. "A baby… Oh, Kelan, I wish my dad was here so I could tell him he is going to be a grandpa!" Trisha choked out a wobbly laugh as she pictured her dad's face when he discovered his only daughter was married to an alien, could shift into a dragon, and was going to give him the grandchildren he always wanted. She hoped he could handle it all without killing Kelan!

Kelan's face lit with a huge grin as he began moving inside of Trisha again. "He will be but not today… Today, you are mine," Kelan whispered against Trisha's lips.

Chapter 14

"How do I do this again?" Trisha asked in frustration.

She was trying to transform into her dragon, only the damn thing wouldn't cooperate. They spent the rest of yesterday into the early morning making love. Trisha was of the firm belief Kelan was determined to make her pay for being gone for almost six days. Not that she minded paying. Personally, she couldn't think of a more satisfying way to repay a debt. They sat on her small pallet early this morning, eating fresh fruit and roasted seeds and discussing the best way to return to the palace. Kelan suggested using his symbiot, but Trisha wanted to try her hand at transforming into a dragon and flying. Kelan's dragon was in obvious agreement as the suggestion was met with a howl of excitement. Kelan actually blushed a bright red as the sound ripped from his throat. Trisha promptly dissolved into a pile of giggles that lead to another session of lovemaking. Now, it was midmorning.

"You need to talk to your dragon," Kelan said again.

"She isn't listening. All she wants to do is coo and curl up around the little light inside of me," Trisha whined in annoyance. "Are you sure changing into a dragon won't harm the baby?"

Kelan laughed. "No, it won't hurt our child. It is natural for us to be able to shift. My mother often talked about shifting when she was pregnant with us just so she could get some peace from the nausea."

"Oh, I am so looking forward to that!" Trisha replied with a roll of her eyes. "Okay, what am I supposed to do if she refuses to listen to me?"

Kelan let a sly grin lift the corners of his mouth. "I could ask my dragon to call to his mate," Kelan said holding back a grin.

There was no need to let Trisha know what would follow if his dragon demanded his mate. His dragon snickered as he moved under Kelan's skin just waiting for his mate to emerge. *Let me call her. I call to my mate,* his dragon growled out in a low, deep rumble. Trisha looked at Kelan with a doubtful look but shrugged her shoulders. At this point, she was willing to try anything.

"Okay, do it. Call her," Trisha said.

Kelan's face broke into a huge, triumphant smile. "Come here," he said wickedly as he held his arms open to Trisha.

* * *

"This is for real, right? You aren't just horny and wanting to get it on again, are you? 'Cause if you are, I think we've more than made up for being apart for the past five days. I really want to try to do this whole dragon changing, shifting, transformation thing," Trisha asked, looking pointedly at the front of Kelan's pants where a rather large bulge was clearly evident.

Kelan chuckled. "Oh, it's for real. Come here," he whispered.

Trisha took a tentative step forward, then another and another until she was in the circle of Kelan's arms. She ran her hands up his chest until she could wind her arms around his neck. Trisha played with the hair on the back of his neck as she pressed closer to him.

"I'm here," Trisha whispered softly pressing a light kiss to Kelan's chin. "Now what?"

"Now this…" Kelan said with a growl. He wound his hand in Trisha's hair, pulling her head to the side as he pressed a hot kiss to the dragon's mark on her neck. *"I want my mate!"* his dragon growled in a deep, commanding voice right before he bit down on the mark, breathing his dragon fire into Trisha.

Trisha stiffened and tried to pull away. Kelan's eyes glowed with burning, gold flames as he let his dragon call to his mate. It was time for him to claim her…in every way. When Trisha tried to resist him, he growled out a warning. He let the fire flow from him to his mate, arousing her to the point she could not deny him.

Come to me. Be with me. I want you, my mate, Kelan's dragon demanded.

* * *

Trisha gasped and tried to pull away from the heat invading her body. She felt the instant response of her dragon to its mate's call. It growled and fought against being pulled away from the tiny spark inside her but was unable to resist the call of the male. She was pissed. She didn't like being commanded to do something against her will. As the dragon fire flowed from Kelan to Trisha, her blood felt like it was beginning to boil with the hot desire flooding her. She could hear the males demanding their mates. The need and desire in their voices increased the flood of arousal inside the females. Trisha felt the familiar tingling that indicated her dragon was coming to the surface. Suddenly, everything seemed to change. Her eyesight became sharper, clearer. She could hear the different insects, as if they were in their own individual little chorus, and smell everything from the plants to the trees to the soft, moist ground.

Kelan released Trisha, stepping back and watching as she began the transformation as her dragon emerged for the first time. *She is beautiful,* he and his dragon thought at the same time. Bronze, gold, and black scales rippled over her. Her face became elongated, changing as she transformed. Her eyes darkened even more with fiery gold sparks flickering in the deep, dark-brown depths. In moments a smaller, more delicate bronze, gold, and black dragon stood in front of Kelan, looking down at him with fire blazing from her eyes. That was the only warning Kelan got before she let out a growl and curled her tail around him, tossing him into a nearby muddy pool of water left over from the storm. Kelan sputtered as he sat up, wiping the oozing mud from his eyes.

He stared at Trisha in shock before asking, "Why the hell did you do that?"

Trisha's dragon snapped her teeth once at Kelan before giving an indelicate snort and leaping up onto a nearby tree, digging her front and back claws into it as she climbed.

Trisha giggled at her dragon's temper. It did not like to be told what to do. It did not like being forcibly taken from the tiny spark it was guarding, and it didn't like the tone of voice her mate used when calling her.

Like I supposed to just roll over and lift my tail, her dragon snorted. *My mate bad as yours.*

Trisha rolled with laughter as her dragon grumbled more about horny males needing to learn to control themselves and how they weren't the center of the universe no matter how much they seemed to think they were as she climbed up the tree to a thick branch about twenty feet off the ground. Her dragon stretched her wings out behind her several times as if she was testing them. Trisha decided the best thing to do at first was just to observe how her dragon did things. It was kind of weird being a part of something else. She knew everything that was going on around her, like she was doing it, but always was a bystander as well. The pilot and the co-pilot all at the same time, Trisha thought with a kind of enlightenment.

You fly good, yes? Her dragon asked as she peered down at Kelan who was struggling to get to his feet, her keen hearing picking up his muttered curses as he slipped in the mud.

Very good... Why? Trisha asked curiously.

We teach mates we hard to get. We play tag and have fun before we mate. Her dragon responded as she blew out a stream of dragon fire in front of Kelan, causing him to fall on his ass in the mud again.

Before we what? Trisha asked startled just as Kelan let out an angry bellow of rage and shifted into his dragon. Kelan's dragon stood glaring up at Trisha's, daring her to move.

Trisha's startled question turned to a squeal of surprise when her dragon leaped off the branch and soared down toward Kelan's, missing him by inches as she snapped her tail at his head. Kelan's dragon roared out at his mate's behavior. Even Trisha could understand his demands for her to obey him. That was all Trisha needed to agree with her dragon that both males needed to be put in their place. The females were not about to roll over, and as her dragon said, "raise their tails."

Kelan's dragon growled in annoyance at his mate's behavior. How dare she challenge him! He was the dominate mate of the pair; she should submit to him. Kelan had a bad feeling as his dragon took over, refusing to listen to him.

I don't think the females like being told what to do. Kelan tried to reason with his other half. *Maybe I was a bit hasty at letting you call your mate.*

My mate. You mate with yours; I want mine! Now! Kelan's dragon roared as he spread his huge wings and leaped up after his female.

Bio lay in the shade of one of the trees enjoying the show the two dragons were putting on. *Yes. Trisha was the perfect mate for all of them.* The symbiot shimmered as it responded happily. It kept its focus on both dragons, watching through the small bands of gold attached to both the males and the females. Soon, the mating would be complete and all would be sated. Bio's huge gold body shimmered in a variety of colors as the essence of his mates flowed through him making him stronger, healthier, and happier than he ever imagined possible.

* * *

Trisha's dragon darted through the thick forest, swerving around obstacles and using her small, sleek body to maneuver between fallen trees. They could hear the males coming up behind them. Their larger body would not be able to squeeze through some of the areas the females were flying. Trisha's mind quickly sped through one scenario after another. They would need to put some distance between them or find a blind spot to just "disappear." Sometimes it was possible to hide in plain sight if you knew what you were doing—and Trisha knew what she was doing. Her coloring matched a lot of the surrounding foliage. If she could find a tangle of vines against the darker outcropping of rocks or a thick covering of the bronze, gold, and black ferns, she would almost be invisible.

Go to the right, Trisha whispered to her dragon. *On the way here we passed an area where we can lie down among the ferns. Our coloring matches it perfectly, and it is thick.*

Trisha felt her dragon shift to the right, swooping under a huge tree that looked like it might have fallen in the storm. Trisha laughed as she heard the roar behind her. Kelan wouldn't be able to see her with the branches still covered with huge leaves. Trisha instructed her dragon to stay low to the ground. They skimmed along the dense carpet of ferns covering the forest floor. Trisha saw a really thick area and knew she could hide most of her dragon in it.

Drop down lightly so that you don't disturb any of the surrounding foliage, Trisha said calmly. She was in the zone, as her daddy would say.

Trisha's dragon dropped down in the thick ferns, folding her wings in and burying her long slender neck down into the ferns, letting the leafy plants drape over her. She lay still, barely breathing and waited. Trisha couldn't resist the smile as she felt her dragon's joy at being out. Trisha let her senses spread out, absorbing the smells and sounds around her. She could hear the males approaching from above her. Her dragon started to stir, but Trisha calmed her.

Patience. If you stay still, they will miss us, Trisha whispered soothingly.

How do you know? her dragon whispered back.

They won't expect us not to still be moving and definitely won't expect us to be out in plain sight, Trisha responded. *I used to do this all the time. As long as you don't move, you probably won't be seen.*

Within moments, the males were past them. Trisha's dragon lifted her head above the ferns just high enough to watch the back of her mate fly by. She giggled as she watched him looking upward into the higher branches instead of down toward the forest floor.

It worked, she breathed in amazement. *Now we play tag?*

Now we play tag, Trisha said.

Trisha's dragon slowly stood up. She swung her head toward the direction the males went, watching them as they flew farther away. With a push of her wings, she lifted off the ground, moving quietly behind them. She kept the larger trees between them so she wouldn't be seen.

There is a waterfall with a small meadow to the west of here about a mile or so. I saw it when I was up in the trees before the storm. Let's head there. It may take the males a little while, but I bet they will end up there. We can hide behind the falls and surprise them when they land. Trisha said as her dragon landed on the thick trunk of a tree, hanging there silently when the big males landed on a branch farther ahead.

I surprise my mate. He not know I tag him till it too late, Trisha's dragon responded with a chuckle. She liked playing tag with her mate.

They waited until they heard the roar of the males again and the crack of a branch as the huge male swung his tail in frustration at not finding his mate. Once the males took off toward the north, the females let go of the tree and headed west, keeping to the shadows as much as possible. Trisha's dragon landed on the edge of a small grassy meadow. There was a waterfall that Trisha estimated to be about three hundred feet high falling into a small pool of water which flowed into a fairly decent-sized stream. Trisha's dragon raised her head, sniffing the air carefully for any predators. When she felt confident there was no danger, she stepped out into the thick purple grass that was sprinkled with thousands of small flowers in a wide variety of blues, yellows, pinks, and reds. Trisha giggled as her dragon swooped down and gobbled up a mouthful of them.

Good, her dragon said.

You know you just left tracks the guys will be able to see. Trisha chuckled.

Want my mate to find me. I tag first, then lift my tail. I do it when I want... her dragon growled back playfully. *...but not make it too easy,* she added with a snicker.

Trisha just chuckled as her dragon rolled around the meadow trampling some of the grass down before she lifted off the ground just enough to flutter over to the rocks near the falls. She carefully maneuvered her way until she ducked her long, slender neck through the icy water. There was a recess behind the falls just big enough for her to fit. Trisha felt her dragon's muscles bunch as she gauged the distance before she jumped, landing on a small, slippery ledge. Trisha's dragon shook from the tip of her nose to the tip of her tail, shaking the icy water off her scales. The water actually felt really good in her dragon form, Trisha thought distractedly. After a few moments they both settled down, curling into a ball and watching through the sheets of water falling. They had a clear view of the meadow. Now, it was time to wait.

* * *

Kelan's dragon was furious with his mate. They traveled several miles north before turning back. It was only when Kelan began working with his dragon, reminding him of some of the tricks Trisha used when he was tracking her that his dragon finally let him have some control back. Once they backtracked, they found where she'd clung to the trees. Kelan chuckled when he realized the hunted had become the hunter. She had been following them. They traced back to the thick foliage where she had lain down. Kelan's dragon growled out about Kelan needing to whip his mate's ass again when he realized he had flown right over her without even seeing her. Now they knew what to look for, they moved slower, with more precision, following the faint tracks.

Kelan paused on a high branch overlooking the small meadow. They could see where some of the flowers had been eaten recently and a spot where the grass was lying down from being trampled.

They are here…somewhere, he said softly to his dragon.

He let his dragon's keen eyesight sweep the meadow carefully. Raising his nose up, he sniffed. He caught the faint scent of his mate but couldn't be sure if she was still here. He wouldn't be at all surprised if she wasn't. She could have made a big circle and either headed back to the small cave where they started or was coming up behind him. Kelan spread his wings and leaped off the branch he was on, landing a few feet from where the grass was trampled. He moved slowly looking for clues and sniffing the ground. His mate's scent filled his nostrils and heated his blood. He wanted her. Kelan's huge head came up, and he let out a loud roar followed by a series of coughs, demanding his mate answer him. When there was no answer to his call, he growled low, letting the sound rumble across the meadow. Kelan lowered his big body down to where his mate had rolled in the thick purple grass and rolled on top of it, marking his scent along with hers. He rolled back and forth for several minutes before getting to his feet with a snarl and stomping over to the small stream to get a drink. Kelan decided he would head back toward the small cave where they'd spent the night before to see if Trisha had returned there. He was just lowering his head to drink deeply from the icy water when a sixth sense warned him he wasn't alone. It came a split second too late.

Trisha's dragon roared out with glee as she tackled her huge mate, knocking him over onto his back and gripping his front claws with hers. She reached down and bit his neck, breathing a small amount of dragon fire into his blood before she sprang away and circled around him.

"Tag, you're it," Trisha's dragon crowed, swinging her tail back and forth seductively.

Kelan's dragon growled low as he rolled back onto his feet. The bite on his neck seeped a small amount of blood, calling to Trisha as she watched it well up before a tiny line ran down. Kelan watched as his mate moved a short distance from him. Water glistened like diamonds on her scales, casting millions of brilliant, colorful reflections off the beautiful body of her dragon. She turned her back to him, swishing her tail back and forth while she looked over her shoulder at him.

"You stare all day or you play?" Trisha's dragon purred to her mate.

Oh boy, Trisha thought as she stared at the flames burning in the eyes of the huge dragon staring back at her. She really hoped her dragon knew what she was doing. *You do, don't you?* Trisha whispered uncertainly.

..*

Kelan's blood flared at his mate's challenge. She was teasing him, daring him, taunting him to come after her…to capture her and take her in the most primal way. He watched as she swept her tail back and forth slowly, lifting it every once in a while. Kelan felt the rumble of a purr start as he imagined what it was going to be like to finally be totally sated. His eyes drooped as he watched his mate lower her head and raise her tail a little higher in invitation. The huge male dragon could not resist such an offer. He moved toward the females with determination. He wanted to fuck his mate. Kelan felt the muscles in his dragon's back legs tense as he prepared to pounce on the smaller female. He knew better than to deny him his mate. He had waited long enough. The huge male lifted his head and roared as he sprang forward to capture his female.

Trisha's dragon contained a little more guts than she ever would, Trisha decided. She was taunting the huge male, teasing him into a frenzy of desire. It was worse than wearing red to the running of the bulls, Trisha decided. The little female dragon just laughed as she swept up into the sky just as the huge male sprang forward. She even had the nerve to tap the big male on the cheek with her tail as she

228 ~S. E. Smith

shot straight up, pumping her powerful wings in an effort to gain enough height that he couldn't grab her. Trisha felt the exhilaration of the chase as she moved through the small meadow, landing in a nearby tree along the edge. She watched as the males turned in a tight circle before launching off the ground with a deep growl of warning. She knew they would catch her this time, and she knew she would let them. She wanted to be completed. She wanted to become one with Kelan more than she wanted anything else in the universe. She leaped off the branch, swooping down, trying to get under the males as they flew at her. The last thing she expected was for Kelan's dragon to reach out with his tail and wrap it under her belly, tossing her up into the air above him. The move caused her to tumble over and over in midair, disorienting her. Trisha's dragon let out a startled cry as she felt herself falling.

Kelan's dragon spun around in a tight circle as his mate leaped up in the air away from him. He snapped at the tail that brushed his cheek, trying to get some type of hold on the frustrating female he wanted to claim. He choked back a laugh as he thought of how much fun he was having and how perfect his mate was for him. He would have been bored with a mate who was not a challenge. His little dragon would always keep him guessing. The huge male even admitted Kelan was right, the females did not like to be told what to do. He would have to remember that whenever he wanted to stir up the fire in her eyes. He would just also have to be prepared for the consequences. He watched carefully as his little mate landed in a tall tree on the edge of the meadow. She stood there, letting out delicate, sexy little coughs and swishing her tail back and forth, almost daring him to try and come get her. The huge male's eyes drooped a little as he thought about what he would like to do with that tail when he caught her.

Kelan's dragon decided it was time to claim his mate once and for all. With a deep growl, he launched off the ground. He was more experienced in dragon form and anticipated the moves his little mate might make. When she swooped down out of the tree intending to duck under him, he waited until the last possible second to reach out with his thick tail and wrap it around her. With a flick, he sent her upward so he could maneuver until he was under her. As she started to tumble back down, he caught her cry of fear. He used that to his advantage as he caught her to his powerful body using his front and back claws to grab her. The little dragon clung to him in fear, her little heart racing as she tried to reorient herself before she hit the ground. Instead of hitting the ground, Kelan's dragon wrapped his tail around hers pulling her even closer until he could impale himself in her hot core. He let out a loud groan as he felt himself slide even deeper with each downward stroke of his wings. Bending forward, the huge male warned the smaller female of his intentions before he bit down on her neck and breathed the dragon's fire into her.

"I claim you. My mate. Yes?" the jade and silver dragon of Kelan groaned out to Trisha's smaller one.

"Yes. My mate. You tag me...always," Trisha's dragon replied, letting her smaller head fall back so the sleek line of her throat was offered in submission.

Kelan's dragon lowered their entwined bodies down into the thick purple grass, never parting his hold on the small, delicate female under him. He continued to breathe the hot fire of his desire into her as he rocked back and forth. He wrapped his tail tightly around hers making sure she was pinned as he claimed her over and over, letting his hot seed pour into her welcoming body. When he freed her neck to roar out his release, he felt the small body of the dragon under his stiffening before she let out a series of soft coughing noises, her body closing around his and holding him to her while her body milked him.

"My mate. My mate. Love my mate," Trisha's dragon coughed out as her small body spasmed.

The huge male looked down where he held his smaller mate trapped under him, feeling the love for her well up and burst through his huge body until he shook with the intensity of it. He would always protect her. He would kill anyone who ever tried to harm her or their child. She was the fire of his blood. The feelings rushing through the huge dragon were so intense he felt his cock harden deep inside the female and coughed out a loud groan as he felt more of his seed flood into her. He wanted his scent so deep there would never be a doubt as to who this particular female belonged to.

Chapter 15

Trisha was exhausted by the time they reached the palace. It was well after midnight before they landed on the balcony outside of their living quarters. They planned to return sooner, but it seemed that both Kelan and his dragon were determined to keep their mates in their line of sight at all times due to the little issue of having to chase them down. Unfortunately, line of sight usually meant being ahead of him which is what seemed to cause the problem. Whenever Trisha's dragon was ahead of the huge male it meant he was staring at her tail which seemed to turn him on. More than once, Trisha's dragon found herself pinned from behind with a huge male buried deep inside her—not that her dragon was complaining at all. Trisha never knew she could be such a horny little slut! Once their dragons were done, it was Kelan and Trisha's turn. They stopped to rest at least four times on the way back, and everytime they shifted back to their two-legged form, Kelan would have her down on the soft grass, bend of a limb...well, okay, two out of the four times it was her tackling Kelan, but hey, fair was fair. Now, all she could think of was a hot shower and a soft bed. Even the hot shower wasn't a prerequisite since their last stop ended with them making love in one of the many streams that ran through the forests. Trisha decided bed was more important as she wobbled on unsteady legs.

Kelan wrapped his arms around Trisha as she stumbled. She was a natural at transforming to her dragon now, and he was amazed at her flying skills. Valdier warriors learned to transform into their dragons at an early age. After their first transformation, they were taught by the more experienced warriors in the art of flying and defense. Not all Valdier males transformed. It was not necessary. There was an increase in the number of males who could during the Three Wars. Their scientists believed it was due to the need for more warriors to protect the females and fight for their species. But since the war and the decrease in available females who were true mates, the number was on the decline again.

Kelan gently laid Trisha's sleeping form in their big bed, carefully undressing her. He let his fingers run through the tangle of long curls, spreading them out across his pillows the way he liked. Even in sleep Trisha turned toward the heat of his hand, seeking his touch. Kelan took a deep breath, soaking in the combined scent of him and his mate. He gently touched the dragon's mark on her neck in reverence.

My mate beautiful, Kelan's dragon said with a contented sigh. The big male was finally sated.

Yes, our mate is beautiful, Kelan replied silently, still staring down at Trisha's relaxed form.

Kelan started when he heard a light knock on the outer door. Calling to his symbiot, he instructed it to watch over their sleeping mate. The golden creature shifted into the shape of a huge dog and jumped up on the bed. It turned several times before lying down next to her. Satisfied his mate would be safe, Kelan stood up and walked into their living quarters. He was shocked when he saw Mandra standing outside looking grim.

"What is it?" Kelan asked, knowing immediately something bad had happened.

"Trelon and his mate were attacked yesterday by Curizan skimmers," Mandra said quietly.

Kelan looked at his brother's face and felt his heart skip a beat. "Is he...are they..." Kelan began.

Mandra was shaking his head. "Trelon is hurt badly but will recover. Creon believes he has found Trelon's tiny mate, Cara, but is unsure if she survived the attack. Trelon is still unconscious. I know you two are very close and hoped you could be with him when he awakes. He will not be happy when he finds his mate may not have survived," Mandra finished roughly.

Kelan nodded. He sent a message to his symbiot to take care of and protect their mate. It replied with a wave of warmth. Mandra quietly explained what happened while they walked to Trelon's living quarters where his symbiot and the healers were working on repairing the damage done to Trelon's body. He couldn't help but think of Trelon's tiny mate. How could anyone want to hurt something so precious? Okay, so he thought about it a time or two on board the *V'ager* when she was doing all her little experiments, but it wasn't like he would ever have really done anything. Even he admitted she was just too damn cute to hurt. His only hope was she was also resourceful and fast.

..*

Trisha woke late the next morning. She let her hand stretch out to feel for Kelan, sitting up when all she encountered were cool, smooth sheets. She frowned as she looked at the side of the bed which had obviously not been slept in.

"Kelan?" Trisha called out into the silence of their living quarters.

Her hand went to her throat as doubts assailed her. What if he changed his mind? What if all he wanted to do was trick her into coming back? No sooner had the thoughts formed in her mind than she pushed them away. Kelan was *not* Peter. Kelan loved her, really loved her. He didn't just want to use her. Trisha started when she found herself being pushed back by a massive gold head. When she was trapped flat against the pillows, Bio stood above her in the shape of a huge cat and stared down at her intensely before letting its huge tongue go to work on her face. Trisha squealed as the huge golden tongue lapped at her face and shoulders causing her to giggle uncontrollably.

"Stop! Bio…stop!" Trisha begged as it continued to cover every inch of her face, neck, and shoulders. "I give up! I promise…I give up!"

Bio snorted as it brushed one more time against Trisha, leaving delicate strands of gold wrapping around her neck and twisted in her hair. It would not let her feel the pain of the one who hurt her before. Bio thought of going to his mate's planet and eliminating the male who hurt his Trisha. Bio moved slowly off Trisha but not before sending images to Kelan and his dragon of their mate's fear. It shivered as it received a response from both of them. They would not be leaving her planet without first visiting the male who harmed their mate. Bio snickered as it curled up on the end of the bed to watch over Trisha. Their mate did not need to know all of their plans. Some things were best left to the males to take care of.

Trisha sat up again, pushing her long curly hair out of her face. "I don't know what that was all about, but it definitely woke me up," Trisha said with a soft smile. "You know I love you, don't you, big guy?"

Bio shimmered a variety of colors and the tiny strands in Trisha's hair moved so her hair seemed to float all around her. Trisha laughed as she felt the tiny ribbons of gold began to dance through her hair, combing it out, then weaving back and forth to braid it.

"Wow!" Trisha whispered in awe. "Who needs a beautician when they can have you?"

Bio snorted before lowering its head back down to the bed and closing its eyes. It felt Kelan's rapid approach toward their living quarters. Kelan would not allow his mate to doubt his feelings for her.

Trisha was just stepping into the cleansing unit when Kelan appeared. He stood at the doorway watching her intently. Trisha turned and splayed her hands on the clear glass, returning his heated gaze.

"I love you," she said softly, unable to hold back expressing her feelings. "I missed you."

Kelan's eyes darkened as he stared at his mate. "There has been a situation. I was called away."

"What happened?" Trisha asked softly, stepping aside as she watched Kelan slowly removing his clothes. Her body heated at the idea of their bathing together. It would not be the only thing they did.

"My brother Trelon and his mate were attacked yesterday afternoon," Kelan replied, stepping into the cleansing unit. "I don't have much time, but I needed to see you, touch you," Kelan murmured.

"Cara…?" Trisha asked frightened.

Kelan shook his head. "We do not know yet. Creon is organizing the search for her. We believe we have found where she is," Kelan did not add that there was an excellent possibility she might not be alive. He would not say anything to Trisha until he knew for sure.

"Oh, Kelan," Trisha whispered as she moved into his arms. "Your brother…will he be all right?"

Kelan's arms tightened around Trisha's slender frame, pulling her tight against his body. "Yes. Physically he will be. It depends on what has happened to his mate as to whether he will survive," Kelan said quietly.

He wouldn't lie to her. His arms tightened as he remembered how he felt when Trisha disappeared. At least he knew after a short period she left on her own accord. He shuddered to think what it would have been like if she was taken or…worse. He pressed a kiss against Trisha's forehead before moving slowly down the side of her face where he stopped with his lips hovering above hers.

"I love you, *mi elila*. You are my true mate. Never doubt my love or the love of my dragon and symbiot," Kelan said before he crushed his lips to hers.

Trisha moaned as she wrapped her arms around Kelan's neck. She would never get enough of him. She let her fingers tangle in his hair, trying to get closer as she rubbed her breasts against the light coating of hair covering his broad, muscular chest. She whimpered when she felt the heat rising inside of her. It wasn't as bad as when he bit her and breathed the "dragon fire" as he called it, but it was still a hot, burning desire that left her achy and needy. Kelan seemed to understand the fire burning inside of Trisha. He pulled back slightly and looked down at her for a moment before he said anything.

"I am going to take you over and over. I need to feel how alive you are. I need to imprint my scent into your soul, Trisha," Kelan whispered, looking for her consent.

"Oh, baby, you say the sexiest things sometimes," Trisha whispered against his lips with a faint smile curving her swollen lips.

Kelan groaned as Trisha's lips parted, letting him taste her warmth. His breath caught in his throat as she sucked on his tongue. All he could think about was how wonderful it would feel if she wrapped her lips around his throbbing cock. As if she could read his mind, she pulled back and gave him a soft smile. His eyes drooped, and he braced his hands against the wall as she slid down his body until she was sitting on the bench inside the showering unit. He lowered his head, shielding her from the spray and watched as she wrapped one hand around his hard length and used her other hand to gently cup his sack. Kelan couldn't hold back the deep growl as he watched Trisha slowly open her mouth. She brought his cock almost to her lips, pausing to look up at him. Sliding her tongue out, she ran it over the tip, circling the swollen head before sliding it into her hot mouth. Kelan's hands curled as the look and feel of her almost made him explode. He would never last at the rate they were going. Kelan rocked his hips back and forth as Trisha's hand tightened around his length. He let her take as much of him as she could without choking before pulling back out. A shiver went through him as he felt Trisha's hand move between his legs so she could run her nails along his buttocks. His breathing increased to a pant as he fought against the pull of his climax.

"Trisha, stop," Kelan choked out, watching his cock disappear again and again in her mouth as she tilted her head this way and that to take as much of him as she could. "Stop, *mi elila*, or I will come down your throat."

Trisha's hum of pleasure at the thought sent the last of his control spiraling outward. His body clenched as the vibrations of her enjoyment rocked through him. With a loud cry, his body jerked as he spilled his hot seed into Trisha's mouth. His head fell back, and his hands splayed on the wall as he forced his trembling legs to support him as she continued to drink from him, sucking hard to get every last drop. Kelan couldn't believe how intense the climax was. He slowly sank down onto his knees in front of Trisha and laid his head on her lap. The soothing warmth of the water flowed around them. Kelan turned his head until he buried his nose in the soft curls between Trisha's legs. The smell of her arousal refueled the hunger in him as it called to his blood.

"Lie back," Kelan said hoarsely.

Trisha groaned as she lay back on the narrow bench and spread her legs for Kelan. She closed her eyes and used her senses to absorb his touch. She couldn't suppress the cry that escaped her lips as she arched when he ran his finger along her swollen clit. She wondered if it would always be like this—the need, the craving, the desire.

"Yes," Kelan said softly, making Trisha aware that she had whispered those words aloud. "It will always be there and will grow stronger over time."

Trisha's reply died on her lips as Kelan leaned forward and began sucking on her swollen nub. Trisha gripped the edges of the bench tightly as Kelan forced her legs up and farther apart until they hung over his shoulders. She was panting by the time he moved his fingers to join his mouth. She could feel the rough texture of them as they moved in and out along the soft walls of her vagina. He would pump into her, then replace his fingers with his tongue before doing it all over again. She swore at one time his tongue was even longer as it moved deeper inside of her, touching her sensitive spots to the point she couldn't contain her cry as her orgasm swept through her, coating his mouth with her essence.

Trisha thought they would be done now that they were both sated. She forced her eyes to open as she felt Kelan move from between her legs. When she looked up, it was into flaming eyes filled with undeniable desire. Kelan wanted his mate again. Only this time, he would take her over and over. Trisha gasped as Kelan jerked her up until she was standing on shaky legs. He growled at her when she would have moved away to give him more room. Before she realized what he intended, she was turned until she was facing the wall of the showering unit. Kelan ran the soft soapy cloth over her neck and shoulders, down along her back all the way to her ankles. When he moved back up he stopped at her ass. He pressed her legs until she was forced to spread them. Trisha shuddered as he ran the cloth up over her ass, spreading her cheeks as he did it. Trisha trembled as he ran a finger around the tight ring of her ass. Kelan stepped into Trisha, keeping his finger against her as he used his other hand to wrap around her and wash her breasts, belly, and finally, her pussy.

Trisha was so hot she didn't know if she wanted to push back against the finger on her ass or forward against the ones pressing against her pussy. She groaned in frustration. How could she want both at the same time? Kelan was a master at turning her inside out and upside down. She never thought of exploring the darker desires of lovemaking with Peter, but with Kelan she wanted to not only explore it, she wanted to experience it. With a cry of frustration at the teasing, Trisha pushed back against Kelan gasping as his thick finger pushed past the tight rim.

"Kelan..." Trisha moaned desperately.

"I will never leave you, Trisha," Kelan muttered softly as he pushed another finger past the rim to join the first. "You are mine, Trisha. I will hunt you down wherever you go. I will track you to the ends of the universe and farther if necessary. You are mine for always," Kelan whispered as he pressed a kiss against the dragon's mark on her neck.

He moved down to her shoulder and pressed another kiss to it. He would mark her again. As he claimed her, he would put his second mark on her so she would always know he would be there for her. He pushed his fingers deeply into her pussy at the same time as he pushed them deeper into her ass. When she threw her head forward with a moan he bit down onto her shoulder, breathing dragon fire into her blood. He gently pumped her as he breathed, feeling the heat building until she started to struggle. He pulled back at the last moment before she climaxed, licking the small wound before blowing a heated breath over it so the shape of a small dragon appeared. He smiled as he watched the shape form. She was his.

"Lean over and grab the bench. I want to fuck your ass at the same time I fuck your pussy," Kelan said thickly.

Trisha was beyond thinking. She was into pure feeling at this moment. She whimpered when Kelan withdrew his fingers from her pussy but kept the ones burning and stretching her ass in place. She leaned forward, placing her palms flat against the carved stone and spreading her legs as far as she could. She cried out as Kelan pushed his thick, heavy length into her. She was so swollen with need again she didn't know if he would even fit. She whimpered again as the pressure built until her swollen, hot walls seemed to welcome him.

"Hang on tight," Kelan said through gritted teeth as he began pumping in and out of her.

Trisha let her head hang down as Kelan began a pattern of pushing into her ass while pulling out of her pussy and then reversing it. He added another finger, causing Trisha to feel even fuller than before. She panted as the burning and pressure built. She needed relief and soon. The fire building inside her was about to ignite her blood if she didn't do something.

"Faster," Trisha choked out.

Kelan increased the speed, slamming into her until Trisha's climax exploded around him. As Trisha clamped down around both his cock and his fingers, he felt his own orgasm burst from deep inside him. He pulled his fingers out of her and leaned over Trisha's heaving back as she sobbed out her pleasure. He wrapped her tightly against him, enjoying the way her vaginal walls milked his cock over and over as he pulsed in her.

"Oh, *mi elila*. You are so beautiful," Kelan groaned out as he held her tight and rocked against her, thinking if he hadn't already planted his seed in her womb he would have done so today.

Chapter 16

Trisha stared out the window at the two dragons lying quietly in the small garden far below. It was a month since Trisha and Kelan returned from the forests to find out that Cara and Trelon were attacked by Curizan and, more disturbing, Valdier warriors. Kelan's brother, Creon, found Cara hiding in a small cave at the base of a mountain. Trisha knew how afraid of small, dark places Cara was and couldn't imagine anything more horrifying than for her littlest sister to be buried alive for three days.

Trisha explained to Kelan about Cara's claustrophobia. He was trying to help his brother. The first two days after their return, Kelan spent most of his time sitting with Trelon. He came back to their living quarters briefly to rest, and as he put it, with a need to know his mate was safe. Sometimes they would make tender love when he came, and other times it was rough and explosive. Afterward, she would hold him while he slept for a couple of hours before returning to his brother's side. She saw a little of Abby but none of Ariel or Carmen at first. Once Cara was found, Kelan soberly explained she was in her dragon form and both were not well. It seemed Cara had buried herself so far inside her dragon none of them, including Trelon, could reach her. After Trisha pressured Kelan, he finally admitted if Cara did not return soon both his brother and the female she considered to be a sister would perish, for a dragon could not live long in a half life. Trisha insisted that she, Ariel, Carmen, and Abby be allowed to visit with Cara daily in the hopes their familiarity would bring Cara's "human" self out. So, far nothing was working.

Trisha turned as Kelan's mom walked over to stare out the window with her. Morian stared down over the garden where her son lay next to his mate. She wrapped an arm around Trisha's waist, hugging her. While Trisha hadn't said anything yet, Morian knew her new daughter would soon be blossoming with Kelan's child.

"Is there anything we can do to help her?" Trisha asked quietly, staring at the heartbreaking sight. She fought back tears as she watched Trelon's dragon tenderly scoot closer to Cara's tiny one, wrapping one of his big wings around her to shield her from the sun.

Morian watched as the tiny dragon's head turned to rest her cheek against the huge male's chest. Tears formed in her eyes as she watched Trelon care for his tiny mate. If something wasn't done soon, they could lose both of them.

"I think it is time to have a talk with my daughter," Morian responded with soft determination as she turned and walked out the door.

Trisha stood watching the pair and praying that some miracle would occur. Her heart leaped as she saw Kelan approaching Trelon's dragon. He said something, and she watched as Trelon transformed back into a man. They were having some type of heated discussion when Trisha noticed Morian in the garden with them. Whatever she said must have worked. Within moments, Kelan was pulling a very reluctant Trelon down the path toward the wing of the palace that held the offices.

Trisha studied Morian as she requested refreshments from a servant. She secretly wished her dad could meet Kelan's mom. She thought back to the list she and her dad wrote that day long ago about all the qualities he was looking for in a woman. Trisha swore Morian met every single criteria. She was strong yet gentle, wise, elegant, determined, caring, beautiful, and Trisha loved her, something she could honestly say she had never felt toward any other woman her dad ever dated.

Trisha frowned as she tried to imagine what Morian could be saying to Cara. She knew it must be something because Trisha could see the difference in the body language of Cara's dragon. It was like Morian was saying something that was tugging at the tiny dragon's heart. Trisha continued to watch in fascination as Morian calmly took a sip of her drink before she set it down and stood up.

Trisha gasped and her hand flew to her mouth as she watched Cara's dragon shimmer for a moment before disappearing. In her place was Cara's tiny figure, crouched down on the ground. Trisha felt the tears course down her cheeks as she watched Morian gently cradle Cara's small form in her arms, rocking her back and forth before helping her to stand. A smile tugged at the corners of Trisha's lips as she followed the woman who created a "miracle." Trisha leaned her head against the glass so she could follow the two delicate figures until they disappeared inside the palace. Yes, if she had to choose a woman for her dad, it would be Morian Reykill.

* * *

"Morian, what did you say to Cara to bring her back?" Trisha asked quietly a few hours later.

Kelan was in an emergency meeting with Zoran, so Trisha asked if Abby and Morian would like to have late afternoon refreshments with her while she waited for him to finish. There were two important things she learned since living on Valdier. One, they liked to eat—a lot—and two, they enjoyed eating dinner late, very late. Trisha was going to have to work out constantly if she continued to eat the way she was.

No, you eat for three. I need food. You pick. Her dragon snorted a reply as she rolled over and snuggling up to the tiny spark that seemed to be growing rather rapidly.

Trisha rolled her eyes. Her dragon was perfectly content to make love, eat, and cuddle the tiny spark. She didn't have to worry about getting a big butt; she already had one!

I hear that. My mate like my butt...and my tail, her dragon purred in response. *You mate like you butt too.* She giggled.

Morian raised her eyebrow when she noticed Trisha turning a bright red suddenly. "Are you well, Trisha?"

Trisha fanned her face as she replied. "Damn dragon."

Morian's chuckled as she imagined what Trisha's dragon was saying. "Yes, they can be a bit pesky at times," she sobered as she took a sip of her tea. "To answer your question, I simply told her the truth. Trelon was dying, and she was the cause of it. If she didn't want him to die, then she needed to come back to him. You see, without your other half there is no life."

Trisha and Abby stared at Morian for a moment, absorbing what she was saying. "Are you saying if one of us were to die, then the other would die as well?" Trisha asked quietly.

Morian nodded. "That is precisely what I am saying." Morian looked at Abby first. "When Zoran claimed you on your planet he knew he could never leave you behind. It would have killed him and you, if he had. You were not the only one changed during the exchange. While Zoran, Trelon, and Kelan were able to give you the dragon's fire, the chemical which allows your body to be transformed into a dragon, in exchange he must also give to you his essence, what he is made of. This is how you are accepted by not only him, but his dragon and his symbiot."

Abby looked at Morian with huge blue eyes. "He told me we were one."

Morian nodded again. "Yes. You are both halves of a whole, incomplete without the other." Morian turned to look at Trisha. "My son should have explained this to you. When you ran away, he had no other choice but to follow you. He would never stop…never," Morian said firmly. "This is why he cannot return you to your planet. Your body is different now but even more is your need to be near each other. Over a period of time, when one true mate dies, the other mourns the loss until the will to live is no longer there."

"But, I don't understand. What about Zoran, Trelon, and Kelan's father?" Abby asked.

Morian smiled softly as she remembered her mate. "I loved him dearly, but he was not my true mate. Ours was a match to form one strong clan. We both came from royalty, descended from the gods and goddesses themselves. Over time, we came to love and respect each other. At first, I thought to join him in death, but I still had much to live for. I have five wonderful sons and hoped, with good cause, that one day I would have five wonderful daughters and a house full of children once again. It was not my time. Not yet, anyway," Morian said softly.

"Did you ever think you would find your true mate?" Trisha asked thinking once again of her dad.

Morian was about to respond when a knock came at the door. A messenger quietly handed Morian a note before bowing and quickly leaving. Morian stood up with a calm smile and held out a hand to Abby.

"I think now might be a good time to go see how Cara is doing," she said with a small, secret smile.

Trisha and Abby looked at each other before shrugging their shoulders. Sometimes Trisha got the feeling Morian was a little clairvoyant or something. She seemed to know stuff before it happened. It would have freaked Trisha out except then she would have to be freaked out about loving an alien, dragon-shifting hunk who was BFF with a gold symbiotic creature.

And he likes your butt too, her dragon whispered mischievously.

Trisha tripped as her dragon added that last little tidbit. *Oh, shut up!* Trisha growled silently as her face heated up again. She needed to find out from Kelan if there was any way to block her dragon from their lovemaking sessions. From the laughter of amusement her dragon was giving, she had a bad feeling the answer was a big, fat *no*.

* * *

Trisha and Abby watched as Cara moved back and forth. They snuggled up on the couch not long after they came in with Zoran and Kelan. Abby explained that Ariel and Carmen were on an adventure with Mandra and Creon. Trisha giggled when Abby mentioned she hoped the brothers remembered to bring the two sisters back.

Trisha watched as Cara paced back and forth, biting a fingernail and casting quick glances at the bedroom where Trelon was unconscious. They encountered Zoran and Kelan rushing to Cara and Trelon's living quarters just as they rounded the corner. Zoran quickly explained something happened to Trelon but he didn't know what, as the message he received was sketchy at best. Trisha glanced at Morian when she chuckled under her breath. Trisha relaxed when she noticed amusement rather than concern in Trelon's mom's eyes. She knew something everyone else didn't.

Trisha listened as Cara explained what happened again right before Trelon passed out on her. When she heard the part about Cara expecting twins, she couldn't help but think the males on Valdier must be pretty potent. It didn't take long for Trelon, or Kelan for that matter, to knock up Cara and her. She was curious if it was natural. So much for wondering if they were a compatible species, Trisha thought with amusement.

Not knock up! her dragon growled in disagreement. *Give us their seed. Males choose when female get seed.*

Well, excuse me. They seem to have no problem giving out their seeds. Trisha responded dryly. She wondered if Zoran had "given his seed" to Abby. The palace would never be the same with three hormonal women in it all at once.

"So, I think he took that really well," Abby was saying calmly. "Zoran knew before I did that I was pregnant. He seems to think we are having a boy."

Well, that answered that question. "Better you two than me," Trisha blurted out before she could stop herself. She blushed, looking toward the other room. "I mean…well…it's not like I…oh, hell," she said before she looked down at her drink in confusion.

She wasn't ready to admit she was pregnant too…not yet anyway. She wanted to let her dad know first. Trisha sniffed back the sudden tears that threatened at the thought of him. Damn hormones, she thought in dismay. It was tearing her up inside knowing her dad was going through hell not knowing that she was alive and well. She needed to talk to Kelan again. She needed to go get her dad soon. It was already almost three months since she and the others disappeared. She shuddered as she thought of what he must be going through. Trisha jerked back to the present when she heard Cara squeal.

"You too? This is going to be so much fun. We can teach the kids all kinds of things, and it will be like they are cousins because of course they are, but you know what I mean," Cara babbled excitedly.

Trisha looked at Cara bouncing up and down and finally shook her head. She was really beginning to feel sorry for Trelon and totally understood why he passed out. "Cara, girl, you have to either sit down or stay in one spot for a moment. My head is swimming trying to keep up with you."

Cara plopped down between Abby and Trisha. "So, you're having a boy and I'm having twin girls," Cara said, then turned to Trisha. "So, what's the story with you? Is Kelan giving you a hard time? You know, Abby and I can roast people. Do you need us to roast him for you?"

Trisha laughed. The thought of seeing Kelan running through the palace with his pants on fire was very tempting, though. "No, I think I can handle him. We just don't see eye to eye. He likes to command; I like to ignore. It makes life interesting."

She didn't mention things were much different now than they were on board the *V'ager*. Now, instead of ignoring him, she couldn't keep her hands off him. The only things they didn't agree on were him not telling her everything that was going on, waiting to go get her dad, and when to tell everyone she was expecting. He was so excited about their expecting a child he wanted to shout it from the balcony of their living quarters. Trisha wanted to tell her dad first. If it was one way to motivate him to return to her planet for him, so be it. She wasn't doing it just to be mean. She felt she owed it to her dad for all the love and support he always showed her. He stood beside her throughout all the doctor appointments and physical therapy after she kicked Peter out for cheating on her.

A loud roar pulled her out of her thoughts. Trelon stood in the doorway looking decidedly disheveled. His eyes were glued to Cara's tiny form. Trisha's lips curved as she saw the love and devotion in his eyes. The rest of them didn't even exist for him; he only had eyes for Cara. Trisha's eyes flew to the tall figure standing behind Trelon. Kelan's gaze was fixed on Trisha. She could see the same emotions in his eyes. She stood up, fighting the need to go to him. Trisha's gaze swung to Cara as she talked out loud to herself about wearing only Trelon's shirt while he wore only his pants so they could save on laundry. Yes, she thought, she was definitely feeling sorry for Trelon.

Cara looked at everyone and shrugged. "Well, a girl's got to think about stuff like that when she's going to have a family," she said to no one in particular.

Trisha watched as Kelan reached out a hand when Trelon seemed to sway on his feet again at the mention of the family. "Out! Everybody out now," Trelon roared.

Trisha's gaze jerked over to Cara in concern. Morian walked out from behind Trelon, shooting him a dark look before she walked over to Cara. Trisha stood aside as Morian leaned close to Cara, giving her a hug and whispering in her ear. Abby gave a small murmur of protest when Zoran wrapped his arm around her and started to pull her toward the door.

Trisha raised her eyebrow at Kelan when he came to grab her arm. He was looking at her with a heated gaze, telling her with just a look he wanted her again. Trisha couldn't help the smirk that twisted her lips. Valdier warriors were a horny bunch! She shook her head at him in amusement. Kelan threw his arms up in the air with a curse before he bent over and picked Trisha up in his arms, ignoring her squeal of protest. He let his hand slip down until he could rub her ass as he turned toward the door.

Yes, your mate like your butt, her dragon whispered in glee.

Oh, shut up. Trisha giggled as she wrapped her arms around Kelan's neck and pressed her lips against his throat.

Chapter 17

Trisha smiled when she heard Kelan enter their living quarters. She'd spent the last two weeks hanging out with Abby and Cara, when Cara could sneak away from Trelon. She loved going down to the market with Abby. Trisha learned a lot about Abby and couldn't help but admire her quiet strength. She reminded Trisha a lot of what Morian must have been like a few centuries before. Trisha couldn't help but be stunned to learn the life expectancy of a Valdier was much, much greater than a human. Perhaps that was why the males were able to decide when to have children. The fact it was difficult to have them with anyone other than their true mate was another bonus. It was a very effective way of maintaining the population, Trisha thought. Trisha sent Bio out earlier to play with several of the symbiots of the warriors. Poor Bio must be tired of constantly babysitting her, Trisha thought compassionately. Trisha spent most of her mornings in the bathroom looking at the bottom of the toilet. She was having major morning sickness at some of the strangest times. Unfortunately, while a symbiot could heal just about any injury, they were powerless against morning sickness. This was one thing she was going to have to cope with all on her own.

Kelan was a sweetheart. He would bathe her forehead and neck with cool water until the nausea passed. Then, he would carry her back to bed and feed her their version of saltine crackers until she felt better. The whole time she was trying to nibble on the crackers and keep them down, he would rest his hand over her belly murmuring words to the baby like it could understand him. Trisha was a little concerned about how fast the tiny spark seemed to be growing. She could already tell there was a slight swell to her belly.

Kelan finally talked Trisha into seeing the healer and talking to his mother. Trisha did fine with the healer, listening carefully as she explained that the baby was very healthy and her dragon was doing a good job of caring for it. She suggested a few changes in Trisha's diet and encouraged her to eat more. It was when she and Kelan finally told his mom that she broke down in an avalanche of tears. Kelan promptly swept her up onto his lap and rocked her as she sobbed out how she wanted to tell her dad about the baby and how guilty she felt and she was going to be such a horrible mom because she didn't know anything about raising babies. It took Kelan almost ten minutes to finally calm her down. Morian sat patiently throughout Trisha's tearful outburst. When she finally calmed down to a pile of undignified sniffles and hiccups on Kelan's lap, Morian handed her a cup of strong, hot herbal tea.

"It's...it's...the hormones," Trisha hiccupped as she took a sip of the tea.

Kelan looked worriedly at his mother. *"Dola,* Trisha has been very sick. Is this natural?"

Morian chuckled. "Yes, but I believe it is slightly worse for a human female. Cara and Abby have also complained about the sickness...and being very emotional."

"I'm already starting to show!" Trisha sniffed out. "I shouldn't be showing this soon. I'm only about two and a half months. I don't think I should even be showing until I'm about four or five months." At least the few girls she knew didn't seem to show until around then.

Morian leaned back in her chair and looked puzzled. "But, you will be almost ready to birth by then. A female only carries their young for six months. How long does a female carry on your world?"

Trisha paled as she thought she would be giving birth sooner than she expected. "Nine…" she cleared her throat. "Nine months," she whispered.

Morian nodded as if suddenly understanding. "That may be why it is so difficult for you. Your body is not used to the changes in it so quickly. I will mention it to our healers and see if there is not something that can be done to help with the nausea. I'm afraid, though, it is something the females of your world will have to endure."

Kelan's mouth tightened as he thought of his mate's discomfort. "There will be no more children until they find something," he said stubbornly. He would not let his mate suffer through this again.

Trisha gave a watery laugh. "If you think this is bad, wait until the delivery. I expect you to be there through the whole thing, big shot. If you think this is bad, you haven't seen anything yet."

Kelan turned pale at the thought. "Valdier warriors welcome their children after they are born. They are not expected to be present during the birthing. That is for the females."

Trisha looked at Kelan with a raised eyebrow. "Oh, you are going to be there, my Valdier warrior. If you can decide when to plant your seed inside me and be there for the fun part, you can be there to see the fruit of that fun." Trisha's mouth firmed into a no-nonsense line as she glared at Kelan.

Trisha's dragon rolled with laughter as she pictured the big warrior's face. *Your mate going to be like Cara's. Have big pillow ready when he pass out.*

Morian chuckled as she watched her son and his mate. She was so happy to see a female who was just as strong-willed as her son. She did not doubt that Kelan would be right beside his mate when their child decided to come into the world.

They visited for another hour before Kelan saw Trisha's eyes drooping. That was another thing, she thought sleepily, she was always tired now. Trisha was asleep by the time Kelan carried her back to their living quarters.

* * *

Kelan carefully tucked Trisha into their bed. He didn't bother removing her clothes as he didn't want to take a chance of waking her. He could see the dark shadows under her eyes. He worried carrying his child was too much for her slender frame. He shuddered at the thought of anything happening to Trisha or their child. It wasn't often, but there were times in their history where a female perished while giving birth. He needed to believe what the healer and his mother told him, that what his mate was going through was natural.

Kelan leaned down and pressed a kiss to Trisha's forehead. He promised Zoran he would meet with him and Trelon this afternoon to go over some of the information they were receiving from Creon and Mandra. So far, his brothers were able to find out a few leads to what his uncle, Raffvin, was up to. Kelan gritted his teeth in frustration. He couldn't wait until the bastard he once called family was dead. Creon discovered their uncle was behind the death of their father. His greed for power knew no end, nor did his cruelty. Information coming in showed many of his elite army was forced to fight for him in order to protect their families. Mandra went to meet with Ha'ven's brothers in an effort to discover where Raffvin was holding them. If they could secure the families, most of his army would crumble. Zoran had already killed one of his minions, Ben'qumain. Ben'qumain was Ha'ven's stepbrother. Ha'ven and his brothers found out, almost too late for the two younger brothers, that Ben'qumain murdered their father and disguised it as an accident. It was only when he tried to have the two younger brothers killed and failed that they discovered the extent of his treachery. Now, with their spies deeply embedded in Raffvin's forces, they hoped to discover where he was and eliminate him once and for all.

Creon mentioned he might have a lead as to where the Sarafin king might have been taken. It was suspected that Raffvin was behind that as well. If Raffvin could cause a war between the Valdier and the Sarafin, he could undermine the strength of the royal family and attack when they were spread out across the galaxy. Creon was going to pursue trying to find and rescue King Vox before it came to that. It was always good if you were the one to rescue the leader of a warrior species, even if it was one of your people who did the kidnapping. Neither of the brothers mentioned the females with them, and Kelan could only hope they didn't leave them on some out-of-the-way spaceport somewhere. He didn't think Trisha would ever forgive him if her two sisters didn't return in one piece.

Kelan instructed the two guards outside his living quarters to protect his mate at all costs. Each nodded respectfully. Kelan vaguely wondered if he should instruct them to have their symbiots with them but decided it wasn't necessary in the middle of the palace. The security was tightened since Cara's poisoning. Kelan frowned as he thought of that incident. It didn't make sense. No one else was harmed that night almost three months ago. His mind ran through possible scenarios, trying to think of who would have wanted to harm Trelon's little mate. He was so deep in thought he wasn't looking where he was going when he turned the corner.

"Oh, my lord," N'tasha said softly with a deep curtsy. "I am so sorry. I should have been looking where I was going."

Kelan held onto N'tasha's arms gently where he grabbed them to prevent her from falling. "My apologies…I was not looking where I was going. How are you, Lady N'tasha?" Kelan asked politely as he took a step back. Personally, he'd never liked his brother's lover, but who was he to complain, considering his dragon and his symbiot never liked any of his.

"I am well, my lord. I hope you have a pleasant day. Are you meeting with your brother, Lord Trelon?" she asked quietly, looking at him intently.

"Yes, I am and with Zoran. N'tasha…" Kelan began. It was really none of his business but he felt a thread of loyalty to the tiny human female who meant so much to his brother.

"Yes, my lord?" N'tasha responded in the same calm, quiet voice she always used around him.

Kelan frowned before he shook his head. "It is just…my brother…you are aware he has a true mate now," Kelan said firmly.

N'tasha bowed her head so he couldn't see her eyes. "Yes, my lord. I am very happy for him. I do not wish to cause any trouble." She raised her head and looked Kelan in the eye as she finished the last of her reply.

Kelan studied N'tasha for a moment before nodding his head again. "Very good. I wish you a good day."

Kelan couldn't quite shake the feeling that he had missed something crucial in the exchange with N'tasha. Shaking his head at his growing paranoia, he strode down the corridor leading to the outside gardens. He would cut across them to get to the conference wing.

..*

Trisha yawned. She didn't realize she had been so tired. Opening her eyes slowly, Trisha frowned at the ceiling above her. Where was she? This wasn't the ceiling of their living quarters. Trisha turned her head, trying to clear the fog from her brain. She slowly sat up, putting her hand down on the thin, coarse blanket covering the small cot she just woke up on.

Everything seemed to spin crazily for a few moments before things slowly started to stay in one place. It looked like she was in some type of small holding cell of some kind. Trisha shook her head, moaning as it caused everything to spin again. She placed her hand on her belly and closed her eyes, calling softly to her dragon.

Are you and the baby all right? Trisha asked softly.

Her dragon rolled over groggily. *Where are we?*

I don't know. How is the baby? Trisha asked worriedly.

Our baby is sleeping, her dragon replied as she curled up protectively around it.

Trisha stood up, looking around the small room. There wasn't much in it, not even a bathroom. She pulled the thin mattress covering the cot up and saw there were metal slats holding it up. They were a possibility. Trisha let the mattress fall back down into place and walked unsteadily to the door. There was no panel on the inside. She ran her hands along the frame and the outside of the door. It looked like once something was placed in the room the only way to get out of it was if the door was opened again. Trisha looked along the ceiling, nothing. Not even a vent. Moving along each wall, she carefully ran her hand over the flat surface. No openings, nothing, nada, Trisha thought as she eliminated each possible escape option. Moving back to the cot, she sat down heavily as a wave of nausea washed over her. Trisha leaned her head between her knees and tried to breathe through it.

Please, not now, she begged silently. *Please, little one, work with your mommy for now and stay quiet until I can get us out of this mess.* Trisha's dragon cooed to the baby trying to keep it still as it began to move.

Trisha was still leaning over when the door opened to her small cell. She was too busy fighting not to throw up to even look at it. She continued to breathe deeply through her nose and rocked back and forth.

Trisha started when she felt a cool hand along her cheek. She risked looking up and was surprised to see the young face of a male. He wasn't a Valdier. While his hair was long and a thick black like the Valdier warriors liked to wear it, his facial features were different. His nose was a little broader and his eyes weren't gold, they were more of a yellow color and were slanted at the corners.

"Are you unwell?" the young warrior asked softly.

Trisha nodded her head briefly. She didn't want him to know she was pregnant. She didn't know what they might do to her if they found out. She needed to protect her baby.

"Can I…can I have a drink of water?" Trisha asked hesitantly.

The warrior looked at another man standing in the doorway. The man nodded and disappeared. The young warrior kneeling in front of Trisha laid the palm of his hand against her cheek briefly and closed his eyes. After a few moments, Trisha could feel warmth flowing through her. When the young warrior opened his eyes they were almost glowing.

"That should help. The medicine they used will not harm you, your dragon, or your child. It will prevent your dragon from emerging, though," he said just as quietly as before. "I am called Jaron. I was a healer for my village before I was 'recruited.'"

Trisha listened as he spoke softly to her. "Where am I? How did I get here?"

Jaron looked up as the other warrior appeared. He took the small cup of water from him before he said something to the man in a dialect Trisha's translator didn't decipher. He nodded once, and the man smiled gently at Trisha before he turned to look out toward the corridor. Jaron took a sip from the cup before he held it to Trisha's lips. Trisha understood it was his way of showing it was not drugged. She took a thankful sip, moaning softly as it soothed her parched throat.

"You are on board a Class Two freighter bound for a primitive moon just on the other side of Quitax," Jaron said quietly as he continued to hold the cup for Trisha.

Trisha frowned. Was she supposed to know where this Quitax was? "Where is that, who took me, and why?"

Trisha asked, beginning to feel better now that the nausea passed.

Jaron was about to reply when the man in the corridor cleared his throat suddenly. Jaron shoved the cup under the cot and stood up quickly taking a step back from Trisha. Trisha was about to stand when she saw Jaron shake his head once. She sank back down onto the hard surface of the cot and waited. She had a feeling she was about to get the answers she was seeking, and she didn't think she was going to like them.

An older version of Abby's mate Zoran stepped into the small room along with two other men holding some type of weapon. Jaron immediately lowered his eyes and stood back against the wall. The small room was positively claustrophobic with the four huge males in it now. Trisha debated as to if she should play the strong, silent type, the batty bimbo, or the weak female. She quickly decided the weak female was less likely to get her killed right away.

Good...good...don't like man. He bad...very bad, her dragon whispered, frightened, as she curled even tighter around the tiny spark next to her.

"So, you are finally awake," the older man said coldly. "Which mate are you?"

Trisha let her hand shake as she pushed her long curly hair away from her face as if she was still confused. "Mate?" she asked faintly.

The man's eyes narrowed and his lips tightened. He took a step forward and slapped her hard across her face. "I don't ask questions twice," he snarled.

Trisha sat stunned as the blow to the side of her face sent shards of pain through her head. She could taste the blood in her mouth and bit back a curse that rose to her lips. She let her hair fall over her injured cheek as she fought the urge to nail the big asshole between the legs.

"Answer or the next time will be more painful," the man said coolly.

"Kelan...Kelan is my husband, my mate, as you call him," Trisha said with a tremor in her voice. She kept her head down slightly so the asshole couldn't see the hatred blazing from her eyes. "Why...what do you want from me?" Trisha asked in a whisper.

"I want nothing from you but to kill you. With your death, your mate will die an even slower one. As for the why..." the man said in a voice that must have been made of ice water. "I should have been the True King of the Valdier. Morian Reykill should have been my mate, not my brother's. I was the oldest son. Now, it is time to reclaim my place."

Trisha looked up into the cold black eyes of the man. She frowned. All the Valdier had gold eyes. She never saw any of them with another color. "Why are your eyes black?" Trisha blurted out before she could stop herself.

The man lunged at her, grabbing her by her neck and lifting her off her feet. Trisha grabbed at the hands crushing her throat. She couldn't breathe as he slowly squeezed, shutting off her airway. She struggled to loosen his grip, but it just seemed to make him angrier.

"My lord, you mentioned using her as bait. She will be of no use to you if she is dead," Jaron reminded the man who was slowly strangling her.

Trisha was beginning to see spots and knew she was just moments from passing out when he threw her back against the wall. Trisha hit the wall toward the back of the cot and bounced down on top of it, where she lay gasping for breath and holding her throbbing throat.

"I am Raffvin Reykill, True King of the Valdier. Once that mongrel mate of yours comes for you, I will watch you both die. I want to watch as each of my brother's bastard sons slowly dies as they are forced to watch as their mates are killed in front of them. My eyes are black, bitch, because of the wrong done to me so long ago by the gods and goddesses. Their deceit at choosing my brother over me has blackened my heart, but soon...soon that will change as I take what should have been mine from the start," Raffvin snarled as he wiped his hands on a piece of cloth he pulled from his pocket.

Trisha watched in horror as Raffvin wiped his hands on a cloth obviously stained with blood. She shivered as she tried to swallow. Her cheek and throat throbbed with the heat of the damage done to them. She stared blankly as the obviously insane man turned, muttering she was not to receive any food or drink. Jaron cast a regretful look at Trisha before he and the other man who was still standing outside the room were forced to leave. Only after the door shut tightly behind everyone, leaving Trisha blissfully alone, did she allow herself to sink the rest of the way down onto the cot and let silent tears drip onto the coarse covering. She closed her eyes, checking on her dragon and her baby before she sent out a silent prayer for Kelan to find them in time to protect them. It wasn't until she felt a familiar heat against her cheek and around her throat that she opened her eyes and felt with her fingers. The thin gold threads slipped from where they had woven themselves throughout her hair. Now, the tiny gold threads of symbiot from Bio formed into a slightly thicker one and began moving over her throat and cheek, healing them.

"Thank you," Trisha whispered softly as she began thinking more calmly.

Her dad always taught her that one day she might have to save herself. It was his job to make sure she was ready to do that. Trisha remembered her dad saying it didn't matter if you were a male or a female when it came down to fighting for your life. You either knew how to fight to live or you died. Trisha smiled; her dad made sure his little girl knew how to fight to live. "Thank you, Daddy," Trisha whispered softly.

* * *

Kelan was listening with half an ear to Zoran and Trelon talking about a new defense system Trelon was developing for some of their smaller warships. He and Trelon already tested the prototype on two of the Class Four warships several months ago so he was fully abreast of what Trelon was talking about. Zoran turned and asked him if he thought it was feasible to go ahead with production of the system and have it installed in the over one hundred warships. Kelan was about to reply when a faint wave of unease swept through him. It must have hit Zoran and Trelon even harder, because both of his brothers turned pale. All three men jumped to their feet and were already heading for the door when a warrior burst through it.

"My lords, the females are in danger," Lurr growled fiercely.

Kelan was through the massive doors before Lurr even finished his sentence. Zoran and Trelon were behind him. All four men ran through the corridors, bursting out into the open gardens and cutting through to their living quarters. Kelan skidded to a halt just as N'tasha and four men appeared from the palace living quarters. He heard Zoran's and Trelon's roars of rage when they saw their mates draped over the shoulders of two of the men. Out of nowhere, two of the palace guards swung around toward the group cutting off the man carrying Abby. One of the warriors grabbed Abby while the other sliced through the stomach of the man holding her, letting the dead body drop while he carried her to Zoran. N'tasha turned a glare full of hatred toward Trelon before smiling savagely as she raised a blade to her throat and drew an imaginary line across it. Before they could do anything, N'tasha, the man next to her, and the one holding Cara disappeared in a transporter beam.

"NO!" Trelon roared in protest.

Kelan watched in horror as his brother's mate disappeared. He was about to rush to his living quarters to check on Trisha when Bio exploded into the garden growling and hissing in fury. He closed his eyes as he sent out his senses to the tiny symbiot on Trisha. He could feel nothing.

"Zoran..." Abby sobbed as she lay cradled in her mate's arms, shaking. "They took them. They killed the guards and they took them."

Zoran rocked Abby gently in his arms. "Who else did they take, Abby?"

But Zoran already knew as he studied both of his brothers' faces. He gripped Abby tighter as the full extent of the brutal attack washed over him. If they did not rescue Cara and Trisha, he knew he would lose his two youngest brothers. He snarled out a command to several warriors to see to the bodies of the warriors just as Trelon's symbiot exploded into the garden. Both of his brothers' symbiots were snarling and hissing in fury at the attack on their mates. Kelan vaguely heard Trelon shout out that Symba could sense the symbiot on Cara. Within seconds, Symba transformed into a sleek Valdier fighter and was lifting off. Kelan moved as if in a daze. Why couldn't he sense the symbiot on Trisha? He left her safe in their living quarters with guards, he thought distractedly. She was wearing several pieces of symbiot on her arms and around her neck. Why didn't they respond to him? Kelan growled out a command to his symbiot as he began running toward his living quarters.

He and Bio rounded the corner sliding to a halt when they saw the red and gold splattered walls. Bio jerked as if a megawatt of electricity had been discharged into it. It moved slowly forward making a howling sound unlike anything Kelan ever heard before. Kelan moved slowly forward staring in disbelief at the fragmented remains of the guards and the lifeless gold threads of their symbiots. Never in the history of their kind had a symbiot been destroyed. Now, the gold remains were scattered all over the floor and walls of the corridor outside his living quarters. What could destroy something made of pure energy?

Several warriors rounded the corner, freezing in horror at the sight that met them. "My lord..." Lurr said quietly staring at the sight. "Your mate?"

Kelan looked with dread at the door leading into his sanctuary. "I...I don't know," he whispered.

"Let me go first," Lurr said starting to move around Kelan.

Kelan put his hand out to stop him, shaking his head slowly. "No, it is my right, my responsibility to see to my mate," he croaked out in dread.

Lurr took a step back and bowed his head slightly. Zoran asked that Lurr be with Kelan until he could be there himself. He was instructed to protect Kelan, even if it meant from himself. Lurr would do as his king instructed.

Kelan forced the door to his living quarters open, ignoring everything but what was inside. He forced himself to enter the room. Everything looked just as he left it. There were no signs of a struggle in the living area. He moved slowly toward their sleeping area where he left Trisha sleeping peacefully only a couple of hours ago. His hand trembled as he forced himself to open the door which was now closed. He remembered leaving it open when he left, he thought. Bio was beside him shaking with aggravation as if it was aware of what he might find.

"My lord…" Lurr started to say.

"*No!*" Kelan said harshly. "She is my mate…she is my mate," he said again, his voice fading at the end as if it was too difficult to say anything more.

Lurr once again took a step back and waited as Kelan drew in a deep breath. Kelan stared at the door willing Trisha to still be in their bed sleeping. He pushed open the door and forced himself forward toward the bed. He started shaking uncontrollably when he saw it was empty, the covers tossed back and lying half on the bed and half off of it. As he drew near, he caught a glimpse of gold lying motionless on the tangled covers. Kelan and his symbiot both let out a howl of unimaginable pain as they stared at the lifeless symbiot belonging to Trisha.

* * *

Zoran walked across the room studying Kelan. Lurr gave him a complete report on what was found outside of Kelan's apartment. They knew whatever was used there had not been used in his own apartments. From the little Abby was able to tell him, N'tasha seemed to be in charge of the abduction of Trelon's mate and the death of his personal guards. She had demanded that both Abby and Cara remove their symbiot. Abby complied simply because there was no place for her to hide it. Cara was able to hide some of hers which was why Trelon's symbiot was able to track her location. Kelan returned immediately, ordering the *V'ager* be readied for immediate departure.

"I'm going to kill the bitch after I find out what she has done with my mate," Kelan said calmly.

Zoran studied his brother. The icy control he was renowned for was clearly evident. Kelan moved with precision as he ordered the transporter room readied and all essential personnel to be on board for immediate departure.

"We need to find out what weapon was used to kill the symbiot. This could be devastating to our people if it falls into the wrong hands," Zoran said, placing his hand on Kelan's arm as his brother turned and gave another order.

Kelan's eyes swung first to Zoran's hand, then to his face. His face cut in stone, Kelan replied coolly. "I know my duty, brother. I will fulfill it before I leave this world."

"Kelan..." Zoran said softly. "We do not know that your mate is dead. She is a fighter. You said yourself she was trained as a warrior by not only her people but her father. She will find a way to survive until you reach her."

Kelan stood frozen in place for half a second before Zoran saw a flicker of hope flare. "She is unbelievable. Gunner said as much when we were tracking her through the forests," Kelan replied hoarsely.

Zoran smiled. "She has much to live for. She will need you to be there for her."

Kelan nodded before adding, "And for our child."

Kelan saw Zoran's look of surprise before he nodded grimly. "Go to her. Track her down and bring her back."

Kelan stood on the platform to the transporter and gave a sharp nod. Within moments, he was striding out of the transporter room on the *V'ager*, quietly giving orders. He had a bitch to kill.

Chapter 18

Trisha watched carefully as the five men settled into their seats and strapped down. Jaron sat to her right, and the man who was in the corridor the first day she awoke was sitting to her left. Trisha didn't recognize the other three men, but they didn't look like they were going to be considered "friendly." Jaron was able to slip Trisha food and drink over the last four days of her confinement. She kept it hidden under the cot just in case someone else came in. She was also fortunate they didn't feel threatened by her or feel the need to search her. She developed a bad habit when she worked for Boswell of carrying her Leatherman micro with her everywhere. Because the uniforms didn't have pockets she used the one that came naturally for women, she hid it between her breasts in her bra. It was like picking up your keys or wearing earrings, she naturally tucked it away no matter where she was. It came in handy removing several of the metal slats out of the bottom of the cot in her little prison cell. She used the rough edge of the cot to slowly sharpen the ends of three of the slats to razor sharp. She tore some of the sheeting and wrapped it around one end as a handle. Now, she was equipped with three sharp knives. She would use them without mercy the first opportunity she got. She slowly observed each man in front of her, cataloging which hand was dominant, where there might be a weakness in their uniforms, which foot they stepped forward on first, how they shifted, what kind of weapons they carried and where. She listened as Jaron asked one of the men some questions about the small moon they were going to be landing on.

"I heard this moon is very dangerous. The few colonists who tried to settle were forced off because the animals who inhabit it broke through all their defenses," Jaron said. "Where are we landing that will be safe?"

One of the men with a deep scar across his cheek smiled cruelly. "No place is safe. We won't be there long, though. Just long enough to stake the female out for dinner."

Several of the men looked at Trisha and laughed. Trisha looked down so they couldn't see her roll her eyes. Given the natural inhabitants of the moon and these guys, she would take the moon any day. She turned her focus back to the conversation. She halfway wondered if Jaron was trying to tell her something.

"I thought Lord Raffvin wanted the female alive until her mate found her? How can that happen if she is staked out on the planet?" Jaron asked hesitantly.

Another of the big men laughed. "Well, you see, that is where you and Terac are useful. You two will be staying behind to make sure she doesn't get eaten until Raffvin is ready. If you screw this up, you can forget ever seeing the people of your little village again." All three men laughed at that.

Trisha decided she had enough. She turned to Jaron and smiled innocently. "Do you know how to fly one of these things?" she asked quietly.

Jaron shook his head in resignation. "No, I don't, but Terac does. Why?"

Trisha smiled as she unfolded her arms. She'd popped the restraints on her seat shortly after takeoff. The other men still wore theirs so they were at a disadvantage. She decided she needed to neutralize the three men across from her and the pilot of the shuttle. They would be entering the orbit of the moon in approximately three minutes from what she was able to gather. There would not be enough time for Raffvin to deploy a strike force before they could land. Once on the ground, she would disappear until Kelan could find her. There was no doubt in her mind that she could survive. The thick forests were home to her.

Raising her arms, she launched herself across the narrow aisle, slicing through two of the men's throats and kicking out her leg at the third. She rolled, slamming her elbow into Scarface's nose just as he pulled his laser pistol up and shot out wildly. Trisha used her body to prevent him from unlatching his restraints. He reached a beefy arm out and was able to get it around her waist and began squeezing her. Trisha could feel the pressure on her ribs as he threatened to snap them like toothpicks. She rolled one of the knives in her hand until the handle was facing upward and the point toward her body. She slammed her head back against the nose she already broke, listening as the bones crunched even more. She heard the man roar out in rage and pain, but she got the desired effect she was looking for—he loosened his hold around her ribs long enough for her to drive the four-inch blade between his ribs and twist. She felt his jerk of surprise as she twisted around, slashing with her other hand across his throat. Blood splattered her as she cut through the thick artery in his neck. Trisha glanced at the other two men she'd attacked first. One was already dead, and the other was in the last stages of the death throes.

"Remind me never to make you mad," Jaron whispered in shock.

"No shit," Terac croaked out in agreement.

Both men were staring at Trisha with admiration and a little apprehension. Trisha was about to reply when she was thrown to the floor as the shuttle suddenly lurched to the side. Terac was already undoing his restrains and moving to the front. The wild shot from the last man Trisha attacked had ricocheted, striking the pilot in the back of the head and killing him instantly. Terac let loose a string of curses as he struggled to get the pilot out of the seat.

"Some of the controls are fried. Get strapped in, we are going in for a bumpy landing," Terac shouted as he tried to get control of the shuttle as it hit the outer atmosphere of the moon.

Jaron undid his restraints and helped Trisha back into her seat. He quickly redid her straps before strapping himself back in. He leaned forward and placed his hands lightly on Trisha, letting them move slowly over her.

"What are you doing?" Trisha asked puzzled. She was shaking as she came down from the adrenaline rush.

"Checking to make sure you are not hurt. I want to check your baby as well," Jaron said quietly as he leaned into her.

Trisha closed her eyes and focused inward. *Are you and the baby okay?* she asked her dragon urgently.

Mate whip your ass, yes. I tell mate whip your ass, her dragon snarled. *You scare me! You crazy! I tell mate whip you ass for scaring me. Our baby is safe, but I scared!*

Trisha laughed as her dragon continued to give her holy hell for attacking those men and not waiting for Kelan to come save them. She ignored Trisha when Trisha calmly told her cussing in front of the baby probably wasn't a good idea. Her dragon simply snapped her teeth at Trisha and growled out low after that. The intense vibration of the shuttle brought Trisha back to their current predicament.

Terac yelled for Jaron to come help him. Jaron looked panicked for a moment before he fumbled with his restraints. Trisha laid her hand over his briefly before she undid hers.

"I'll go. I was a pilot on my planet. Maybe I can help," Trisha murmured as she moved past Jaron.

Jaron gave Trisha a weak smile of thanks. "I've never been up in a warship before until I was captured by Raffvin's forces."

Trisha just smiled as she moved to the front. She stepped over the dead body of the pilot and slid into the seat beside Terac. She quickly strapped in and pulled an ear piece on.

"Tell me what to do," Trisha said calmly.

"Grab the controller in front of you. The holoscreen will show the surface of the moon as we break through the cloud cover. Keep it steady as I try to find an area clear enough to land," Terac said tersely.

Trisha let all her training as a pilot and test pilot flow through her. There would be time enough to have a meltdown when she was safe in Kelan's arms. Until then, she had a job to do—stay alive and keep the men with her alive. Trisha focused on the view on the holoscreen and keeping the nose up and the shuttle level as they broke through the thick cloud covering.

"There looks like a place just big enough for us to possibly land in eight-point-three vectors. Trisha, do you think you can keep the nose up while I try to keep us upright? The left burner is working at only twenty percent."

"You get us there and down safely, and I'll not only keep the nose up, but I'll give you a big kiss, darlin'," Trisha said with a determined smile.

No kiss! Lips only for mate! No kiss...no kill...no fighting...no crashing...no...no...no! her dragon roared as she tried to wrap as tightly as she could around the spark inside Trisha.

Trisha frowned. *Damn! That little spark is getting bigger fast,* she thought in wonder.

No thanks to you! I take care of our baby! You too rough! her dragon snapped right before the little spark popped her dragon in the nose. *See! You teach bad habit!*

Trisha felt warmth flood through her at the fight in her little spark. *That's it, baby. I'll show you all the really cool things my dad showed me when you get a little bigger. Just wait until we get grandpa here. He'll have you out swinging from the trees and playing tag before you know it.*

Terac looked at Trisha funny when he heard her peal of laughter as her dragon groaned at having both Trisha and Trisha's dad corrupting the little spark she was trying so hard to protect. *Yes,* her dragon thought sourly. *Trisha mate need to whip her ass.*

Chapter 19

"Do you have anything?"

Kelan looked at his younger brother's face. Trelon's face reflected his determination to get his mate back. Kelan nodded. He would remain focused on saving his brother's mate. He could only pray to the gods and goddesses his would be with her.

"A cloaked ship appeared on our surveillance a few moments ago. They had to uncloak to transport. It was N'tasha, Trelon. Abby says that N'tasha and six men killed two of her guards before taking them hostage. Symba and Goldie killed two in Zoran's living quarters, and the guards were able to kill the one holding Abby. She is fine." Kelan didn't mention the fact that Zoran went ballistic when he saw the blood staining the front of Abby's tunic. Zoran was beside himself until the healers and his symbiot assured him she was unharmed.

"According to Abby, they have Trisha, as well as Cara," Kelan choked out. "Abby says N'tasha plans to slit Cara's throat as soon as the 'True King' is done with her. She said N'tasha wants to leave Cara where you can find her. She didn't know anything else about Trisha. N'tasha didn't say where she had been taken."

Trelon paled and let out a curse. "Cara must have some of Symba's symbiot on her since she seems to know where to go. I will find them, Kelan."

"I'm leaving now. I have the *V'ager* ready to go. Send me constant updates so we can intercept," Kelan said. His eyes flashed in rage at the idea of Trisha being held captive. If she or the baby were harmed in any way he would destroy every man and woman responsible before he joined her. There would not be a place in any galaxy they could hide. He would track them down and slit every one of the bastards' throats.

"I will. Trelon out." Trelon knew the pain his brother was feeling as it flashed across his eyes. N'tasha signed her own death warrant when she threatened their mates.

* * *

Kelan instructed his crew to keep him posted on any transmissions they intercepted. His best crew was aboard and ready for a fight. To harm one Valdier was to harm them all. By now, all the warriors and their respective symbiotic were aware of what happened outside of Kelan's living quarters. The fury and passion of both the warriors and their symbiots could be felt throughout the entire warship. They wanted revenge, and Kelan would let them have it. Kelan turned when his helmsman reported he was receiving a signal from an old Curizan warship.

"Sir, it is the same as the one the tiny human used when she sent Lord Trelon's PVC out," the helmsman said with a grin. He remembered being on duty when they started receiving all the incoming requests for that particular piece of data. He and the other crew members laughed when they found out what she was sending. What made it even better was when Jarak told them she thought it was a plumbing video. After that, the crew started making bets on what she would get into next and how long it would take before she got caught.

Kelan nodded stoically at the helmsman and told him to get Trelon on the view screen. "We have a visual of the warship. We have also been receiving a continuous signal from the warship. It looks suspiciously like the one your mate sent out before. I have a feeling they are having as much trouble keeping her locked up as we did," Kelan said with a strained smile before continuing. "I've instructed the crew to send a disruption pulse to knock the engines off-line. The new system you installed should work at bypassing their shield briefly. It is a good thing the cloaking device only works when the ship is stationary. We need to find out how it bypassed our defense system, though. I have a feeling N'tasha's hand might have been in that, or we have more spies among our ranks," Kelan finished harshly.

"It is something we'll have to look at after this is over. Right now, I just want to get our mates back. It won't take them long to realize we are here. Those aboard better hope they have not harmed a hair on either of our mates or there will be nothing left of that warship," Trelon snarled.

Kelan responded with a cold smile. "Once I have my mate back there will be no mercy for any of them," Kelan turned as one of the men called out on the bridge of the *V'ager*. Nodding, he turned to Trelon. "No mercy."

Trelon nodded to Kelan. "No mercy."

286 ~S. E. Smith

Kelan ordered four energy bursts to be directed at the Curizan warship on the view screen. Kelan and his symbiot were already heading for the transporter room. They would be among the first to board as soon as the shields were knocked off-line. The *V'ager* was over five times the size and more than ten times more powerful than the Curizan warship. Personally, he didn't give a damn what happened to the warship once their mates were safely back at their sides. He forced himself to think logically. Zoran was right. They needed to find out what type of weapon could kill their symbiot. Their essences and the essences of their dragons and symbiot were entwined; to destroy one would destroy all three.

Kelan nodded to the other men who were already in position and waiting with their symbiots by their side. He looked at the view screen mounted to the wall of the transporter room, watching for the signal to know when it was safe to transport. The powerful energy bursts struck the smaller warship in strategic places, one near the bridge knocking out their top energy cannons, two at the stern, knocking the engines off-line, and one to the starboard side cannons. Kelan watched as the Curizan warship seemed to glow for a moment as the energy bursts hit the outer hull. Seconds later, the lights began to flicker and die as the engines were taken off-line.

Kelan gave the command for the golden Valdier fighters to proceed to attack. With a nod to the warrior at the controls of the transporter, Kelan and a group of elite warriors were beamed into the docking bay of the Curizan warship. Kelan rolled as soon as his feet hit the solid flooring of the docking bay. He heard shouts of surprise from the warriors inside. Two of his team members quickly secured the doors leading into it. Kelan exchanged laser fire with one Curizan warrior, shooting him in the head while rolling for cover as three more began firing at him. The warriors on the Curizan ship were no match for the fury of the Valdier warriors and their symbiots, many of which had transformed into werecats and bear beasts. Blood soaked the docking-bay deck as one by one, each warrior who did not surrender immediately was killed without mercy.

Kelan turned as one of his warriors blew the hatch, opening it to allow more Valdier warriors to board. Trelon was the first face Kelan saw. Kelan was having a difficult time trying to keep control of his dragon as he was too agitated.

Need my mate. Need hold my mate. Find my mate, his dragon roared, pushing against his skin. Jade green and silver scales rolled over his arms, chest, and neck as he fought for control. He knew his eyes were already changed as everything was sharper and clearer.

Kelan reminded his dragon he was not made for fighting on warships. *You are too large to maneuver in the tight confines of the rooms and corridors of the warship to find her, and you know what happens when dragon fire is used in space. It does not go well with the oxygen mixture on a warship*, Kelan said, trying to calm his dragon enough that it would not be a hazard to their mission. Dragons and warships usually meant an explosion where nothing survived, not even the dragon. *Patience...we will find her. She must be on board. We will find her and take her home.*

Kelan moved back so his brother could step aboard the warship. He tried to clear his throat, but the words still came out gruffly, his voice deeper and harsher with his dragon so near. "Your mate has been very busy. Our team has detected multiple random shutdowns of the systems aboard. Since they are still occurring, I believe we can safely say they have not caught her yet."

Kelan listened as Trelon let out a sharp chuckle as he thought of the mischief his little mate was causing for her captors. Kelan moved away, heading for the docking bay doors which were reopened. Valdier warriors and their symbiots were swarming the warship. Kelan ordered any man who fought at all to be executed without mercy. The only one he wanted alive was N'tasha. He would be the one to kill her... But only after she told him where his mate was. He did not care if their enemy was a female. She committed treason when she acted against the royal family. The penalty was death.

Kelan moved stealthily through the corridors fighting beside the warriors who would lay their lives down for their people. They took the ship one level at a time. Kelan was surprised to find many of the levels were already under control—by the warriors on board. The crew of the warship was at a crucially low level to start with, and the surrender of almost half the warriors came as a surprise until he was informed many were there as prisoners themselves. The only warriors who fought back were members of Raffvin's elite force.

* * *

N'tasha let out a long string of expletives as the lights dimmed before going out. The eerie glow of the emergency lights kicked in as all power to the warship was knocked off-line. A short time later, N'tasha screamed out in frustration as all the men on the bridge walked off. The tiny human bitch had escaped her cell and was causing malfunctions through the warship's systems. She should have killed the bitch when she had the chance.

Nothing is going as I planned. Raffvin left me to rot in space with a bunch of idiots! she fumed. *I am in command of this ship. I tell them what to do! I am the one who organized everything over the past year and gathered information on the defense systems Trelon was working on. If Ben'qumain hadn't let Zoran escape none of this would be happening! Zoran Reykill brought back those foul alien women, one of whom captured Trelon's heart. She is the reason my warship is now dead in space.* N'tasha muttered insanely under her breath.

N'tasha pulled a laser pistol out of the storage compartment in the officer's conference room off the bridge and checked the charge. Zoran killed her lover, Ben'qumain. Ben'qumain promised her royalty, power, a chance to rule Valdier as his queen if she helped him kill the royal family. Now, it was all in ruins. The only thing left was to find Trelon's tiny bitch and kill her. With her and the other one Raffvin ordered taken dead, at least two of the brothers would be sentenced to a slow, agonizing death. It was the beginning of the end of the royal family. If she was lucky, she would be able to use one of the escape pods to get out of this mess. Raffvin would not be happy but he never was anyway.

N'tasha was exiting the conference room when some sixth sense warned her she wasn't alone anymore. Her eyes jerked around the dim interior of the bridge. She started to raise the arm holding the laser pistol when she felt a huge, clawed hand wrapped around her throat.

Kelan leaned forward and whispered in her ear. "Where is my mate?" Kelan asked softly letting one of the tips of his transformed hand pierce the soft skin of N'tasha's throat.

N'tasha whimpered. "I don't know."

Kelan's grip tightened enough that N'tasha gasped as she could feel the claws sink deeper into her flesh. "I won't ask again."

N'tasha nodded her head. As the grip loosened, she jerked her arm around firing wildly with the laser pistol. Kelan roared in outrage as the blast scored his lower leg. He used his grip on N'tasha's neck to pick her up and toss her across the room, watching dispassionately as her body hit the far wall with a loud thump. His dragon was beyond furious. Kelan let it surface, shifting as he moved toward N'tasha who was moaning on the floor. Kelan's symbiot divided into two, forming gold armor over Kelan's dragon while a smaller section changed into a smaller version of a werecat. It moved silently to N'tasha, its body shimmering in aggravation as she tried to crawl to where the laser pistol landed several feet away from her.

Kelan's dragon moved swiftly, grabbing the pistol with his tail and launching it in the opposite direction. N'tasha, realizing she was doomed, whimpered as she scooted back against the wall. She was surrounded by a furious dragon on one side and his werecat-shaped symbiot on the other. She knew there would be no mercy. Her thoughts flew to Raffvin, and her hatred toward him and all men blossomed as her insanity finally overtook the last rational thoughts in her diseased brain.

It was Raffvin who convinced Ben'qumain to attack Zoran. Raffvin who insisted he was the "True King" of Valdier. Ben'qumain was the stepbrother of the King of the Curizans. He was too stupid to realize Raffvin was just using him and his resources. It was Raffvin who convince Ben'qumain to use N'tasha. She should have killed them both months ago! Instead, she made plans of her own to destroy Raffvin and the Valdier royal family. She wanted to show Ben'qumain that she was a powerful force who would hand-deliver Valdier to the Curizans. She should have made sure the poison she gave the tiny bitch killed her! The bitch should have been dead after she blasted a ton of rocks on her. Now, not only would N'tasha be the one to die, but the human females were all still alive unless Raffvin managed to kill the one he took. It wasn't fair! She was the one who was supposed to rule!

"My lord…" Gunner's voice broke through the haze of red covering Kelan's mind as he moved toward N'tasha, who sat rocking on the floor muttering to herself.

Kelan's head swung around, and he let out a roar at Gunner who stood inside the door to the bridge, Palto and

Kor next to him. All three men stood their ground, studying the furious dragon as if waiting to see if Kelan could get control back. He let his gaze shift back to the figure on the floor again, and he snarled in a deep, low rumble letting the heat of his breath roll over her.

Calm, Kelan repeated over and over to his dragon. *Calm. We need to know where Trisha is. We cannot do that if you eat her.*

I don't eat filth, his dragon snarled back. *Where my mate?*

Let me shift back and I will find our mates, Kelan promised gently. *I promise, my friend. I need her, too.*

Gunner let out a deep breath as Kelan's form shifted back to his two-legged form. "Sir, the warship is secure. All warriors who surrendered have been taken to the docking bay. Do you want us to escort the female down there?"

Kelan continued to stare at N'tasha as she muttered incoherently on the floor. "No, I will escort her myself. Make sure all data records have been uploaded to the *V'ager.* I want to know everything that was ever recorded, sent, or received from this ship."

"Yes, sir," Palto said, barking out the orders in his comlink.

Kelan reached down and jerked N'tasha up. He felt his symbiot moving over the wound on his leg and felt it as the tissue resealed itself. Wrapping one hand around her neck and gripping her wrists tightly in his other hand, Kelan ignored N'tasha's cry of pain as he pulled her in front of him.

"Move," he growled in a low voice. "Either on your own two feet or I drag you by your arms."

N'tasha whimpered and continued to talk in disjointed sentences as she moved in the direction of the docking bay. It took a few minutes before he finally understood what she kept repeating under her breath. "At least one bitch is dead. At least one bitch is dead," she kept saying under her breath. Kelan didn't know who she was talking about, Cara or Trisha. The closer they got to the docking bay the colder it seemed his heart turned.

"Where is my mate? Where is Trisha?" Kelan snarled as he jerked on N'tasha's arms.

Kelan's eyes flew across to where his brother was standing. In his arms was his tiny mate. Unable to stand it any longer, Kelan jerked brutally on the wrists he was holding, pulling N'tasha's arms far enough back he could hear the joint protest at the strain.

"Where is she?" Kelan thundered, ignoring N'tasha's screams of pain. "I will show you no mercy unless you tell me where she is."

N'tasha's head came up, and she stared at Cara and Trelon with hatred in her eyes. She gave an insane cackle before replying, "She's dead! She's dead and so are you! At least I killed one of you. Do you want to know how I killed her? I made sure she screamed as I cut her into little pieces."

Kelan roared out in pain. The hand he wrapped around her neck tightened as his rage and grief overwhelmed him and his dragon. With a quick twist, he snapped N'tasha's neck, letting her lifeless body fall to the deck. He vaguely heard Cara's cry of horror before she buried her face in Trelon's neck with a wild sob. He took two steps before his knees gave out, and he sank to the floor with his head hanging and his breaths coming in harsh gasps. Kelan could hear his dragon's howl of despair and feel the icy chill from his symbiot, both testaments to their grief at the loss of their mate. Kelan drew in a shuddering breath, wondering how his heart still beat when it felt so shattered.

One of the older men who had surrendered pushed forward from where the group was being detained. The crew of the warship was skeletal at best. The warship needed at least a hundred men to run at full capacity. There were half that many on board. Out of the fifty men, thirty surrendered peacefully.

Dulce walked forward with the man. "My lord, this man says he has information about the other human female who was captured."

Trelon nodded to Dulce before looking at the man through narrowed eyes. "Speak."

"My name is Dantor. The other men and I were brought aboard to serve—" Dantor nodded in distaste at N'tasha's prone figure on the floor. "—the female against our will.

Raffvin has members of our family and has threatened to kill them if we do not do what he wants. We could not disobey since there were also members of his elite army on board. I wanted you to know that we regret any harm that has come to your mate, but we had no choice." Many of the men standing behind him, Curizan and Valdier alike, were nodding in agreement.

Trelon cut his hand through the air. "I don't care about your excuses. You said you have information about the other human female that was taken," he said harshly. He only cared about the information on his brother's mate, nothing else at this time.

Dantor cleared his throat. "She is not dead," he began softly.

Kelan's head jerked up at the softly spoken words. He stared at the man for a moment wondering if he heard him correctly. He slowly climbed to his feet. "What do you mean she is not dead?" he demanded. When the man didn't answer fast enough, Kelan strode over and gripped the front of Dantor's shirt tightly in his fists.

"What do you mean she is not dead?" Kelan repeated, shaking Dantor until the other man's head snapped back and forth. Kelan could feel his own strength mixed with his dragon's as he fought to contain his impatience at know if what he was saying was true.

Trelon reached out one hand and rested it on Kelan's shoulder. "Hear him out before you end up killing him."

Kelan jerked back, releasing Dantor's shirt. He drew in a breath as he fought for control. "Tell me," he demanded hoarsely.

Dantor nodded stiffly. "A second group on a smaller ship captured her and was taking her to a primitive moon just on the other side of Quitax. They were told to hold her there until we could pick her up. We were supposed to leave Valdier and travel straight there where we would meet at a predetermined site."

Chapter 20

Trisha gritted her teeth as they pushed through the cloud cover, fighting to keep the shuttle level as Terac worked the thrusters trying to compensate for the damage. She kept her mind focused on the holoscreen in front of her. She vaguely heard Terac swearing under his breath and bit back a chuckle. It seemed it didn't matter what species you were or what planet you came from, cussing in stressful situations was a universal relief from it.

"Hang on. This might be a little bumpy, but I think I have it under control enough to get us down," Terac called out through his teeth.

Trisha let an image of Kelan form in her mind. She pictured him the last time they made love. How beautiful and strong he looked as he held her tightly in the cocoon of his body. She let the warmth of those memories invade her until nothing else mattered but him, his love, his touch. Trisha heard her dragon's mournful cry as she called to her mate. She missed him just as much as Trisha did hers. They really were one, she thought. Reaching out, she briefly let go of the controller with one hand so she could stroke the thick band of gold woven around her throat. It had formed back into a necklace, dissolving from the threadlike strands it was hiding in throughout her hair, right after she killed the three men in the back. She focused on Kelan and sent a heartfelt plea for him to know how much she loved and missed him. She quickly grabbed the controller again when she felt the shuttle shudder and begin to tilt.

"Get us down, Terac," Trisha said quietly above the rattling and groaning of the stressed metal. "My mate will be coming for me, and he would be pretty pissed if I'm not in one piece."

Terac laughed. "I think I would be pretty pissed too. I pledge to keep you safe until your mate comes for you, Trisha."

Trisha grinned. She had a feeling it was going to be more like her keeping the guys alive, but she didn't think now was the time to point that out. Terac yelled out in triumph as he pulled the shuttle over the last section of trees with little more than a scrape against the tops of them. He quickly cut the thrusters and dropped the landing skids. The shuttle groaned but stayed level coming into the small clearing at a slower speed as Terac reversed the boosters. The shuttle hovered for a moment before it settled down with a soft thump.

Terac yelled out a war cry as he shut down all systems. Trisha was laughing and crying at the same time. She quickly undid her restraints and threw herself at Terac, kissing his cheek and giving him a hug as she whispered her thanks. Trisha's dragon growled out a warning when Terac turned his head and gripped Trisha's face between his hands. He looked at her for just a moment before he sealed his lips to hers. Trisha jerked back before he could deepen the kiss, flushing a rose color as she backed away embarrassed.

"I'm sorry," she whispered. "I didn't mean to give you the wrong idea."

Terac grabbed Trisha's hand as she started to turn away. "You didn't. But I couldn't resist a small taste. It reminded me we were alive," Terac said with a crooked grin.

Trisha looked deeply into Terac's eyes and knew he was just saying that to spare her from feeling uncomfortable. She could see the interest in his eyes. Flushing again, she smiled uncertainly before giving him a small nod. They would act like the kiss never happened.

Whip his mate's ass, Kelan will. Kill man for touching his mate, my mate will! I say no kiss! No lips on other males! Mate whip your ass! Trisha's dragon snarled as she paced around the tiny spark that was thankfully sleeping through all the excitement.

Oh, give it a break! Trisha snapped back irritably. *It was only a simple kiss, nothing more, and like he said, it was just a way of saying thank-you for being alive. Now, go lie down if you aren't going to be nice!*

Trisha's dragon growled out dire warnings if that man so much as looked at her again. Trisha tried to ignore the grumblings, but some of them were pretty damn funny. Like when her dragon growled out she was going to light his cock up like a candle. The visual image was just too much for Trisha's overtaxed stress zone, and she collapsed in a fit of giggles while Terac and Jaron looked at her in puzzlement.

"Hormones," Trisha responded to the looks they were giving her. She sobered enough to add, "We need to get rid of the bodies but as far away from the shuttle as possible. The smell of the blood will draw predators to it. In addition, we need to get all traces of blood off of us and our clothing. Predators will scent it and track us down. Next, we need to see if there is any way to camouflage the shuttle. I'm sure Raffvin isn't going to be too happy when he finds out his henchmen aren't coming back. Personally, I don't want to be a sitting duck waiting for him to blow us up." Trisha was already moving through the shuttle pulling out several survival packs and looking for weapons and additional supplies that would be of more use than a burden. She let out a cry of delight when she found several sets of clothing. Hers were covered in blood, and she would need to change and clean up as quickly as possible.

"Is there any information on the types of hostile plants and animals on this moon?" Trisha asked turning to see Jaron and Terac studying her in fascination.

"Not much. It is just known as being extremely dangerous. None of the colonists who tried to settle here survived from my understanding," Jaron said quietly as he saw Trisha sorting through the survival packs. "What are you doing?"

Trisha glanced up and saw both men standing in the aisle watching her. "We probably don't have much time. We need to work together to survive until my mate comes for me. I know how to survive in the forests. I can keep you alive, but I need you to trust me, listen to what I tell you, and follow my instructions to the letter. If you don't, you could get us all killed," Trisha said calmly, looking both men straight in the eye so they would understand she meant what she said.

"How…?" Terac asked curiously. "How do you know how to survive?"

This female fascinated him like none he ever met before. He wanted her as his mate. He wanted to claim her, but he knew she would not hesitate to kill him if he tried. None of the females of his village, or the few from the city where he trained as a pilot, ever captured his attention the way this one did. She was exotic with her long, curly hair of spun gold colors. She was smaller boned than the females of his world, but she was a fierce warrior. She proved that when she killed the three mercenaries Raffvin hired to raid his village and steal his people. She did not fall apart when he needed help with flying the shuttle, and now she was letting them know she could keep them safe on a moon known for its savagery. What surprised him the most was—he believed her.

"My father taught me," Trisha said softly with a warm smile curving her lips. "And no one is better at teaching someone how to survive in the wilderness than my dad," she added with confidence and pride.

Within moments, the two men worked to carry the bodies of the four dead men out and away from the shuttle. Trisha quickly changed and carried the bags she sorted through into the nearby trees. Using one of the long blades, she cut branches and began dragging them back toward the shuttle. It wouldn't be the best cover in the world, but it would buy them a little time. Luckily, the shuttle was close to the tall trees. She had a third of the shuttle covered by the time the guys returned.

"Clean any blood off of you. If there is any on your clothes, change. Make sure there isn't a trace on you," Trisha said as she moved to gather more branches.

She was bending over when a sharp pain cramped her stomach. Trisha gasped as the pain radiated outward. She started to straighten up, but another cramp hit her and she went down on her knees with a cry, her hand flying to her stomach.

"Jaron!" Trisha cried out.

Jaron came out of the shuttle pulling a clean shirt over his head. He ran over to where Trisha was kneeling on the ground holding her stomach. Trisha looked up with terror shimmering in her eyes.

"Please, help me," Trisha whispered as another cramp hit her.

Trisha tried to focus inside her. *What's wrong with our baby?* she whispered urgently. Her dragon was fretting as the tiny spark inside her seemed to be moving in distress. *Our baby needs help. We need our symbiot.*

Trisha reached up and gripped the thick gold band around her neck. *Please help our baby, please!* Trisha could feel Jaron's hands on her stomach as he lowered her down onto the ground. Terac came out of the shuttle and ran over to them. He gently lifted Trisha's head up until it rested on his thighs. Brushing her hair gently away from her sweat-dampened brow, he let his fingers trace over her jaw as he watched Jaron splayed his palms over Trisha.

"Relax, Trisha," Jaron said calmly as he closed his eyes. "I'm just going to check on the baby. I should have done this as soon as we landed."

Trisha let her eyes fly up to Terac who was smiling in encouragement down at her. "If there is anything wrong, Jaron can heal you. He is one of the most powerful healers I have ever seen," Terac said softly, stroking his fingers soothingly over her face.

Trisha nodded. She could feel the symbiot moving down under her shirt to curl over her abdomen as well. It didn't seem to mind Jaron's touch, as if it realized Jaron was trying to help her. Trisha focused deeper until the tiny spark inside her was the only thing she saw. Her dragon was curled back around it, soothing it and stroking it gently.

What happened? Trisha asked her dragon.

Our baby was frightened. Her dragon cooed softly. *He good now. Good man make him better. Symbiot make him better. You be more careful.*

He? Trisha whispered in awe as the tiny spark seemed to reach out for her. *Oh my god, he is so beautiful!*

Yes, our baby boy so beautiful, her dragon agreed.

Trisha could actually see the warm light of Jaron surrounding the baby and healing a small tear in the amniotic sac. Warmth filled her as the symbiot moved down alongside him, checking and healing any contusions as well. The symbiot was small, but alongside Jaron it seemed to radiate strength. She could see a small part of Jaron brush up against it, and it glowed for a moment before it moved deeper. Trisha came back out of her trance when she heard Jaron's deep voice again.

"There was a small tear, but it is healed now. You must let us do the heavy work, Trisha. You focus on keeping us alive, but we will do any physical labor, especially the heavy stuff; otherwise you might lose your child," Jaron said firmly as he stood up. He swayed for a moment before Trisha saw him grit his teeth and straightened his shoulders.

Terac leaned over, kissing Trisha's forehead before he carefully helped her to stand up. Trisha was shaky from the fright of what just happened. She didn't think she had ever been this frightened, not even during the helicopter crash that almost took her life or when the doctors told her she might never walk again. She laid her hand protectively across her stomach. She would do whatever it took to keep the precious bundle inside her safe.

"Okay," Trisha said, thankful the horrible cramping was gone. "We need to finish covering the shuttle, then move out. I would like to put a couple of miles between us and the shuttle before it gets dark. We will need to find shelter as well."

"There are the remains of the small colony to the east about a half-day's hike," Terac started to say but stopped when Trisha shook her head.

"No, that is the second place Raffvin would look. Or at least it would be if I was tracking someone," Trisha said. "We need to do the unexpected. There will be plenty of places where we can find shelter, even if we have to build it. We need to move as carefully as possible. We will lay out some false trails toward the abandoned settlement to throw off anyone looking for us. Do you have a holovid of the moon?" Trisha asked. "I can look at it while you two finish covering the shuttle."

Terac nodded handing Trisha a device. "Tap the screen. You'll see where it will project a holovid of the moon's surface."

Trisha smiled her thanks and moved toward the shade. She sat down gingerly under the trees near the packs she set out earlier. Looking over the holovid, Trisha zoomed in, studying it carefully. To the southwest was a set of small mountains. There were thick forests between the meadow where they landed and the small mountains. A river cut through the center. Trisha glanced up at the trees. They were not as tall as on Valdier or nearly as thick, but they would be of some use for moving above the ground. When Kelan came for her, he would know to look for clues. She showed him the signs her dad taught her to leave, Native American symbols, so he could follow her without anyone else knowing. She would leave the cryptic messages for Kelan. She didn't have a single doubt he would come for her.

Once Terac and Jaron were finished covering the shuttle, they sealed it tightly and headed toward Trisha. The plan was to start toward the abandoned settlement leaving obvious tracks. After two hours, they would "disappear" and work their way north, then circle around back to the southwest toward the mountains Trisha picked out. They would rest once each hour for ten minutes. Terac and Jaron both argued it was too much for Trisha in her condition, but she promised she would stop and rest more often if she felt even the slightest twinge. Neither was happy, but they bowed to her determination. Setting off, they moved at a steady pace. Trisha observed her environment for clues to both hostile plants or animals and helpful ones as they moved through the thick forests. Trisha left a mark indicating where she was hiding her first cryptic message as they entered the forest. She hoped Kelan would find it and remember the symbols she was using so he could track her.

Chapter 21

Kelan's mouth firmed into a straight line as he looked at the image his symbiot was showing him. The old Class Two freighter and a newer Curizan warship were stationary not far off the second moon of Quitax. He would need to be use caution coming in. Fortunately, unless either ship contained technology he was unaware of, they would be unable to detect his symbiotic fighter. It was a living creature and not detectable by their radar equipment. It was another advantage the Valdier had over the Curizans and Sarafin.

"Take us around to the far side of the moon in a moment," Kelan told his symbiot. "I do not want to chance them having technology we are unaware of, especially after what happened outside our living quarters."

Kelan could feel the rage that ran through his symbiot at the reminder of the death of the new symbiot forming as part of Trisha's protection and the destruction of his two guards' symbiots. Kelan knew the information had already been sent on to the Symbiots' Queen. Even now, he could feel changes occurring in his symbiot as if it was evolving to another level. He would investigate it once Trisha was safely at his side and they were on Valdier. Kelan closed his eyes for a brief moment, drawing a picture of Trisha in his mind as he thought of how close he was to seeing and touching her again. He refused to believe anything else was a possibility. Once she was by his side again, he would bind her to him and never let her out of his sight again.

Kelan's dragon rumbled in agreement. *Want my mate,* he growled out softly.

Kelan's eyes snapped open. He needed to find out if Trisha was on board one of the ships or on the moon's surface. He reached for the small device his brother Trelon gave him before he left the *V'ager*. Trelon used some of the modifications his mate devised when she was messing with their communications systems to improve intercepting signals at varying ranges. Trelon developed a handheld device using Cara's calibrations and some of the crystals. Trelon hoped it would allow them to "listen in" on transmissions sent between two warships. He'd tested it on some of their small warships already. Kelan set the device and waited to see if he could find out any information about his mate. After several moments, a transmission signal was picked up.

"*New Kingdom I*, this is the *Tri-twin*. Request for open communications," a deep voice said. Kelan's eyes narrowed, and his mouth tightened as he listened to the transmission being sent from the freighter to the Curizan warship.

"This is the *New Kingdom I*. Authorization approved for communications. Request current status report on the female," a disembodied voice replied to the *Tri-Twin's* request.

"Twelve men confirmed dead. No sign of the female. Current hunters are in process of returning to ship to ship," the *Tri-Twin* replied. "Repeat. Twelve of our men confirmed dead. Eight from the hunting parties sent down, four confirmed remains from the shuttle. No confirmation of the female's body or of the other two missing men."

"*Tri-Twin...*" the disembodied voice started to reply before a deep snarl broke through the transmission. Kelan would recognize the voice of his uncle anywhere.

"Send more men down! Find me that bitch and bring her to me. I want her alive so I can tear her heart out while she is watching. Find the other two men who are with her and kill them as examples for not following orders," Raffvin snarled.

"Sir, the moon's predators are extremely dangerous after dark fall," a new voice from the freighter replied. "We—"

"Captain, I suggest you do what you are told, or I will blow that tub you call a freighter to the moon's surface to join the others. Do I make myself clear?" Raffvin bit out coldly. "Find the female." The transmission signal ended.

Kelan fought back a wave of relief at knowing Trisha escaped, followed by terror at knowing she was down on a moon known for its savage predators. Kelan sent a command for his symbiot to take them to the far side of the moon. They would circle back around. He would focus on finding where the shuttle they were talking about landed. Trisha would have left him some type of message.

..*

Several hours later, Kelan stood in the dark watching the small group of men. It appeared there were only four hunters left alive. All four shifted nervously around a small fire, peering out into the darkness. Kelan's keen eyesight could pick out the partially covered shuttle. The covering of branches over it screamed Trisha. Kelan let a cold smile curve his lips. He motioned for his symbiot to shift into a werecat. He would kill three of the men immediately, saving one for questioning. He listened intently for a few minutes so he could determine which one would give him the most information in the least amount of time.

"Is the captain sending anyone else down?" one of the men asked nervously as he pushed more wood into the fire.

"No," came the short response from a huge man with several scars across his face. "Bastard can't afford to send any more. He's lost half his crew. If he sends any more he won't be able to handle the freighter."

Another man spit in the flames. "He left us to die in this stinking hole. Should have taken the credits and run at the last spaceport. That other bastard is crazy. He's going to get us all killed."

The last man stood up and stretched. "Yes, well, I plan on having a piece of the bitch's ass before I die. She is a fine-looking specimen. I'll enjoy listening to her scream out my name before I hand her over to Raffvin." The other men laughed as the man imitated what he would do to Trisha.

A low growl escaped Kelan's throat at the threat to his mate. He let his dragon's fury wash over him as he moved out of the shadows. All of the men jumped to their feet as the low growl rumbled through the dark meadow. Two of the men started to raise their laser rifles, but they never made it. Bio, in the shape of a massive werecat, struck with deadly precision, slicing through skin, tissue, and bone, severing both of the arms holding the rifles. Screams ripped through the air as Kelan breathed out a wave of dragon fire, igniting the men on fire as Bio turned to the scar-faced man. The man who threatened to rape Trisha stumbled backward in horror, away from his burning companions. He turned and ran for the dark forests. Bio looked up with a hiss from where Scarface's body lay twitching on the ground, the contents of his stomach spread out in a grisly, bloody twist of organs across the blood-soaked ground.

Kelan growled out in a low voice as he shifted back to his two-legged form. "He's mine."

Bodor pushed through the thick branches, ignoring the cuts and scrapes to his face and hands as he tried to get away from the creatures that killed the other men within a matter of seconds. He tripped several times and fell. The last time he fell, he didn't even bother getting up, he just started crawling until he was pressed against a large tree. He gasped for breath, trying to still his racing heart so he could hear any sound. Pulling a long knife out of a sheath at his waist, he slowly stood up, listening. The forest itself seemed to realize there was a predator fiercer than anything currently living on the moon. Bodor ran his sweaty palm down his pant leg. He strained to hear the slightest noise. He was about to slide back down against the tree when four gold arms wrapped around him, pinning him to the tree.

Kelan stepped out of the dark shadows, staring dispassionately at the man as the front of his pants turned dark and the rancid smell of urine filled the air. Kelan let one of his hands shift until the long, sharp claws of his dragon protruded where his own fingers had been. Bio, in the shape of a pytheon, had one golden arm wrapped around the man's mouth, preventing him from screaming.

Kelan sent his symbiot a brief command to release the man's mouth. "Where is she?" he asked coldly.

"How the fuck do I know? Dead probably," the man replied hoarsely. "Everyone who has been sent down to this miserable moon has died."

"How long has she been here?" Kelan asked. He knew the longer she was on the moon the more likely it was she was not alive. Kelan drew a long, deep cut down the man's face when he didn't answer fast enough. "I won't ask twice," Kelan said softly.

Bodor whimpered as blood poured down his face, the metallic scent filling the air. "Four days. We've been searching for her for four days."

Kelan looked at his claw for a moment before he drew it down the man's other cheek. "Who are the men with her?"

Bodor started sobbing as pain and fear radiated out from him. "How the hell should I know? Wait...wait," Bodor pleaded as Kelan pushed a claw into his shoulder. Gasping around the pain, he panted out, "They were supposed to stake her out so the predators would eat her alive. Raffvin wants her mate to find her as she's being eaten. Please, please let me go. I've told you everything."

Kelan rotated the claw, listening as the man screamed in pain. "No, you haven't. Was she harmed?" Kelan gritted out. He needed to know if the crew harmed his mate. If they had, he would hunt every one of the bastards down and kill them. *Kill them anyway*, his dragon snarled. Kelan felt Bio's agreement wash through him as a flash of the dead symbiots flared in his mind.

"No..." Bodor whispered hoarsely, "...not that I know of. The two bastards with her might have done something, I don't know. What's the bitch to you anyway?"

Kelan pulled the knife hanging uselessly from the man's hand. He let his hand shift back until it was normal, staring at it for a moment before he looked at the man again with flaming gold eyes.

"I'm her mate," Kelan growled out right before he buried the knife through the man's heart and into the tree.

Kelan took a step back, letting his head fall back until he was gazing at one of Quitax's other moons. He felt his symbiot reshape into a werecat. He didn't even bother to turn and look at the body pinned against the tree. It would be gone by morning. Any number of the predators in the surrounding forest could probably already scent the fresh blood and would come to investigate it. Kelan was not afraid of them for there were few predators fiercer than a full-grown Valdier male dragon and his symbiot.

Kelan let his eyesight remain enhanced by his dragon. *We need to find out if Trisha was able to leave us a message.*

It took almost an hour of hunting, but Kelan found the hidden message. His legs went weak as he read what she wrote. She pointed him to where she hid a rolled-up map. Kelan gazed down at the symbols she taught him. In the dim light of the fire circle, he pulled up a holovid of the moon's surface. Glancing back and forth between the roughly drawn map on the leaf and the holovid, Kelan let out a loud roar. She was alive, and she was moving to the southwest toward a small group of mountains. She would leave him another clue at the fork in the river. It was the last line on the map, written in Valdier, which pulled the roar out of him.

I love you, my true mate. Come for me and our son.

Chapter 22

Trisha was working on building a small fire in a knot in the tree they were using for the night. It was their fourth night on the move, and they were finally at the foot of the small mountain range Trisha wanted to get to. After the first day, the men realized Trisha really did know how to survive in the thick forests, predators, obstacles, and all.

At first, the men were serious when they said they would protect her and take care of her. They quickly reorganized the survival packs before they left the meadow giving her one that was practically empty. It took several miles before the men threw their hands up in the air when they realized Trisha was better at hiking through the forests than they were. They rested for the designated ten minutes on the hour, and at every stop Jaron would check on Trisha and the baby to make sure they were doing well. They covered almost six miles before Trisha stopped suddenly, looking around and listening. The two men stood silently watching the surrounding forest, trying to see what Trisha sensed. Trisha suddenly motioned for the men to start climbing. Trisha went up first, followed by Jaron. Terac was almost to the first limb when a massive creature burst through the undergrowth charging at him. It resembled a cross between a rhinoceros and a Komodo Dragon to Trisha. She realized instantly the thick hide would protect it from any laser fire. Dropping down onto the branch above Terac, she and Jaron gripped Terac's arms and pulled him up as fast as they could. Even so, they lost one of their survival packs as it was ripped off of Terac's back. Trisha said it was actually a good thing that it happened as anyone following them would think they didn't survive. After that, they decided to use the trees as much as possible and began their turn to the north.

* * *

That was three days ago. Earlier this afternoon they finally made it to the fork in the river not far from the mountains. Trisha laid out a series of rocks and branches as a message for Kelan. If he remembered the symbols, it would lead him to the map she left in the hollowed-out section of a rock near the river. Trisha closed her eyes and let her thoughts drift back to the last time Kelan held her in his arms. Kelan was above her, moving slowly deep inside her. His arms were wrapped tightly around her, cocooning her against his hard length as he pulled almost all the way out before pushing back into her deeply. She remembered looking up into his eyes and thinking there could never be anything more beautiful than belonging to him. He made her feel loved, protected, needed. Trisha bit her lip as she opened her eyes and stared at the tiny flicker of flames beginning to burn in the dry moss. Tears burned the back of her eyes as she gently gripped the thin strand of gold around her neck and sent a message for Kelan to find her and their baby soon. She missed him so much.

Releasing the gold thread, she looked up and smiled at the two men working on building their sleeping platform. She remembered giggling at them the first night she showed them how to make one. She explained it served many purposes. First, it would protect them from the elements. Second, it provided some protection from the insects and other creatures of the night and helped keep them less visible from the ground. Third, she pointed down toward the ground and reminded them it was a long, long way to fall out of bed. It began to rain later that night and the guys agreed it was nice sleeping in a warm, dry bed. Neither one of them admitted to her it was more because she was curled up in between them. Trisha was blissfully unaware of the effect she was having on the two men.

"You know it is an impossible dream," Jaron said quietly as he threaded thick, broad leaves through the branches they tied to the top of their sleeping platform.

Jaron noticed how protective and attentive Terac was of Trisha. He also noticed at night when they took turns sleeping that Terac waited until Trisha fell into an exhausted sleep before he would pull her close against his warm body and wrap his arms protectively around her. He made sure he woke before she did, knowing she would be uncomfortable with his desire to be her mate. Jaron couldn't blame Terac. He watched as she bent awkwardly forward to blow on the dry moss. She was the most unusual female he ever met. He smiled softly as she sat back and rubbed her lower back. In the last few days her stomach had swelled with the child she was carrying. She seemed to glow with an internal beauty.

"I am not the only one dreaming," Terac said as he glanced at Trisha out of the corner of his eye. "I would take her for my mate in a heartbeat if she would have me," he replied sadly.

It did not bother Terac that Trisha was rounded with another warrior's child. He would raise it as his own if she would have him. He often lay at night with her wrapped in his arms wishing it was. At first, her dragon did not like the two men so close to Trisha. It was only when Jaron was checking on the baby that Jaron conveyed the need to protect Trisha and keep her warm during the frigid nights. It was the honest caring of the men that allowed her dragon to finally let Trisha get some much-needed rest. Terac worried she was pushing herself too hard. He pushed up and walked across the thick branch to where Trisha was kneeling.

"You should rest for a while," Terac said quietly. "Jaron and I have finished the sleeping platform."

Trisha smiled her thanks but shook her head. "It will be dark soon and all of us will go to bed. I'm good. Dinner should be ready soon. Want to guess what we are having?" Trisha teased as she rubbed her lower back again.

Jaron grinned as he came over. He flicked a look at Terac who nodded and moved around behind Trisha. Jaron chuckled as Trisha let out a startled yelp before she finally relaxed back against Terac who was gently massaging her shoulders.

"Hum, how about roasted kocta nuts and fresh fruit?" Jaron said as he used a branch to turn the large nuts in the hollowed-out knot in the tree.

At first he thought Trisha was nuts for lighting a fire in a tree but he soon realized she looked for shallow indentions in the tree, then coated it with layers of mud or clay creating a type of burning bowl. She insulated the bottom with wet moss first so it would not heat up. Both he and Terac asked Trisha a million questions about her world. The females there were so different from any they ever heard about. It was when she talked about her father that struck Terac the hardest. The love and admiration for him was clearly evident.

They put the fire out as darkness descended, not wanting to take a chance of anyone seeing it. Trisha was in their sleeping platform unbraiding her long hair. Jaron surprised Trisha with a comb he whittled on the second day. He even proudly showed her all the wood shavings he carefully rolled up in a leaf for their fire later that night. Now, it became her nightly ritual to unbraid the long length and comb it out before re-braiding it for the night. She was just starting to comb through the long strands when Terac entered the platform and slipped around her quietly.

"Let me," Terac said softly.

"Terac…" Trisha started to say but stopped when Terac laid his fingers gently against her lips.

"I know," he said sadly. "Let me have this memory…please?"

Trisha bit her lip to keep it from quivering. She gave Terac a small, crooked smile before turning her back to him. He and Jaron were so good to her. How could she deny him this little joy?

Terac ran the comb slowly through Trisha's hair enjoying the feel of the silky strands as they tried to curl around his fingers. He let his fingers touch the tight curls, pulling them up slightly to see them glitter in the bright glow of one of Quitax's other moons.

"I've never seen this color hair before or felt any so soft and curly," Terac murmured under his breath.

Trisha giggled. "My dad thought it was a nightmare when I was little. I was always running through the woods, and sometimes I would get tree sap in it. He would spend hours trying to get it out."

Terac laughed as he began to braid the long length. He felt Trisha's surprise at his knowledge of braiding a girl's hair. He wove the strands in and out.

"I have two little sisters, Jetta and Mia. They are nine and eleven," Terac said quietly as he pulled the strands together. "They would often beg me to braid their hair before they went to bed at night when I was home from my training."

"Where are they now?" Trisha asked curiously.

She was about to turn, but Terac began massaging her shoulders and lower back again. She felt herself start to melt as the constant exhaustion she fought pulled on her. She didn't bother resisting as Terac gently pushed her down onto the moss-covered bed. She moaned softly as he rubbed a particularly stubborn knot on her shoulder.

"They are with my older brother and his wife on Subtera Spaceport in the Bovi galaxy," Terac replied enjoying the feel and sound of Trisha's soft moans and groans and wishing they were for a different reason. "Our parents were killed during the attack on our village. My father tried to prevent Raffvin's men from taking them and my mother. They killed him in front of them. Jaron and I were out hunting when we saw the flames and smoke. We hurried back as fast as we could but another group of Raffvin's men captured us before we got to the village. My mother hid the girls but stood guard over their hiding place. Raffvin's men raped and murdered her."

Trisha turned and looked up at Terac with tears in her eyes. "Oh Terac, I'm so sorry." She sat up and gave him a hug. "How did your brother know where to find them?"

"Another woman from our village who was hiding near the river found them. She notified my brother. I was able to speak with him briefly after I was transferred to the freighter to guard you," Terac said. He brushed a strand of loose hair away from Trisha's face, letting his hand gently cup her cheek where a single tear slipped down it. "You are so beautiful," he whispered.

Trisha's eyes widened as she realized Terac was about to kiss her again. She shook her head and placed her fingers against his mouth. "Terac, I love Kelan. He is my true mate and will come for me. I belong with him," she whispered.

Terac closed his eyes and pressed his lips against Trisha's fingers. "I could always hope. Sleep now. You are exhausted. Tomorrow will be another long day, and you and the baby need your rest."

Trisha looked hesitantly at Terac before she scooted back down and rolled over so her back was to him. After a few minutes, Terac saw her breathing even out as she slipped into a deeper sleep. He lay down beside her and wrapped his arm tightly around her, splaying his hand over her swollen belly protectively. Jaron came in a few minutes later and looked at both of them. He quietly scooted in and curled his fingers in Trisha's to let her know they were there, protecting her.

* * *

Kelan reached the river just as it was getting dark. He quickly found the message and map Trisha left for him. He followed the tracks the two men and Trisha left. He knew others searched for her, but they would never find her. It took all of the skills he learned from tracking her the first time through the woods of their home world in addition to the clues she left, to follow her. He continued to be amazed at her resourcefulness. She covered her tracks well.

Two hours later, Kelan studied the high tree where he could scent his mate. She was here. Kelan fought to hold in the growl at the scent of the other two males with her. He would kill them if they touched or harmed her in any way. Bio changed into the shape of a pytheon again, using the six legs to move silently up the tree. Kelan climbed up the other side until he came to the branch Trisha was on. He could clearly see the small platform built against the sturdy branches. He knew it was not something anyone of their worlds would know how to build so it must be one of Trisha's designs. He moved silently along the branch until he came to the small, narrow opening. What he saw inside sent his blood to boiling.

Chapter 23

Terac jerked awake when he heard the low, menacing growl. He froze as he instinctively pulled Trisha's smaller body closer to his protectively. Jaron was staring at the entrance to their small platform. Terac's eyes swung to the small, narrow entrance, as well. Twin gold flames burned with hatred as it returned his stare. The growl sounded deeper, more dangerous as Terac pulled Trisha's sleepy form up and back from the heated breath and sharp teeth.

"Wh-what?" Trisha mumbled in a confused, sleepy voice.

She had been dreaming of Kelan. In the dream, he came for her, holding her tight against his hard body. She remembered running her hands up and over his broad chest and tangling her fingers in his long, black hair. They were just getting to the good part when she was dragged out of it. Why did the best dreams always get interrupted at the worst possible times? Trisha wondered grumpily.

Terac slipped his hand over Trisha's mouth to quiet her. He scooted back, pulling her with him, his hand wrapped protectively around her baby. The creature in the entrance grew more agitated the farther he tried to take her. It let out a deep, angry snarl and pushed its huge head farther into the platform.

Trisha's eyes widened as she saw the jade green and silver scales of Kelan's dragon. His huge head and glowing gold eyes snapped her awake in an instant. Trisha let one of her hands come up to pull Terac's away from her mouth. When she went to move forward, Terac tightened his hold.

"It's okay," Trisha said softly, never taking her eyes off the huge dragon's head glaring murder at Terac. "I know him."

Terac reluctantly released Trisha, pulling his arms from around her as she scooted forward toward the creature. Trisha reached out and gently touched the tip of one nostril letting her fingers move over the silky scales until she rubbed her thumb along its lower lip.

"Tag, you found me," Trisha whispered. Her eyes were glued to the burning gold flames.

Within seconds, strong arms wrapped around Trisha and pulled her from the platform. Kelan did not stop until he was up against the trunk of the tree. He kept his arms tightly, but gently, wrapped around Trisha, holding her while he drew in shuddering gasps of air. Trisha wrapped her arms around his huge body holding him just as tightly as her swollen belly would let her. She kept running her fingers through his hair like she had done in her dream.

"I knew you would come for me," Trisha sobbed quietly against Kelan's chest. "I knew you would find me."

Kelan ran his hands up and down Trisha's back, over her hair, and back again. He finally pulled away far enough to seal his lips over hers in a kiss that spoke of his fear, his longing, and his love for her. They were both shaking by the time he pulled back with a low growl.

"You smell of the other males. Did they harm you?" Kelan asked harshly as his voice deepened with his dragon's rage at the scent of other males on his mate. He didn't ask if they touched her. He saw the possessive way both males were lying against her, especially the one who pulled her away from him.

"No, they saved my life...and the life of our son," Trisha said, pulling Kelan's hand around and over her swelling belly. "They protected us and cared for us until you could come for me."

Kelan's eyes flew to the two men standing on the thick branch behind Trisha. They stood quietly near the platform where the three of them had been sleeping. Kelan's eyes missed nothing. He saw the looks of longing and pain on their faces as they watched him holding his mate. But, he also saw understanding and acceptance. They knew Trisha was his mate. Kelan studied both men for a few moments more before he bowed his head in appreciation for their help and protection of his mate.

Jaron cleared his throat. "My lord, I am called Jaron. I am a healer for my people. Terac and I were both taken forcibly from our village. Many of our people were killed, including Terac's parents. We would be honored if you would accept our help in seeking revenge against the wrong done to you and your mate, as well as to the many innocent victims from our village. A Lord Raffvin is to blame for your mate's capture."

"He is no lord. He is a dead man," Kelan growled out. "My symbiot, my dragon, and myself wish to thank you for your protection and care of our mates. I accept your help. I have already contacted my warship to come for us. Are there others on board either ship forced there against their will?" Kelan hated the idea of destroying innocent lives, but he would do so if necessary. He would not let his uncle get another chance to harm Trisha or his brothers' mates again.

"No, my lord. Jaron and I were kept because of our usefulness. Jaron is a gifted healer, and I excel as a pilot," Terac said in a voice devoid of emotion.

Kelan nodded. "The *V'ager* should be here within a few hours. It was waiting for my signal. When it comes there will be payment for the injustices done."

Jaron took a step forward, nodding. "My lord, if you would like I can check on your mate and your child again. I try to do it several times a day. Your mate came close to losing the child once."

"I'm fine," Trisha said as she snuggled into Kelan's warmth.

Kelan looked down at Trisha in concern and splayed his hand over her belly. He called for the symbiot on his wrists to check on Trisha and the baby. That should have been the first thing he did, Kelan thought in disgust. Bio, who was crouched silently on a branch above them, slowly lowered its massive gold body down onto the branch putting itself between Kelan and Trisha and the other two men. Both men took a tentative step back when Bio reshaped into a werecat. Bio moved until it was pressed against Trisha's back. Kelan let his senses focus inward until he could see Trisha's dragon curled around the tiny form of his son. Trisha's dragon growled softly at the intrusion before purring as she scented her mate.

Kelan stared in wonder at the tiny sleeping form. Bio assured him Trisha and the baby were fine. The thicker symbiot wrapped around Trisha's waist dissolved as it felt Bio. Bio absorbed the tired strands and sent fresh bands out for Trisha's arms and around her neck. Kelan briefly sent a wave of warmth and love over the tiny form snuggled safely within his mate. His dragon purred as it sent the image of stroking to his mate. A low rumble escaped Kelan's chest as his dragon pushed to be closer to his mate.

Kelan refocused on Trisha, pulling her close again and brushing his lips against the dragon's mark on her neck. "My dragon wants his mate," Kelan growled out softly against Trisha's neck.

Trisha giggled as the warmth tickled her neck. "Now?" Trisha whispered back, blushing.

"Now!" Kelan smiled, happy to have his mate in his arms again. "Come with me."

Trisha pulled back and looked up into Kelan's face. "But…" She glanced over her shoulder.

"Come with me or I will take you in front of them," Kelan warned as his voice deepened with need. "I need to feel you, Trisha, and so does my dragon. It is not something that can be denied this time."

To come so close to losing their mates was more than either male wanted to live through again. The fear escalated in a need to reconnect physically and emotionally with their mates. Trisha needed to understand it was a part of their genetics to ensure their mates were safe. Not only that, the scent of the other two males on Trisha was driving both Kelan and his dragon nuts! He needed to put his own scent on her before he lost control and killed the other two males.

Trisha watched as Kelan's eyes deepened again to the flaming gold. Jade green and silver scales were rippling across his neck and up along his cheeks. She could see the struggle and finally realized it was the scent of Jaron and Terac which were causing Kelan to be upset. It was like that with some animals back on Earth. Trisha let her hand slide over Kelan's cheek before she took a slight step backward. Trisha turned and looked at Bio.

"Protect my friends until we get back," she whispered softly before she called to her dragon.

Trisha felt the change sweep through her as her dragon eagerly came to the surface wanting her mate. Terac and Jaron both stared in awe. Where Trisha once stood, now a delicate bronze, gold, and black dragon of incredible beauty sat, her wings glittering like tiny stars in the moonlight. Trisha turned toward the two men and stood up. She carefully walked over to them, balancing her large weight as she moved. She lowered her head first to Jaron who tentatively reached out and ran his fingers over her small head. Trisha reached out with her tongue and gave him a lick on his face. It was her dragon's way of saying "thank-you" for saving her and Kelan's child. Trisha then swung her head over to Terac who stood gazing in awe and wonder at her. She pushed her small head against his chest gently. When she raised her head again she let out a purr. Trisha's dragon knew Terac kept Trisha warm at night and would do anything to protect her and her baby. She no longer felt threatened by his presence around Trisha because she knew he was a good man.

"I thought you were beautiful before," Terac whispered softly as he ran a hand over one of Trisha's delicate ears. "You are just as beautiful as a dragon and more remarkable than any woman I've ever met. I am glad I was given this chance."

Kelan's dragon growled in warning when Terac leaned forward and kissed Trisha lightly on her snout. "Go with your mate. He needs you," Terac whispered again with a small chuckle as Kelan puffed out a hot breath in discontent at his mate's affection for the other two men.

Trisha turned her head and with a low purr launched herself off the thick branch sweeping down through the forest. She headed to the river not far away, knowing Bio would protect her friends, and Kelan and his dragon would protect her and their child. She felt Kelan's dragon flying right behind her. She giggled when she heard him purring. He was definitely a tail guy, she thought, as he nipped at her tail as she purposely swished it back and forth. She broke through the trees and lifted her wings as she softly landed on the grassy area near the bank. She barely had time to close her wings before Kelan's large form covered hers. He wrapped his tail around hers pulling it to the side as he slid into her hot core, impaling himself as deeply as he could go with a loud roar. Kelan lowered his head to grip Trisha's neck as he began rocking back and forth. Trisha lowered her neck and pushed back against the thick length moving deeply inside her. She let out a small series of soft coughs as she cried out her joy at her mate's possession of her.

"Kelan!" Trisha cried out in dragonspeak.

Kelan groaned as the sweet taste of Trisha washed over and through him. *"Mine, Trisha. Never again do I want to know the fear of you being taken from me."* Kelan's groan turned into a series of roars as he felt his mate's hot channel swell around him, locking him to her as she spasmed in her climax. The tight grip was more than the huge male could handle, and he came hard inside her, pulsing as his hot seed flooded his mate's womb. Kelan threw his head back, wrapping his wings around his mate as he held her under him, locked to him as one.

"I love you," Trisha murmured softly as she felt the weight of the huge male move off of her a few minutes later.

"I love you more, mi elila. My true mate," Kelan replied running his rough tongue over the scales on Trisha's neck where he bit her during their mating. *"Tell me what happened,"* Kelan requested softly.

Trisha turned her head until it was resting against his huge chest. She was curled up in the tall grass, one of Kelan's large wings wrapped around her. Her dragon was enjoying the feel of the big male and wasn't in a hurry to let Trisha shift back to her two-legged form. Trisha wasn't in a hurry either, considering nighttime was the most dangerous time to be out in the open, especially near a water source. She lifted her head and sniffed the air for predators. The only predator she could smell was Kelan.

Puzzled, Trisha looked up at Kelan. *"Why aren't there any predators nearby? I can't smell anything but you. All the other nights we could either see or hear some of the larger predators moving under the trees we were in."*

Kelan chuckled. *"I am a larger predator. Few creatures want to tangle with a full-grown Valdier dragon. They seem to understand we are not something they want to fight with. Now, tell me,"* Kelan said as he brushed his snout against Trisha's small head. Mentally he braced himself for what she might tell him. The man he killed said she was not harmed, but the faint image of Raffvin striking her from the weak symbiot that was on her before spoke of something darker.

"I don't know how I ended up on the freighter. The last thing I remember was you kissing me. When I woke up, I was in a small cell on the freighter. Jaron said something about the drug someone gave me not harming me or the baby, but it would prevent me from shifting. He checked me out to make sure the baby and I were all right. It's strange, but he can just put his hands on me and heal me. A man named Raffvin came in shortly after I woke up. He's crazy." Trisha shivered as she remembered his dark black eyes staring coldly at her. *"He almost killed me, but Jaron was able to talk him out of it. He didn't want me to have anything to eat or drink but Jaron and Terac made sure I*

did. About four, or is it five, days ago—I can't remember now, so much has happened—anyway, Jaron, Terac, and three other men plus the pilot of the shuttle were supposed to bring me down to this moon and stake me out. Jaron and Terac were told to keep me alive long enough for you to find me. Raffvin wanted you to find the predators having a shish kabob of me." Trisha smiled as she thought how proud her dad would be of her for keeping her head and using the skills he taught her.

Kelan snorted in anger at the danger his mate had been in. *"How did you get away?"*

"My dad taught me to keep my cool and be resourceful." Trisha rubbed her head against Kelan as she continued. *"I keep a little Leatherman micro in my bra. I used it to remove some of the slats from the cot in my cell. I sharpened them into knives. Once on board the shuttle, I released my straps right after takeoff. None of the men thought it was necessary to tie my hands or feet. I guess they thought one small human female was nothing to worry about."* Trisha smirked as much as her dragon form would allow. She raised her head and blinked her long, dark lashes at her mate innocently. *"They were wrong. When we were close enough I thought Raffvin couldn't send a strike force until it was too late, I attacked the three men. I was able to kill two almost immediately. One of the guys got off a shot but it hit the pilot, taking care of him so I didn't have to worry about him. I was able to break the guy's nose and did a headbutt into him when he grabbed me trying to break my ribs. Dad always told me if you hit something right on the tip of the nose it hurts like hell, and they'll*

loosen their hold while they see stars. It worked! He loosened his hold enough for me to drive my knife into his ribs before I slit his throat."

Kelan tightened his wing around his tiny mate and looked up at the stars in a prayer of thanks to the gods and goddesses for protecting her. Then he looked down at his mate and growled out, *"I'm so proud of you, but if you ever do anything like that again, I'll whip your ass."*

Trisha's dragon coughed out in glee as she suddenly sent images to her mate through the symbiot around their necks letting him know exactly what happened through images. Trisha tried to stop her but her dragon was determined her mate know exactly what happened in minute detail. Trisha could feel Kelan's temper rise as the images flooded through him. She knew the exact moment when her dragon shared the kiss Terac gave her after they landed. Kelan's snarl would have scared off any predators within a fifty-mile radius. He even started to get up but the next images of Trisha in pain and frightened as their son struggled flashed into focus. Trisha heard Kelan's cough of distress at the knowledge he came very close to losing both Trisha and his son if not for the care of the two men with her.

"Maybe I won't kill them yet, but if either one of them ever kisses you again..." Kelan started to growl out at Trisha. She stopped him by running her tongue along his lips.

Kelan wrapped his tail around hers, flipping her over onto her back and positioned his big body over hers. He lowered his head until their snouts touched. Trisha's dragon coughed out softly, begging her mate to claim her again. She let her front claws wrap around the upper arms of Kelan's dragon while she stretched her tail out and wound it around his, moving both of them gently back and forth. She could feel Kelan's thick cock lower from the slit and push against her. Her dragon arched under the big male, opening for him as she used her back claws to pull him forward into her. Both dragons called out as they became one in the age-old call of mating. Kelan let his dragon take over, rocking and driving into his mate over and over until both were totally sated. Kelan grinned at his dragon's sigh of contentment and joy. It was the first time he let go totally and just became his dragon. His dragon sent a heated breath of love and warmth over his exhausted tiny mate who was curled up under his wing sound asleep. Kelan reached out to Bio to see how the men were doing and if it had heard anything yet from the *V'ager*. The *V'ager* was just entering the galaxy and would be within range in approximately two hours. The men were talking quietly and were safe. Bio sent one large predator running when it tried to knock the men from the tree, but otherwise everything was quiet. Bio sent a wave of warmth and affection to Kelan and his dragon for caring for their mate.

Anytime, my friend, anytime, Kelan responded silently.

Chapter 24

Kelan gently nudged Trisha's sleeping form to wake her. The *V'ager* was going to be transporting them up and was already attacking the freighter and the Curizan warship. Gold Valdier fighters were already deployed, and the *V'ager* was sending out disruption bursts. Kelan looked at the two men as they came out of the forest with Bio by their side.

"Is it time already?" Trisha asked sleepily. She was already exhausted all the time now, and Kelan's dragon and hers didn't let her get a lot of rest last night. She felt like she could sleep for a week if given the chance.

"Yes, the *V'ager* will transport us up shortly. How are you feeling?" Kelan asked as he helped Trisha to stand up.

Trisha started to answer when she turned deathly pale. She covered her mouth and ran for the edge of the river where she knelt down and vomited. Kelan moved quickly beside her, holding her as she tried to empty the contents of an already empty stomach. Trisha moaned in embarrassment at the thought that the three men were watching her puke her guts out.

"Leave me alone for a few minutes," Trisha groaned out as another wave of nausea hit her hard. She doubled over again.

"Never again will I let you out of my sight," Kelan said gently as he dampened a piece of his shirt to wipe across Trisha's forehead and the back of her neck.

"Perhaps I can help," Jaron said as he knelt down next to Trisha. "Sniff this."

Kelan looked suspiciously at the small green leafy plant Jaron was rolling between his fingers. "What is it?" he asked, pulling Trisha a little closer to his body.

"It is a plant I recognized from my planet. It has been used for centuries to help the women during their pregnancies. The smell will help alleviate the nausea. I found it as we were coming to the river. I should have looked for it before," Jaron explained calmly, holding it out for Kelan to sniff first.

Trisha moaned as she leaned against Kelan. "Give it to me if it works. I feel terrible."

Kelan sniffed the plant and was surprised by the pleasant smell. He carefully took it from Jaron and held it under Trisha's nose. Almost immediately the nausea dissipated. Trisha leaned back weakly in Kelan's arms and sent a grateful smile to Jaron.

"Thank you," she whispered.

"My pleasure," Jaron responded with a grin. "My mother swore by it."

"Look!" Terac said pointing up to the sky where a large fireball was shooting across it. "It looks like what's left of the freighter."

Kelan watched grimly as the huge fireball exploded into smaller pieces as it fell through the atmosphere of the moon. He looked at Bio who showed him images of the *V'ager* attacking both the freighter and the Curizan warship. The warship was trying to flee. Kelan growled out a silent command for Bio to notify the *V'ager* there were five of them to transport and their location. Within moments, a bright light engulfed them.

..*

"Status report!" Kelan shouted above the alarms. "Someone shut off the alarms. I want a full report now."

Kelan picked Trisha up in his arms and strode through the doors of the transporter room. She would have to be content in the officer's conference room off the bridge since he did not want her more than a few feet from him. He listened intently, making slight changes or asking questions as the lift took them up to the bridge. Once there, he carefully lowered Trisha to her feet.

"Go with Kor. He will show you to the conference room. There is a large couch there. It is not as comfortable as our living quarters here, but I cannot have you far away from me," Kelan explained gently as he ran his hand down her cheek.

Trisha nodded. She understood he was needed here. Trisha smiled as Kor came up and waited patiently while Kelan brushed a kiss over Trisha's lips. Kelan turned to Kor with a nod before shouting out orders. Trisha turned one last time to see Jaguin explaining something to Kelan. He glanced up and smiled at her before turning his attention back to Kelan. Trisha felt her love for her warrior swell as she noticed how the whole atmosphere on the bridge seemed to change when Kelan walked in. Here was a man used to giving orders and expecting them to be followed. He was a true leader of men. She started when she felt Kor gently touch her arm.

"Thank you," Trisha said softly as she turned and walked into the conference room.

Kor showed Trisha where the cleansing unit was and where Kelan kept some of his clothes. "He spent a lot of time here from what I hear, when he first met you," Kor teased as he laid some blankets on the couch.

Trisha blushed as she remembered how stubborn she was at first. "It did him some good," Trisha retorted humorously.

Kor just laughed and explained he was to guard her. He apologized for any inconvenience but it would be necessary for him to remain in the room with her at all times. Trisha raised her eyebrow and asked if that included the cleansing unit while she took a shower. Kor's face turned a dull red as he responded he felt she would be safe long enough to bathe, that is, unless she needed help washing her back. It was Trisha's turn to turn pink. Kor laughed as Trisha mumbled something about males and their sense of humor.

* * *

Trisha tried to stay awake, but after a nice warm shower in the cleansing unit and the wonderful meal Kelan had delivered to the conference room, she couldn't keep her eyes open. She and Kor talked about the forests on the moon and some of the things she did to survive while she ate, but he finally encouraged her to lie down and rest. Trisha was asleep before her head even hit the pillow.

Kor looked down in wonder at the amazing alien female from Earth. He knew Kelan planned to take Trisha back to Earth as soon as they were finished with the Curizan warship. Kelan already made sure the coordinates were programmed into the navigation system for the location of Trisha's father's home in the place called Wyoming. Kor looked up when the doors to the conference room slid silently open. Kelan's eyes immediately sought out his mate. His face softened as he walked over to her sleeping form.

"How has she been?" Kelan asked Kor quietly, not wanting to wake Trisha up.

"Good. She fell asleep shortly after she ate. What happened with the Curizan warship?" Kor asked in return.

"Destroyed. It took longer than I expected. They had some new technology we were not aware of but luckily so did we. We sustained minimal damage to the port side and repairs are underway," Kelan murmured.

"How many warriors did we lose?" Kor asked.

"Two warriors," Kelan said soberly. The weight of responsibility was heavy when he lost any of his men. The two lost were wounded too severely for their symbiots to heal them fast enough. It didn't happen often, but it did happen. They were in the section damaged on the port side and were crushed, dying almost immediately.

"Was Raffvin killed?" Trisha asked softly, causing both men to start.

"You should still be asleep," Kelan reproached softly as he knelt next to the couch and ran the palm of his hand along her cheek.

Trisha smiled sleepily and yawned really wide. She tilted her face until her lips were pressed against his palm and licked it. "I'm not tired anymore."

Kor laughed and stood up. "I think I'll go check in with Jaguin unless you have further need of my services, my lord."

Kelan never turned his gaze from Trisha's as he responded. "No, I think I have this."

"Until later, my lady," Kor said as he moved to the door.

"Kor," Kelan called out as the door opened.

"Yes, my lord?"

"Make sure we are not disturbed unless we are under attack," Kelan said with a small grin.

"Yes, my lord. Not even if your brother's mate was on board," Kor laughed as he exited the conference room. Bio moved to lie down in front of the door to make sure no one interrupted his mates.

"So, what's on your mind, my lord?" Trisha asked softly as she walked her fingers up Kelan's chest.

"I need to clean up before I make love to you," Kelan groaned against Trisha's lips.

"I could help you," Trisha whispered back.

Kelan pulled Trisha up growling when he realized the only thing she was wearing was one of his shirts. "This is all you had on with Kor in here?" He growled.

Trisha laughed as she saw the flames of jealousy flare in Kelan's eyes. "Honey, I have dresses back home that cover less than this."

"You'll have to bring them back with you," Kelan murmured against Trisha's lips as he kissed her deeply.

It took a moment for her to understand what he was implying. Trisha tore her mouth away from Kelan's and looked at him with tears in her eyes. She opened her mouth but nothing came out at first. It was almost like she was afraid to voice her hope.

"Do you…" Trisha began. "Are you saying…?"

Kelan cupped Trisha's face between his big palms and pressed a gentle kiss on her lips. "We are going to get your dad. He needs to know he is going to be a grandpa," Kelan murmured gently, referring to the name Trisha used when she talked of wanting her dad to know she was with child.

"Oh, Kelan!" Trisha gasped as she flung her arms around his neck and buried her face in his chest. "Thank you! Thank you! Thank you!"

Kelan laughed as he wiped the tears from Trisha's face. "I can think of a way you can thank me," he whispered devilishly.

Trisha's face lit up as she began pulling at the ties holding his shirt on. "So can I," she whispered back before running her tongue over one of his nipples.

Kelan shivered at the feel of Trisha's tongue on his extended nipple. Gods and goddesses, he would never get enough of her. He found her even more desirable rounded with his child. His cock grew long and heavy at the thought of sliding in and out of her. He wanted her desperately. Kelan quickly pulled the shirt Trisha was wearing over her head and pulled the rest of his clothes off, stumbling when Trisha reached down and cupped his heavy sac in the palm of her hand.

Kelan groaned and picked Trisha up, chuckling when she squealed out she was getting too big and heavy for him to carry her. He strode into the cleansing unit. With a swipe of his hand the cleansing foam made quick work of cleaning the dirt and sweat from the moon off his body. Kelan was about to reach for the door when Trisha sank down to her knees in front of him and pulled his thick cock into her mouth without warning.

"Goddesses' bosoms!" Kelan roared out at the feel of her hot mouth wrapped around him.

He splayed his hands on the wall behind her and leaned into her mouth. Kelan closed his eyes, trying to hold back as waves of intense pleasure pulsed through him as Trisha moved her head back and forth. When she pulled almost all the way out and waited, his eyes opened, and he stared down into her dark-brown ones. A small smile curved the corner of her mouth as she pulled his cock out of her mouth so she could lick the tip. Kelan's eyes widened at the erotic picture she made as she licked and sucked him. He could feel his sac drawing tighter but was unable to break the hypnotic hold the sight of her sucking his cock created. He felt the shaking begin in his legs and move up as he lost control.

Moaning, Kelan wrapped one hand in Trisha's hair, holding her head still while his cock pulsed, sending his hot seed down her throat. He watched as she swallowed. She never took her eyes from his, watching how he changed shape and color as he came. When she drank the last of it, she licked him clean before slowly standing up again. Kelan wrapped his shaking arms around her, loving the feel of her soft, silky skin as it moved against his.

Trisha turned her head into Kelan's throat and whispered softly, "I love you, my true mate."

Kelan was about to reply when he felt Trisha's sharp teeth pierce the skin of his throat. He groaned out deeply as she began breathing dragon fire into his blood. His hips moved back and forth in rhythm with the waves building. When she licked the wound on his neck, he growled out it was her turn now. Trisha threw her head back and to the side welcoming the claim of her mate. She tensed and groaned loudly as Kelan bit down on the opposite side of her neck from the dragon's mark. She felt the heat of his breath as he began sending the dragon's fire through her.

He was marking her again as his. Trisha half thought at the rate Kelan was marking her there wouldn't be a place uncovered by their first anniversary.

"Kelan!" Trisha cried out as the first wave hit her hot and fast.

"Turn around," Kelan groaned out. "I want to take you from behind."

Trisha turned and spread her legs. Her pussy was throbbing with need. She almost came when Kelan pressed two of his fingers inside her to see if she was ready for him. Her vaginal walls clamped down on them, greedy for more.

"Gods, Trisha!" Kelan moaned. "Your body wants mine."

"I know, damn you. Do something!" Trisha sobbed out as another wave washed over her.

Kelan aligned his swollen cock with her dripping pussy, pushing her forward slightly so her ass was higher in the air. He swore one day he would take her beautiful ass. He pushed forward, groaning as his cock fought to push through the swollen folds of her pussy. He had to grit his teeth to prevent the moan of pain as she wrapped around him so tight he thought he would explode from how good it felt.

"Faster!" Trisha begged as she pushed back.

"Trisha, if I take you any faster I won't last long, and I want you to come before I do," Kelan muttered as he tried to control the building wall of heat in his cock.

"I need you!" Trisha whimpered pitifully. "Please, Kelan. Faster, harder."

"Fuck!" Kelan said loudly as he gripped her hips tightly between the palms of his hands.

Kelan began rocking his hips harder and faster. Sweat beaded on his brow as he fought his own release, wanting Trisha to come first. The sight of his cock disappearing into her swollen nether lips and her moans of pleasure were too much for him. Kelan let one of his hands move to her ass. He massaged it gently before he lifted his hand, bringing it down in a sharp slap against one cheek. He felt Trisha's start of surprise, then felt her push back against him for more. Kelan raised his hand and let it fall again over the slightly rosy imprint of his first slap. Kelan gasped as he raised his hand and brought it down a third time on the same spot. Trisha cried out wildly when she climaxed at the same time as the sting of his slap warmed her ass. Kelan jerked deep inside Trisha as her hot channel squeezed his cock, milking every last drop of his seed from him. They were both panting and shaking as the wave crested. Kelan lay across Trisha's back holding the two of them together, one hand wrapped to hold one of her full breasts in his hand while the other lay protectively over the bump of their son.

"Do you think we can make it to the couch without separating?" Trisha asked curiously.

"Let's see," Kelan chuckled as he lifted Trisha just enough to walk.

"Oh, my god!" Trisha whispered in awe as she felt Kelan push deeper into her with every step.

Kelan chuckled as he felt a fresh wave of pussy juice coat his cock. She liked that, he thought wickedly. Kelan set Trisha down on her hands and knees on the wide couch. He could sense the wave of dragon fire building again in both of them. It was as if two huge waves were on a head-on collision course. Kelan pulled partially out and began moving with the wave, ebbing and flowing in and out of Trisha as if he was part of the tides. The movement caused a ripple effect in both of them. Trisha rocked back and forth with him, letting his cock slide deeper and deeper into her with each crash until the rhythm was as wild as some of the storms on Valdier.

"Now…" Kelan groaned as one particularly strong wave crashed over both of them. Kelan roared out as Trisha screamed, the heat seemed to scorch them both as it passed back and forth between them.

Kelan collapsed next to Trisha on the couch, spooning her exhausted body against his without pulling out. He never wanted to be separated from her again. Kelan wrapped his arm around Trisha's belly, letting his hand rest over her swollen stomach.

He pressed a kiss to Trisha's shoulder. "I love you, *mi elila.*"

"I love you, too," Trisha said laying her hand over Kelan's. "So, you never did tell me if Raffvin is dead."

Kelan sighed as he tiredly thought of how to answer his mate. "I hope so. I want to believe he is, but there is no way of knowing for sure. The Curizan warship was destroyed. We destroyed fighters trying to escape."

"But…?" Trisha asked looking over her shoulder into Kelan's worried eyes.

"But, there was an unknown signal on our sensors. We did not have a visual and there didn't seem to be anything, but it was there. My gut tells me Raffvin escaped," Kelan said quietly.

"Then I believe he escaped. My gut feelings have saved me too many times to not take them seriously," Trisha replied, laying her head back down on Kelan's forearm and snuggling back against him. "We will just have to be careful and wait for him to show himself."

Kelan pressed a kiss to the new dragon's mark on Trisha's neck. "How did you get so smart?"

Trisha giggled as Kelan's hot breath fanned out against her neck and shoulder, tickling her. "My dad," she responded softly. "You're going to love him, and he is going to love you in return."

"How do you know this? You don't think he will be mad that I kidnapped his only daughter, took her far, far away from her world, and planted my seed in her womb?" Kelan asked curiously.

"No," Trisha said, yawning and snuggling closer. She let her eyes drift shut.

"Why not?" Kelan asked, unable to let her fall asleep without telling him why she didn't think her dad would want to kill him. He would have killed any man who did the same to his daughter.

"Because you make me happy and whole," Trisha whispered faintly.

Kelan lay still, listening as Trisha's breathing deepened, telling him she had fallen asleep. He made her happy and whole. Kelan was just about asleep when he felt something kick the palm of his hand. He pressed his hand over Trisha's swollen belly and sent a wave of warmth through the symbiot on both of them to his son, calmly telling him to settle down and let his mommy rest. Tears burned the back of Kelan's eyes as he felt a tiny wave of warmth return to him in answer.

Epilogue

"Are we there yet?" Trisha asked for the hundredth time in the last two hours.

"Almost…just another hour," Kelan grinned as his mate paced back and forth nervously.

"Are you sure we should beam down? Is it safe for the baby to get its molecules all scrambled?" Trisha asked again.

"It is very safe," Kelan replied…again.

"Are we there yet?" Trisha asked looking at Kelan and biting her bottom lip anxiously.

Kelan laughed out loud and so did the half-dozen other men on the bridge. They spent the last two weeks almost exclusively in his living quarters on board the *V'ager*. The first night was fine in the conference room, but the couch was much too small for many of the things he wanted to do with Trisha. He grinned as he thought of how creative they'd gotten. He especially liked having Bio create straps to tie her down while he fucked her over and over.

His dragon even got a chance to have fun with his mate. Trisha had him move all the furniture in the living area to the sides of the room one night so her dragon could be with her mate. Kelan remembered Trisha snapping at Gunner when he barged in thinking something was wrong when he heard Kelan's dragon roar. Kelan's dragon chuckled as Trisha snapped and snarled at an embarrassed Gunner who quickly backed out of their living quarters with an apology.

Kelan had to soothe his riled mate with several additional lovemaking sessions before she was ready to forgive Gunner. It took him a little longer to soothe Trisha from her embarrassment and convince her Gunner didn't see anything. Gunner took one look at the warning in Kelan's eyes and swore on his own life he saw nothing but Kelan's wings. Trisha finally nodded shyly before smiling in relief at Gunner. Gunner swore he never saw anything more beautiful than Trisha's eyes shining with relief and shyness. He would never admit the incident caused him to return to his own quarters where he had to relieve the pain of his swollen cock caused by the erotic picture of the two entwined dragons.

Now, Trisha waddled—it was the only way Kelan could describe her—back and forth. When she turned pleading eyes to Kelan he couldn't stand it any longer. Taking her hand gently in his, he stated it was time for them to go to the transporter room. He laughed as Trisha practically dragged him off the bridge.

"What if he's not there? What if something happened to him while I was gone?" Trisha asked anxiously. "What if...?"

Kelan sealed his lips over his mate's mouth silencing her doubts. "He will be there."

Kelan didn't tell Trisha he sent down Kor and Palto to make sure before he transported Trisha down. That was one of the reasons he procrastinated on taking her down. They were in range to transport twenty-four hours before. He wanted to make sure Trisha's father was in the home she told them about first. He did not want her to be disappointed. Kor notified him that a human male matching Trisha's description of her father arrived home late last night. Trisha had finally fallen into an exhausted sleep by the time the message came in. Kelan wanted her well rested for whatever happened. While Trisha seemed confident her father would approve of him, Kelan was not so sure. For the second time in his life, he didn't know what to do. He was scared to death Trisha's father would try to convince her to stay on Earth. Taking a deep breath, Kelan prayed to all his gods and goddesses for the strength to get through the next few days.

"It's time," Kelan said as he lifted his lips off of Trisha's.

She looked at him with love and excitement shining brightly from her deep, dark-brown eyes. She nodded and nervously stepped onto the platform next to Kelan and Bio. Kelan turned and looked at the warrior in charge of the transporter and nodded. Within moments they were on Earth, almost four and half months since Kelan first arrived.

* * *

Kelan looked at the huge two-story house that Trisha told him about. This was where his true mate grew up. There was a large wraparound porch and an old transport out in front of it. Kelan instructed they be transported to a small wooded area so it would not be obvious to any humans if there should be any around. Kelan started forward when he heard Trisha's soft cry of joy. A huge man was coming out of the house and moving down the steps. Even from this distance Kelan could tell the man was light on his feet for being so large. Trisha moved out of the woods before Kelan could stop her, moving as fast as her rounded shape would let her.

"Daddy!" Trisha cried out, running toward the huge man.

Paul Grove's head jerked up as if he had been shot. His eyes widened as he saw his baby girl running toward him. He took one step, then two before he broke into a run. He opened his arms wide as Trisha threw herself at him, pulling her close in a big bear hug.

"Baby girl," Paul Grove whispered softly as he stared down into his little girl's tear-filled eyes. Paul hugged Trisha again, pulling away only when he felt her rounded belly.

"What…?" Paul asked uncertainly before his gaze caught on the huge, dark-haired man standing near the woods. Paul put a protective arm around Trisha, trying to turn so she would be behind him.

Trisha glanced over her shoulder and smiled at Kelan. She held out her hand for him to come closer. "I tagged him, Daddy. He's mine," Trisha said, smiling up at her dad.

Paul Grove stared down into the beautiful face of his only daughter. There was something different about her—a wholeness that she never seemed to have before. She had found true love. Paul turned his attention to the man walking toward him. He was taller than Paul by a couple of inches but not much broader. He walked with an air of confidence that spoke of leadership and power. Paul took in every detail from the unusual clothing to the long sword strapped to his back and some type of gun at his hip. His hair was almost as long as Trisha's but black as night and straight with two long braids in the front. He wore boots that reached just below his knees and was dressed all in black. Paul took a step back when he looked into the man's eyes. They were not human. There was no other way to describe them. They were a deep, dark gold with black elongated pupils, almost like a cat.

"Daddy, this is Kelan. He is my true mate…my husband," Trisha said hesitantly as Kelan came to stand by her. He gently took her hand in his.

Kelan looked steadily at Paul Grove knowing instinctively the man was sizing him up to see if he was good enough for his daughter. Kelan returned his stare. He was curious about the man who was the father of his true mate. The man who taught her how to survive, how to be strong, and how to fight for what she believed in.

"Daddy," Trisha said softly, waiting until her father looked down at her. "I love him. He took me to the stars and made me whole, just like you said momma made you feel."

Trisha moved back letting Kelan wrap his arms around her and their son. Paul Grove watched the possessive, yet gentle way Kelan looked and held his baby girl. He saw Kelan place a protective hand over Trisha's swollen stomach. He also knew if he wanted to be a part of his daughter's and grandchild's lives, he would have to accept the man she chose.

Paul Grove cleared his throat and gave Kelan a small smile. "Well, son, my daughter once promised me if she ever went to the stars she would take me with her. When do we leave?"

"Oh, Daddy," Trisha breathed out, smiling.

Trisha didn't tell her dad she found a woman up there who might be just what he was looking for. She couldn't wait for him to meet Morian Reykill. Trisha grinned as Kelan stretched out his hand to her father in greeting and watched as her dad pulled him into a big hug instead. It took a trip out of this world to find true happiness, but she found it in the stars. Trisha looked up at the clear blue sky knowing there were stars up there and thanked her mom for all her help. She could have sworn she saw a twinkle in the sky for just a moment before it disappeared.

To be continued…

ABOUT THE AUTHOR

Susan Smith has always been a romantic and a dreamer. An avid writer, she has spent years writing, although it has usually been technical papers for college. Now, she spends her evenings and weekends writing and her nights dreaming up new stories. An affirmed "geek," she spends her days working on computers and other peripherals. She enjoys camping and traveling when she is not out on a date with her favorite romantic guy. Fans can reach her at SESmithFL@gmail.com or visit her web site at: http://sesmithfl.com. Join me for additional information about the books at http://pinterest.com/sesmithfl/s-e-smith/, http://twitter.com/sesmithfl, or http://facebook.com/se.smith.5?fref=ts

Additional Books:

Abducting Abby (Dragon Lords of Valdier: Book 1)

Capturing Cara (Dragon Lords of Valdier: Book 2)

Tracking Trisha (Dragon Lords of Valdier: Book 3)

Ambushing Ariel (Dragon Lords of Valdier: Book 4)

Cornering Carmen (Dragon Lords of Valdier: Book 5)

Choosing Riley (Sarafin Warriors: Book 1)

Lily's Cowboys (Heaven Sent: Book 1)

Indiana Wild (Spirit Pass: Book 1)

River's Run (Lords of Kassis: Book 1)

Star's Storm (Lords of Kassis: Book 2)

Tink's Neverland (Cosmo's Gateway: Book 1)

Hannah's Warrior (Cosmos' Gateway: Book 2)

Tansy's Titan (Cosmos' Gateway: Book 3)

Gracie's Touch (Zion Warriors: Book 1)

6697226R00195

Made in the USA
San Bernardino, CA
13 December 2013